Stories of the Mountains

Selected Short Stories
by
Emma Bell Miles

Stories of the Mountains

Selected Short Stories by

Emma Bell Miles

ILLUSTRATED BY THE AUTHOR

Imaging Specialists, Inc. ★ Sparta, North Carolina
WWW.STARROUTEBOOKS.COM

CONTENTS

Emma Bell Miles was a naturalist, an artist, and an author who lived most of her life in the southern Appalachian mountains.

She was was born on October 19, 1879, in Evansville, Indiana, to Benjamin Franklin and Martha Ann Mirick Bell. By the time she was nine, her family had moved to Red Bank, Tennessee, and later, to Walden's Ridge (now called Signal Mountain) near Chattanooga.

Emma married George Franklin Miles in October of 1901 and they had five children: twin daughters, Jeanne and Judith; Joseph, "Joe"; Katherine, "Kitty" and Mirick, "Mark." Sadly, little Mark died from scarlet fever in 1913 at the age of four.

Emma and Frank had a difficult marriage and separated a number of times. While separated, she would stay at Francis Willard Home "for working girls" in Chattanooga.

In 1897, the Women's Christian Temperance Union of Chattanooga had built the facility. The anti-alcohol group also advocated for woman suffrage.

From the Tennessee Encyclopedia: *"...the WCTU provided fundamentalist Christian women the opportunity to gain significant political experience without stepping beyond the traditional female sphere."*

While Emma's life was one of poverty and hard work, her determination, her faith and her extraordinary intellect allowed her to contend with— if not fully overcome— her adversity.

She used her experience and talent to produce sketches, watercolors, short stories, poems, books— becoming nationally known— and she was beloved throughout and long after her lifetime.

In 1911, Emma was diagnosed with tuberculosis. She entered the Pine Breeze Sanitarium in 1917.

Emma passed away on March 19, 1919, at the age of 39. She was buried at the White Oak Cemetery in Chattanooga.

ABOUT THIS EDITION

The Publisher presents this content unedited except for minor spelling and punctuation corrections whenever necessary.

To the best of our knowledge it is all the work of Emma Bell Miles and in the public domain.

Due to their age, these historical works include certain language and attitudes that may be considered offensive in our time.

All content attributed to the Author is her own opinion of and from her own imagination and has been included for its historical interest.

Content, herein, is not meant to harm or marginalize any particular group of people. The Publisher does not condone hate speech or discrimination in any form.

Reader discretion is advised.

Such a lot of things country women know
which those kept in stupid ease never learn.
If she has dressed the new-born and laid out the dead;
if she can build fires and kill rattlesnakes
and help to cut up the hogs on slaughtering day;
if she bakes bread and sets hens
and harnesses the team on occasion;
if she has ranged the woods in search of a cow
that has hidden her new calf,
fought her way through a winter storm
to help a sister through a bitter trial;
if she knows how to evolve a child's petticoat from a
worn shirt or a little coat from a big one,
how to make the rude mechanism of fire and water
and a few utensils serve the needs of her dear ones, and
perhaps also a deal of rough-and-ready surgery—
if she knows all this she has the truest culture,
the real refinement of sentiment
and ability, infinitely above that of education.

Courtesy of the University of Tennessee at Chattanooga Special Collections.

Emma Bell Miles

Courtesy of the University of Tennessee at Chattanooga Special Collections.

For inspiration, Emma would draw from contrary worlds— the quiet, rural life of Walden's Ridge and the busy environment of town. Journal entries from 1912:

May 24— Back to town. . . Went to Carol's and we talked story plots till after lunch. Met Katherine & sent some laurel to Mrs. Wheatley, who is still abed. Then went to D.V. Stroop's office and asked for a corner in the office to work in. After supper C. & I called on Mrs. Cantrell. We talked about Tennessee laws on women, & as Cantrell is a lawyer, it was very interesting. Then we all went to some moving pictures & had a sundae round in the drugstore. I am tired, but not sick; I have taken heart o' grace with the chance to get some work done.

Sunday 26— Got up an hour or two before any one else and sat writing in the cool, silent house. After breakfast Carol & I went over a story. This evening we walked out on the lighted streets & had some ice cream.

Yesterday, D.V.S. brought my typewriter down for me. Lunched with Mabel. Met Dr. & Mrs. Rathmell & Carol had my photograph taken for the News.

❖

June 7— . . . We expected a drought, but have had good growing weather & the garden looks well. Plenty of onions, lettuce, radishes & mustard.

Saturday, 15— I walked to the post office & called on Mrs. Atlee but she was not at home. Called on Mrs. Chapin. We have beets & beans in the garden now.

Sunday, 16— Spent a couple of hours in the thicket of Woodthrush Hollow, after the others had given up the search, and was finally rewarded by finding one blossom of the Spreading Pogonia, in a clump of fern. Uncle Joe spent an hour or two with us.

[X]

Selected Short Stories

The Common Lot

EMMA BELL MILES

ILLUSTRATIONS BY LUCIUS WOLCOTT HITCHCOCK

THE BIG BOY IN THE DOORWAY WAS HOT AND DUSTY, BUT not tired. It was impossible to be really tired with running free on a morning when all the earth was awake and trembling with the eager restlessness of young summer. His head was carried high, with a deerlike poise; the dark young profile with its promise of early manhood flung up a challenge to greet the world. His gait all morning had been the wolflike pace by which the mountaineer swings the roughest miles behind him.

The woman— she was hardly the mistress— of the big log house was tired, however; she could scarcely remember a time when she had not been so. Life had resolved itself, for her, into conditions of greater or less weariness, and she had learned to be thankful if the weariness were not complicated by rheumatism or other pain. Her day was always long, her night was short; she had no time to think of the sunshine and roses in her own dooryard.

"I come apast Mis' Hallet's," he explained his presence, "and she stopped me to send word that she wants Easter to come and stay with her a spell. I've got a note in my pocket, if I can find it."

Mrs. Vanderwelt read the pencilled scrawl from Cordy Hallet, her married daughter. "Allison," she began, a distressed frown puckering her lined forehead, "if you're goin' by the spring, would you just as soon stop and tell Easter? She's churnin' down thar. Ye might as well carry her a pokeful of cookies."

She filled the boy's hands with freshly baked saucer-wide cookies, scarcely more than sweetened soda biscuit-cakes, and put some into a paper bag for her daughter.

The young fellow might have chosen the highroad, but the sun-dappled path through the woods drew first his eyes and then his feet. Everything was in motion there, tilting and waving in the light breeze; dewdrops glittered still under the leaves; brilliant bits of insect life started out of the sun-warmed loam and rustled with many-legged creepings in last year's dry leaves. On the way he cut a length of hickory, from which the sap-loosed bark could readily be taken, and walked on more slowly, shaping a whistle with his knife, and thinking of Easter, and their days in school. She was not so old as he by several years; perhaps she was not quite sixteen. He had scarce awakened to full perception of her girlish comeliness, but he admired her nervous agility and grace in play. She could run and climb, and play coo-sheepy and hat-ball, as well as any of the boys; that was his way of putting it to himself.

The spring was a dark pool, walled with rock and housed with a structure of logs and hand-riven clapboards. It had

CLOSING THE DOOR OF THE SPRINGHOUSE HE CALLED TIMIDLY

a shelf all round below the surface level, on which jars of milk stood in perpetual coolness. Easter, having finished her task, was nowhere to be seen; her churn stood outside, and new butter floated in a maple bowl of water, set on the rock to cool. Having tested his whistle and found to his delight that it would pipe three or four notes, the boy bent over the water for a while, his eyes caught first by the reflection of his own face and then by the leaping and stirring of sand and tiny pebbles where the vein rose through the bottom. He laid himself flat and drank deeply of the bluish cold water; then, closing the door of the spring-house against stray "razorbacks," he began to look about in the woods. Once he called timidly, "Easter!" but the sound of her name in his own voice rather frightened him, inasmuch as he was not sure he ought not to put a Miss, or some such foolish handle, before it and he proceeded uncertainly into the maple thicket below the spring, not knowing where to search. Then a gleam of blossom flashed between the boles, and he guessed that she would be there.

It was a white-flaming mass of azaleas, delicately rosy as mountain slopes of snow splashed over with the pink of dawn. In the midst sat a girl, drinking the overflowed sweetness of that dripping and blowing bank of flowers: now fingering single branches that lifted into the tender foliage their crowns and pompons, and now drawing all together down against her face in a sheaf of cool, pure petals— drowning her young senses in perfume. She had taken off her coarse shoes to plunge her feet into the dewy freshness of those ferns that in such maple-shaded hollows keep the azaleas company. Easter was too old to go bare-foot, but not too old to delight in the feel of the ancient soil beneath her feet, and in the shining dewdrops on her instep's blue-marbled satin. In after years, when the burden of responsibility bore heavily on her shoulders, she remembered that intermission among the flowers as her last taste of care-free pleasure, her last moments of childhood.

Suddenly, with a soft crash of rending growth, the boy parted the underbrush and came toward her. She gathered herself together with a swift instinctive modesty, tucking her feet under her skirt. "Howdy, Allison?" she greeted him, and "Howdy?" he answered, thrusting the bag of cookies at her by way of accounting for his presence.

She smiled in an embarrassed fashion as she took the poke from his hand. The thought of her bare feet made her unable to rise. The big boy dropped to the ground beside her. He delivered his message and watched her read the note.

"Air you goin'?" he asked, eagerly. "Hit's closer to our house. I ain't seen you since school broke up."

"I reckon so," the girl answered him. And then to relieve the situation she offered him cakes. At that he remembered some May-apples in his pocket and produced them with the awkwardness of big-boyhood. Each was still child enough to enjoy the tasteless fruit of the mandrake simply because it was wild; and to him, moreover, it had all the exaggerated value of a boy's trove. Easter shared her cakes, and theirs was a feast of Arcady. So, too, might the Arcadian shepherds have piped among their flocks; for he tried his whistle again, and she must needs have it in her hands to blow upon it also.

Directly she glanced up and her face brightened. "There's a hominy-bird," she whispered ever so softly. Following her gaze, he, too, saw the tiny creature, swift and brilliant, a flying dagger, more like an insect than a bird. They turned to smile at each other, and as quickly turned away. It poised over flower after flower with a hum as of some heavy double-winged beetle; and ere it could be drunk with sweets a new sound possessed the stillness.

The morning had been vividly many-colored with bird notes. The thrush had waked first, his passionless strain cool as the very voice of dawn; the rest had all carolled of nests and mating, of their lives that were hidden overhead in that trembling world of semi-lucent leaves: keen struggle of life with hunger, brooding tenderness of care for the young, wooing, and quarrelling and fighting, the thousand tiny tragedies and comedies unperceived by human eyes. But now it was a mocker who set the dim, deep-lit shadow a-ripple with the pulsing of his own great little heart, in such wild song as could only come from the wild soul of a winged life— a song of world-old passion, of gladness and youth primordial. Oh, troubadour, what magic is in your wooing? Is it the vast and deep desire of Earth for the returning Sungod— her joy in the year's unutterable glad release, her yearning to the most ancient of Lovers ever young? . . .

Allison drew himself nearer to the girl, and laid his hand over hers. The mating instinct awakens early in the young people of the mountains— cruelly early; we cannot tell why— as a sweet pain that overtakes the exquisite shyness of childhood unawares. She neither looked toward him nor shrank away. Slowly her hand turned until its moist, warm palm met the boy's; and before he knew it he had kissed her— anywhere, any way.

[6]

A kiss is a mystery and a miracle. Easter sprang up, dazed and thrilled, regardless now of her bare feet— conscious only of a choking in her throat and an impulse to burst into the tearless sobbing of excitement. Allison, frightened perhaps even more than she, stood half turned from her, flushed and tingling from head to foot.

At last he found his tongue. "I won't do that no more! I just don't know what made me. . . . Easter, won't you forget hit?"

It was all he could say.

She barely glanced at him. "I won't tell hit," she murmured, and, snatching up her shoes and stockings, fled away, and left him standing so, rebuked, condemned.

Once alone, she flung herself on the ground and hid her face even from herself. This it was, then, to kiss a boy? "Oh dear, why is it like this?" she wept, and crept closer to the ground.

But she had not promised to forget.

When Easter Vanderwelt went to "stay with" her married sister, she planned to come home in time to enter school when it should open, the first Monday in August. There was the half-formulated hope of seeing Allison some-where, sometime during the term, even if he did consider himself too old to attend. So she stacked her six or eight books in the loft room over the kitchen, with an admoni-tion to her brothers not to disturb them in her absence. She had always kept them neat, and the boys should have them when she had learned them through.

But Cordy's baby was a fretting, puny thing; Easter finally consented to forego the summer school and stay on till frost, when, it was hoped, the little ones would improve; and the round of toil soon drove out every other thought. Or did it? Four-year-old Phronie and Sonny-buck, his father's namesake, scarcely out from underfoot, the ailing baby to be tended, preparing cow's milk, washing bottles, wrapping a quill in soft, clean rags to fit the tiny mouth— looking after these was the task of a wife and mother; Easter could hardly devote all day and every day to them without figuring to herself a future of such, shared with— whom?

The children fell ill and needed to be nursed. There were the walls to tighten against winter with pasted layers of old newspapers. Hog-killing time brought its extra burdens. Cordy, a fierily energetic housewife, would set up a pair of newly pieced spreads and get two needed quilts done against winter. In the midst of it all she got an order for rug-weaving from a city woman, and begged Easter to stay through the cold weather, with the promise of a new dress from this source over and above her wage of seventy-five cents a week.

Easter's lot was little harder in her sister's house than at home, and there she had no wages; yet she was glad when at last she could shut the three dollars and seventy-five cents in her hard, rough, red little hand— she had accepted a hen and six chickens in part payment— and set her face once more toward her father's house. Catching the hen and chickens and putting them into a basket made her late in starting. The sun was high when she turned out of the shortcut through the woods into the big road, and she found herself already tired. If a wagon would come along now, with room for herself and her small belongings—and, sure enough, before she had walked "three sights and a horn-blow" along the road, a wagon did. Who but Allison on the seat, and all by himself! She felt rather shy, this being the first time they had met alone since the morning he kissed her, under the swamp honeysuckles: she wished he had been any one else, but when he greeted her with, "Want 'o ride?" she clambered in over the wheel.

He stowed the basket under the seat. "What ye got thar?" he inquired, for the sake of conversation.

"Hit's a old hen that stoled her nest and come off with these few chickens," she answered. "What y' been a-haulin'?"

"Rails to fence my clearin', " he told her with pride. He had recently worked out the purchase of a piece of land. "Hit's got a rich little swag on one ind, and a good rise on the other, in case I sh'd ever want to build. Hit fronts half a acre on the big road, too," he added, shyly, looking from the corners of his eyes at the girl beside him.

Talking thus, as gravely as two middle-aged people, they rode across Caney Creek and into the ridges. "Gid up," he gave the command to the team from time to time; but there was no haste in the mules; their long ears flapped as they plodded, and the wheels slid on through the dust as though muffled in velvet. He began to tell her of his hopes and plans, tentatively, without once looking at her.

"If I'm so fortunate— maybe next winter . . . I've been spoken to about a position in a hardware store in town, and . . . " He did not finish that sentence, but presently went on: "One man told me last week that he wouldn't hire a single man— said they was always out nights, and no good in the daytime." Now Easter knew that Allison was never out at night to any ill purpose, and she smiled a bit wisely to herself. His favorite pose was that of the cosmopolitan, the widely experienced man; but that was pure boyishness. There was a rough innocence about him, despite his every-day familiarity with all the crimes that lie between the moonshine still and county court. What of evil there was in him seemed to have grown there as naturally as the acrid sap of certain wild vines or the bitterness of dogwood bark. The freakish lawlessness of even the worst mountaineer seems in some way different from the vice and moral deformity of cities, as new corn whiskey is different from absinthe.

Under her sunbonnet the girl inquired, demurely, "Why 'n't ye stay here?"

"Oh, I'm jist restless, I reckon. . . . I would stay if I had a home here."

That word "home" laid a finger on their lips for full five minutes. Again he ventured, flicking nervously with his whip at the roadside weeds:

"And Mavity wants me in his new saloon. I seed him when I was in Fairplay last week. The wages is good."

She spoke now quickly enough. "Don't go thar, Allison! I don't want to be— worried— 'bout you."

He turned away to hide a swift change of countenance, slashed hard at the inoffending bushes, and jerked out, in a husky, boyish voice, "What makes ye care?"

She dared not be silent. "Because I know how good you air. Because I don't want to see— a boy like you go wrong."

"I ain't good!" he cried, almost roughly. Then he turned to find her looking at him serenely, silently— not quite smiling. . . .

That was all, but it was almost a betrothal to the two. From this moment she tried to imagine what life with him would be like. The picture she saw clearest was of a low-browed cabin in the dusk; through its doorway, glowing with red firelight, a glimpse of a supper awaiting a man's return.

Mrs. Vanderwelt was as glad to see her daughter home again as was Easter to rejoin the family, but that did not prevent her levying on Easter's wages. The dish-pan had gone past all mending, and the water-bucket had sprung such a leak that it was no longer fit for use except about the stable. The lantern globe was broken. So Easter reserved for herself only the price of eight yards of gingham.

"Ye're jist in time for the dance over to Swaford's," announced her younger sister, Ellender, when, after the supper dishes were washed, they sat down to tack carpet rags. "They're goin' to give one a-Sata'day night."

"You 'uns a-goin'?" asked Easter. Of course the boys would be there, and all the youngsters of the countryside— Allison, too. There are never enough girls to go round in a frolic in the mountains.

It transpired, however, that Ellender had no dress— at least, none that could appear beside Easter's contemplated purchase. So Easter was forced to consider the means of providing eight yards for her sister as well as for herself.

This was on Monday. The sisters walked two miles to the store next day, and chose the double quantity of cheaper goods together. It was white with a small pink figure printed at intervals, coarse and loosely woven as a flour-sack. They stitched all day Wednesday, and finished the frocks Thursday morning. But on Thursday evening they received a letter recalling Easter to her sister's house.

Easter's trembling hands dropped in her lap.

"Cain't you go this time, Ellender?" she pleaded.

"Maw says I ain't old enough to do what Cordy needs. She says you ain't— scacely," the younger sister protested.

"You-all act like you wanted to git shut o' me," Easter almost wept." Cordy can wait three days. I'm obliged to go to this dance."

But she knew it was not so. Only in her pain she struck at what was nearest.

Easter's return found an ominous tremor and strain in her sister's affairs. At first her girl's mind groped vainly for the cause. There was the endless toil of spring house-cleaning and truck-patch, of chickens and cows, with the ailing youngest to tend, and Jim Hallet going softly, outcast by his wife's displeasure, while poor Cordy sat at night mending and freshening all the coarse little garments, scarcely outgrown, putting them in readiness for an expected use.

Oh, it was hard, it was hard on Cordy, thought the girl, pondering this thing of which she had no experience. It was hard; but she had as yet only the outsider's point of view.

Next week she had a surprise. Allison brought his team on Saturday evening, and asked her, "provided she didn't mind ridin' a mule," to go to the dance with him. It was a long way to Swaford's Cove, and she would be fearfully tired to-morrow, but she was accustomed to pay dearly for every bit of pleasure, and did not hesitate. So he came again Sunday week to walk with her to the church at Blue Springs, and later took her to the close-of-school entertainment, where she had the pleasure of seeing Ellender speak a piece, clad in the frock that was the counterpart of her own.

In the midst of corn-planting time the baby died. The weak life flickered out one night as it lay across Cordy's knees. Such was her exhaustion that the physical need of sleep came uppermost, and her grief did not reveal itself till next day.

The little body, cased in a rude pine box, was taken in the wagon to the untended graveyard by the Blue Springs church. Easter and Cordy rode beside Jim on the seat, and three neighbor women were behind in the wagon, sitting in chairs. These, with the Vanderwelt boys, who had helped dig the grave, were the only persons present at the burying. Cordy asked that one of the women should offer a prayer, but they protested that they could not.

"I never prayed out loud— afore folks— in my life," said one. "I wouldn't know what to say."

"If one o' you 'll hold my baby, I'll try my best," faltered the second, after some hesitation. "He's cuttin' teeth, and may not let nobody tetch him but me."

So it proved; and the third, a poor creature of questionable reputation, burst into hysterical sobbing, and answered merely that she did not feel fit.

"I cain't have it so," whispered the poor mother, desperately. "I cain't have my pore baby laid away without no prayer, like hit was some dead animal. Ef nobody else won't say ary prayer— I will."

She stood forth, throwing back her sunbonnet, clasped her hands, shut her eyes tight, and gasped. One could see the working in her throat. They waited. Easter stared at the open grave, shallow, because its bottom was solid rock; the impartial sunshine on the crumbling rail fence, and the little group of workaday figures; the rude stones of other graves scattered through the tangle of briers and underbrush. Then Cordy drooped her head, and whispered, with infinite sadness:

"Lord, take care of my pore baby, and give hit a better chance than ever I had."

"Amen!" Hallet's deep voice concluded with a dry sob, and the three women whimpered after him, "Amen!"

The earth was hastily shovelled in, and the woman who had accounted herself unfit to pray began crying out loud. Presently Jim led his wife back to the wagon.

She spoke but once during the ride homeward. "An' I've got no idy the next 'll thrive any better," she said, dry-eyed. Easter, sitting in one of the chairs back in the wagon, held her peace; so this was what life might mean to a woman.

All next week the bereaved mother went about her work muttering and weeping, until both Jim and Easter began to fear for her reason. But presently the work compelled her thoughts away from her loss. She began to take interest in the milk and the chickens; and she noticed Allison and

Easter. She told her husband one day that those two would make a good match.

Far from a match, however, was the present state of affairs in that quarter. The mountain people have an over-mastering dread of attempting to cope with a delicate situation in words, insomuch that the neighbor who comes to borrow a cup of salt may very likely sit for half an hour on the edge of a chair and then go home without asking for it. And Allison had never kissed her again. But both knew, without having discussed the matter at all, that Allison wished to marry Easter, and that she, although Allison was undoubtedly her man of all men, could not obtain consent of her own mind to agree.

Why?

Cordy awaited her sister's confidence, and at last it came.

"I'm afeared," the girl said, and her eyelids crinkled woefully, her mouth twisted so that she was fain to hide her face.

"You don't need to be afeared," said Cordy, slowly, staring straight ahead of her. "You'd be better off with him than ye would at home, wouldn't ye? Life's mighty hard for women anywhars."

"Well, I don' know," said Easter, doubtfully.

But when, some days after, Allison did formally ask her in so many words, she gave him the same reason for her uncertainty.

"What air you 'feared of?" he demanded at once.

She was silent, terribly embarrassed.

"What is it you're afeared of— dear? Tell me. Won't you tell me?" He put his arms around her. She hid her face on his shoulder and began to cry. "You know I'd never mistreat you?"

"Hit ain't that."

"What, then?"

"I'm just afeared— afeared of being married."

He took a little time over this, and met it with the argument, "Would you have any easier time if you didn't get married?"

She tried to consider this fairly, but there was not an unmarried woman in all her acquaintance to serve as a basis for comparison. Most girls in the mountains marry between the ages of twelve and nineteen. She saw, however, that it was a choice of slavery in her father's house or slavery in a husband's.

Then Allison made a speech; his first, and perhaps his last. "Dear, dear girl, I'll just do the very best I can for you. I cain't promise no more than that. You know how I'm fixed. I've got nothing more to offer you than a cow or two, and a cabin, and what few sticks o' furniture I've put in hit; but that's more'n a heap o' people starts with. Hit's for you to say, and I don't want to urge ye again' your will an' judgment. But I've got a chanst now to go North with some men that'll pay me better wages than I ever have got, and I won't git back till fall; and I— want— you," he said, "to be my wife before I go. I want to know, whilst I'm away, that you belong to me. Then, if I was to happen to a accident, on the railroad or anywheres, you'd be just the same as ever, only you'd have the cows, and the team, and my place. Won't you study about it?"

Easter thought of that for days, in the little time she had for thinking. But she thought, too, of the other side of the picture. Poor child, she had no chance for illusions. Sometimes she felt that she would be walking open-eyed into a trap from which there was no escape save death.

She thought of Cordy at that tiny grave. She dwelt upon her sister's alienation from her husband. Would she, Easter, ever come to look upon Allison in that way?

Yet the time drew near when Allison must go with those who had employed him. The thing must be decided. There came a heart-shaking day on which, clad in a new dress of cheap lawn made for the occasion, and a pair of slippers, Cordy's gift, she climbed into his wagon beside the boy, rode away, and came back a wife.

"But I mighty near wisht I hadn't," she said, thoughtfully, as she told her sister of the gayety of the impromptu wedding at home.

He wrote every week, some three or four pages— a vast amount of correspondence for a mountaineer. At the end of a month he sent her money, more than she had ever had before. His pride in being able to do this was only equalled by hers as she laid out dollar after dollar, economically, craftily, with the thrift of experience, for household things. He had given no instructions as to how the money was to be used; so she bought her dishes and cooking-pots, a lamp, a fire-shovel, and, by way of extravagance, a play-pretty apiece for Suga'lump and Sonny-buck, and even a tiny cap for Cordy's baby not yet arrived.

[17]

"I WANT TO KNOW THAT YOU BELONG TO ME"

Then, one day, taking the little boy with her, she went to Allison's cabin to clean house, put her purchases in order, and make the place generally ready for living in on his return.

She chose a fair blue day, not too warm for work. White clouds lolled against the tree-tops and the forest hummed with a pleasant summer sound. She brought water from the spring and scoured the already spotless floor, washed her new dishes and admired their appearance ranged on the built-in shelves across the end of the room, set her lamp on the fireboard, and then spread the bed with new quilts. She stood looking at these, recognizing the various bits of calico: here were scraps of her own and Ellender's dresses, this block was pieced entirely of the boys' shirts, this was a piece of mother's dress, this one had been Cordy's before she married; others had been contributed by girl friends at school. Presently she went to the door and glanced at the sun. It would soon be time to go back and help Cordy get supper, but she must first rest a little. Seating herself on the doorstep, she began to consider what other things were necessary for keeping house, telling them off on her fingers and trying to calculate their probable cost— pillow-slips, towels, a wash-kettle; perhaps, if Allison thought they could afford it, they would buy a little clock and set it ticking merrily beside the lamp on the fireboard, to be valued more as company than because of any real need of knowing the time of day. Her mother had given her a feather bed and two pillows on the morning of her wedding; Allison would whittle for her a maple bread-bowl, and a spurtle and butter-paddle of cedar; and she herself was raising gourds on Cordy's back fence, and could make her brooms of sedge-grass.

Thus planning, she felt a strange content steal upon her weariness. It was borne strongly in upon her mind that she was to be supremely happy in this home as well as supremely miserable. She ceased to ask herself whether the one state would be worth the other, realizing for the first time that this was not the question at all, but whether she could afford to refuse the invitation of life, and thus shut herself out from the only development possible to her.

Little Sonny-buck toddled across the floor, a vision of peachblow curves and fairness and dimples. She gathered him into her arms and laid her cheek on his yellow hair, thrilling to feel the delicate ribs and the beat of the baby heart. He began to chirp, "Do 'ome, do 'ome, E'tah," plucking softly at her collar. Easter bent low, in a heartbreak of tenderness, catching him close against her breast. "Oh, if hit was— Allison's child and mine—"

On reaching home she kindled the supper fire and laid the cloth for the evening meal of bread and fried pork and potatoes; and it was given to her suddenly to understand how much of meaning these every-day services would contain if illuminated by the holy joy of providing for her own.

She fell asleep late that night, smiling into the darkness, but was awakened, it seemed to her, almost at once. Cordy stood before her, lamp in hand, laughing nervously; her temples glistened with tiny drops of sweat, and her eyes were dark and strange.

"It's time," said she.

When it was over, and they could, in the gray morn, sit down for a few minutes' rest before cooking breakfast. Easter saw Jim approach the bed on tiptoe. His wife smiled, and raised the coverlet softly from over a wee elevation. Tears came into the girl's eyes, and she rose hastily and went to build a fire in the stove.

Beside the wagon road that was the sole avenue of communication between the Blue Springs district and the outer world, Easter sat on the mossy roots of a great beech awaiting her husband's return. Her sunbonnet lay on the ground at her feet, and she was enjoying herself thoroughly, alone in the rich October woods. She was now almost a woman; her abundant vitality had early ripened into a beauty as superbly borne as that of a red wood-lily. She had walked a long way among the ridges, her weight swinging evenly from one foot to the other at every step with a swift, light roll; she was taking time for once in her life to rejoice with the autumn winds and the riot of color and autumn light. How much of outdoor vigor was incarnate in that muscular body of beech towering beside her! Easter's eyes ran up from the spreading base to the first sweep of the lower branches, noting the ropelike torsion under the bark. A squirrel, his cheeks too full of nuts even to scold her, peeped excitedly from one hiding-place after another, and finally scampered into safety round the giant bole. Then through a rent in the arras of pendent boughs she saw her man coming.

His grandfathers both had worn the fringed hunting-shirt and the moccasins; and though he himself was clad in the Sunday clothes of a working-man, he moved with the plunge and swing of their hunting gait. Such a keen, clean face as she watched it, uplifted to the light and color and music of the hour! His feet rustled the drifting leaves, and he sang as he came.

It seemed but a moment's mischief to hide herself behind a tree so as to give him a surprise; but the prompting instinct was older than the tree itself— old as the old race of young lovers.

. . . Suddenly they were face to face. He never knew how he cleared the few remaining steps, nor how he came to be holding both the hands she gave him. They laughed in sheer happiness, and stood looking at each other so, until Easter became embarrassed and stirred uneasily. He drew her hand within his arm as she turned, and, not knowing what else to do, they began to walk together along the leaf-strewn roadside, but stopped as aimlessly as they had started.

To him a woman's dropped eyes might have meant anything or just nothing at all. He scarcely dared, but drew her to him and bent his head. And somehow their lips met, and his arms were about her, and his cheek— a sandpapery, warm surface that comforted her whole perturbed being with its suggestion of man-strength and promise of husbandly protection— lay against hers.

That kiss was a revelation. To him it brought the ancient sense of mastery, of ownership— the certainty that here was his wife, the mate for whom his twenty years had been period of preparation and waiting. And the tears of half-shamed fright that started under Easter's lids were dried at their source by the realization that it was her own man who held her, that he loved her utterly, and that her soul trusted

ON THE MOSSY ROOTS OF A GREAT BEECH SHE AWAITED HIS RETURN

in him. She lifted her arms, and her light sleeves fell back from them as she pushed them round his neck.

"Oh, Allison, Allison, Allison, Allison!" she murmured, as she had said his name over to herself so many hundreds of times; only, now she was giving herself to him for good or ill with every repetition.

Before them lay the vision of their probable future—the crude, hard beginning, the suffering and toil that must come; the vision of a life crowned with the triple crown of Love and Labor and Pain. Their young strength rose to meet it with a new dignity of manhood and womanhood. In both their hearts the gladness of love fulfilled was made sublime by the grandeur of responsibility— by the courage required to accept happiness in sure foreknowledge of the suffering of life.

The squirrel ran down the beech and gathered winter provender unheeded; and yellow leaves swirled round them as through the forest came a wind, sweet with the year's keenest wine.

Published in
Harper's Monthly Magazine - December 1908

A Dark Rose

EMMA BELL MILES

ILLUSTRATIONS BY LUCIUS WOLCOTT HITCHCOCK

Fɪᴠᴇ ᴘʀᴇᴀᴄʜᴇʀs, ɪɴ ᴛʜᴇ ɪɴᴛᴇʀᴠᴀʟs ᴏꜰ ᴀ ʙʀᴜsʜ-ᴍᴇᴇᴛɪɴɢ on Puncheon Camp Creek, were enjoying the hospitality of Brother Zack Lowry, whose big log house was near the place of meeting.

Aunt Sa' Jane, the house-mother, quick and tireless as an ant despite her fifty-odd years, was clearing the dinner from the table in the open entry, and the men, sitting on the long porch, told stories of past revivals.

Luther Estill, youngest of the group, was not listening to the stories; neither was he watching the movements of Aunt Sa' Jane, who, ever since he was cast, a lonely little lad, into her hands, had mothered him. He heard only Averilla in the room beyond. The Sunday "singin' " was really over, and the other singers dispersed to get ready for the evening meeting; but she, who never had any pressing work to do, and seemed always ready for any occasion, lingered alone at the organ. One is supposed, in respect, to sing only

[25]

hymns or pieces of a religious nature where the preacher is a guest; but this girl was choosing songs strange to Luther's ears. "Hick's Farewell" he knew; the "Cowboy's Lament" he had heard; but these ballads, centuries old, of poignant yearning and regret, he had never heard before. Aunt Sa' Jane and his far-away mother had crooned to him— but this new manner of singing, this heart-expression, drew him strangely.

The old voices on the porch droned on, with occasional feeble laughter; but her contralto filled the echoing room with its pleading minors and cadences of passion. What was this that had come like a red flame searing his consecrated life?

From the overheard conversation of several boys, who had been loath to leave Averilla at the organ, he had gathered that there was to be a dance that night, a "frolic," at the very hour of the foot-washing— an open defiance flung in the face of the Church, at the climax of campaign against the devil. Averilla's father, Lark Sargent, had been for years the arch-enemy of the few forces that made for righteousness along the Sourwood Mountain circuit. Now they were soon to be rid of him, for he had sold his land to a mining syndicate and given out that he, with Averilla and her brothers, would move to the Settlement, a valley town, to live; but before they were ready to leave the district he was averse to firing a parting shot. He was flush with the recent sale; there would plenty of cards and whiskey. Let Averilla break up the meeting if she could.

When the song was ended, the singer came out on the porch, swinging her bonnet by the strings. Her dark gaze swept the four elderly preachers' indifferently, but met young Luther's with a smile.

"Who's goin' to conduct the meetin' to-night? You?" she asked, pausing before him. The watchfulness of the four was turned aside by these words, and under their resurgent buzz of talk she added: "Come a piece with me. I've got something to tell you."

He hesitated a moment; then, with a kindling of his dreamy face, took up his hat and followed her out of the yard, while the other preachers looked at one another.

This house had been his home until, being "called to preach," he had ceased to have need of a home. Strange that in all those years he had never really seen this daughter of a neighbor! What was this change wrought by a few months in him— or her?

"I wish't I was a little boy, and could go barefooted in the road again," he said, overtaking her outside the gate. "This white dust feels like velvet."

The powerful scent of mountain-mint and bee-balm came to them, called up from the roadside by the evening air; and fainter, finer breaths came at intervals out of the forest. All afternoon a procession of dazzling thunder-heads had been sailing slowly along the horizon toward a mellow rolling of distant thunder, as marching to the seat of war. Now they were piled, sierras above sierras, opposite the sunset, flushed with pure color from base to peak, and glowing from time to time with a silent excitement of lightnings. Passing the mounded bush that almost buried Lowry's gate, the girl had plucked a belated rose; it glowed now in her musky, heavy hair, matching the vivid softness of her mouth. Each time she turned her face to him in talking, her eyes sang; and she moved with a buoyancy unlike the gait of the ordinary mountain girl, who is apt to be weary in the cradle from her mother's killing toil. She was all music, the lovely thing! Luther was like to forget his office. But along with the duteous performance of ancient rites had descended to him something of the austerity of priesthood. He presently broke upon her rippling chatter, bethinking himself to speak sternly.

"I guess I know what you're aimin' to tell me. I heard Bark and 'Vander and them a-talkin'. You're goin' to have a big dance to-night."

She persisted, however, in speaking as to the boy who was walking a "piece" of the way with her. "Yes; don't you wish't you was comin'? Can't you, anyway?"

He tried to counter with a rebuke— "You'd do much better to come to the foot-washin' "; but he saw it fall on stony ground.

"Come, and we'll learn you to dance," she challenged.

"Why, you know that I'd be turned out of the church next day!"

"Well, you're too young to be a preacher; you've never had your life. Just think, you'll get old and die before you've had any playtime!"

Had not his own heart told him so in the night-watches but lately? Ah, the cooing, lilting singsong of her voice! the bubbling gurgle of throaty laughter! her velvet beauty!

"I wouldn't for anything!"

"Come up awhile and look on, can't you?— after you've been to the meeting."

"No-o; I can't think of hit, Averilla."

Of what use to say no to one who would not take it for answer? His refusal only changed her mood for the worse; her tone became one of raillery, without, however, detracting from the warmth and dearness of her presence.

"How many chickens did Aunt Sa' Jane kill for all you-uns to-day? Two to a preacher is what she 'lows, I think. Let's see"— she pretended to count on her fingers—" all but one of ol' Top-knot's early brood! La! just think how lonesome he'll feel a-flyin' up to roost to-night!

> "Wherever these feet-washin' preachers go,
> They never leave a chicken for to crow-crow-crow—
> They never leave a chicken for to crow."

She peeped around into his face with sweet mischief, laughing; and he could but laugh with her. Tossing her head on her rounded neck, she began to dance along the road before him, singing through the tinted twilight:

> "It was the Lady Alizonde
>   Looked forth from her dark tower;
> She saw the stranger minstrel ride
>   That came to be her wooer.
>   *If you love me as I love you,*
>   *There'll be no time to tarry.*

> "She from her casement lightly cast
>   A rose as dark as sin;
> Your sign of sure defeat, although
>   Against the field you win!
>   *If you love me as I love you,*
>   *No knife can cut our love in two!"*

"Do come down for awhile— just to hear Alf King play the banjo— just a little while! You don't hafto be a good boy all the time. Here's your short cut back to Uncle Zack's barn."

He said good night, but he heard her song all the way back to Lowry's through the dusk of the summer woods:

"If you love me as I love you,
    There'll be no time to tarry—"

There had been a conference, or business meeting, earlier in the day, setting in order the church's affairs; so that now all who sat forward, ready to take part in the foot-washing, were approved members in good standing. But out of Luther, who was wont to throw himself into this work with glad abandon, the joyous sense of fellowship with them had gone and could not be rekindled. He sat only a little apart from the rest, yet as far away in thought as if lost in those caverns of shadow cast by flaring pine torches under the woods behind him. A sibilant buzz of gossip rose above the whispering leaves, for the service was not yet begun. That distant rolling of thunder was coming nearer, though it had brought as yet neither wind nor rain.

So many people gathered here, all bound to him with what he had been taught from babyhood was the highest and truest bond of which humanity was capable— and yet all insignificant, all suddenly worthless, because Averilla the alien was not present. He was astounded that his life's endeavor should have so played him false. He felt that he stood at the parting of the ways, that a choice lay before him— to serve his Lord no longer, or to see his love no more. He would not have been the youngster he was, chosen and flattered for a gift of tongues in things spiritual, if he had not put the matter to himself in somewhat magniloquent phrases.

"Gittin' along todes time, ain't hit?" suggested a brother, after glancing across the space to see that the crowd was "about gathered in."

"Reckon hit'll come up a rain?" asked another. They all peered anxiously at the black sky, but were unwilling to forego the service.

"Maybe the storm ain't comin' here; hit may go round an' swing off down the river. That roarin's mainly the heat on the Side."

"Looks like the devil's bent on whippin' us out if he can," said Brother Brock, who was chosen to conduct the foot-washing. "Hit's done rained us out two meetin'-nights this week." But he took his place— a seat on the rough platform; he crossed one leg over the other, threw back his head, and began to sing:

> "Go, preacher, and tell it to the people,
>   Pore mourner's found a home at last."

He was joined by the "leader" and other singers, and there were not three voices in the crowd that had not caught the strain by the end of the second verse. Like most of the hymns they employed, this one was a sort of incantation, a repetition of a half-dozen lines over and over indefinitely. When Brock had heard enough he rose, and the people became silent, awaiting his direction. He announced in measured ministerial tones:

"We don't aim to protract the meetin' any longer, except that there'll be a baptizin' in Puncheon Camp Creek to-morrow at nine (nine o'clock, didn't you say, Brother

Barlow?). Yes, at nine o'clock: and I want you all to come and bring your families to see these twenty-two dear converts dipped and brought into the fold. And let us all sing and praise the Lord; yes, we'll aw-aw-awl sing and praise the Lord. I further announce that there's to be preachin' in the Blue Springs Church by Brother Rogers to-morrow night, and a experience meetin' Wednesday night; and after that Brother Estill's to take charge and preach there the second Sunday in each month. I reckon that's all the 'nouncements I have to make. Now let us throw ourselves heart an' soul into this meetin' with all sinceriousness; let us not be disturbed nor distracted by the powers of darkness nor the thunder; the Lord will take care of us. Brother Rogers, will you lead us in prayer?"

As a matter of fact, three or four prayed together, at the top of their voices Luther caught scattered phrases of reference to the "pleasures of the weecked," and knew that the frolic at Sargent's was present in all minds as a lure of the enemy to destruction, with Averilla as chief beguiler. Songs followed, a big-lunged, swinging chant in which every soul joined with good will. But to Luther, under the spell of another voice and music in expression of a different aspiration, it seemed for the first time to have no meaning, no immediate connection with anything of vital importance in his life.

> "Oh, we'll lay down the Bible and go home.
> Yes, we'll lay down the Bible and go home.
> We'll lay down the Bible and go home.
> Bright angels standing at the door."

"COME, AND WE'LL LEARN YOU TO DANCE," SHE CHALLENGED

mechanically he sang with the rest; but even while the chapter ordained for this sacrament was being read, the boy was trying to remember the weird and moving melody of the ballad of Lady Alizonde which he had heard that evening. Averilla's words were in his mind all during the sermon— an exhortation the fervor of which well-nigh exhausted its deliverer, and wrought the nerves of the listeners to a keen tension. There was still no rain; but the thunder was crashing now, and the lightning outlined the tossing boughs more vividly at every flash.

"Even so ought ye to wash one another's feet," repeated the preacher again and again. Between the threat of storm and the proximity of Sargent's dance, it was inevitable that a note of antagonism should ring out from time to time. "And what did He do then— yes, what did He do then? He girded Himself with a towel. Yes, He girded Himself with a towel." Here Brock knotted towel about his waist. "You hypocrites and sinners in the back o' the camp can jist laugh if you want to; if do ye're a-makin' fun o' what your Master did; I'm a-doin' jist what He did now— yes, I'm a-doin' jist what He did now."

But there was none to smile at the quaintness of the old ceremony, for all except the faithful and those under close parental or avuncular surveillance were half a mile away, dancing to the banjoes. The bread and wine had been passed, and they had begun to sing,

> "In all humility we now
> Each other's feet do lave,"

when the storm came upon them in earnest, as if by the personal malice of a living thing. Light javelins of rain shot through the tree tops, sounding a patter on the leaves; then heavier spears pierced the roof of the brush shelter. A few drops struck the faces of the sleeping babes, who at once woke and added their wail to the clamor. No mountain man minds a wetting, but among the sisters there was a hasty readjustment of sunbonnets and shawls. Several began to shriek hysterical triumph:

"Glory, glory! My soul's happy!"
"Glory to the blessed Lamb!"
"Amen! O sweet Saviour!"
"Glo-o-ry!"

Brock saw that he must take command of the situation. Not for nothing had he been a competent shepherd for thirty-five years. He held up one hand and shouted: "Let us all walk to Brother Lowry's house, singing as we go, and thar continue the sacrament. Brother Rogers," he added in a lower voice, "if you and Brother Lowry'll holp me, we'll carry these pitchers an' things over." He headed the procession with a torch-bearer, both voicing hallelujahs on the way.

Luther intended to follow with a torch: but such a tide of emotion was surging up in him that he wished intensely to be alone for a few minutes at least. He fell back unobserved into the threshing woods; the darkness, wild now with rain, concealed him instantly. He leaned against the trunk of a big tree that afforded some protection from the force of the wind. But almost before the shouting of the congregation in the distance was covered by the roar of the rain on a million leaf-drums, his feet were bearing him in an opposite direction.

"Where am I going?" he muttered; but he knew. "I am weighed in the balance and found— Send the thunderbolt,

O Master!" He bared his throat and looked into the eyes of the storm, thinking how death would be better than the blight that must follow his course. But he felt the tide rising, steady and certain, its current saying always below the thunder, "Averilla— Averilla— Averilla." He must see her face again— he knew, in the very instant of prayer, that he would see her. The rain lashed forward, screaming; the wind got beneath it and lifted and waved it like a sheet; and so he stumbled on, whipped by desire— now the crash and the torrent! Except for the changing play of colored lightnings through the blaring rain he could not see an inch of the way. The earth under his feet trembled to a short, deep booming, nearly continuous— suggestive of close range, of breathless fighting, of the short-arm jolt, of clinch and break away. He breathed deeply, and was glad of the rivulets that coursed over his shoulders and chest. At last he reached the plain road and fell into the swinging stride of the mountains. At the same time the downpour softened to a steady drumming, and the night became a little less dark. He hastened on until he saw the red glow of light from the doorway of Sargent's cabin.

The revel was now at its height. Rain had driven into the porch all the lookers-on, and he was able to peer unobserved in at the low, square window by the chimney. Already flung far off his usual pivot of thought and feeling, he was still further unstrung by the ring-tump-a-tankle of the banjoes and the singing fiddle. His blood bounded to the rhythm of the dancers' play. There was Averilla with 'Vander Bolton, who was dancing with the Indian-like intensity of the mountaineer. Ah! Her dress, her hair, her gleaming face! The perfume of her flesh, the music of her every motion, the warmth and color and charm of her! . . . And he had neither part nor lot in her life. But, oh, if she would only come out— come with warm hands and ripe lips and a tender word— come out to him! If they two together might leave the merrymakers, and the congregation, too, and go utterly away from both! . . .

Some fellows who had been across during a slack in the weather to the jugs in the "little timber," returning noisily to the cabin, half recognized the face at the window and spoke to him. Instinctively he drew back out of the light; and they, deeming now that they must have been mistaken, filed into the house.

Luther did not return to the window; he was unable to endure the sight of Averilla dancing with the other lads. Instead, he cast himself face down under the rose-bushes. Something gleamed pale in the wet grass here— aces and kings of an unlucky deck flung out in the wrath of a loser; he felt an almost physical repugnance toward these symbols of wickedness. But the elder roses, rain-weighted, shattered in a purple drift across his hot temple and cheek, and their scent was that of the dark one in her hair.

Something rustled in the crape-myrtles near him, and he warily got to his feet. Her voice called his name, ever so low. Through his body passed a soft, swift, tingling shock, as if one had touched him unexpectedly. He did not answer at once, but she had seen the movement, and laughed a little.

"Bark 'lowed he seed ye, or somebody powerful like ye, at the window. I'm sure glad you came! I can't stay out here with ye— there's hardly girls enough to make up a set, and they'll come lookin' for me; but you come on in— a little while! Come dance with me." She even drew his arm.

He was able to answer her with firmness, "No." Yet he lingered. And she. Presently he went on, and his voice tense, but truly toned on every word:

"I have this to say to you— you come with me."

She looked at him, wondering.

"The meeting breaks to-night, and to-morrow I'm going on into the valley."

"You'll be back to the baptizin'. "

"I'll not be back to no baptizin'. "

"You'll preach at the Blue Springs church."

"I'll not come back to you again, never no more."

"Then," she pouted, "I'll go to town with pap, and never come back her more, neither."

He was silent. Averilla pursued imaginary advantage.

"If you'll stay, I will. You hate to go!"

"I've got a work to do."

"Ah, what's that? Why?"

But it was his turn now. "Come with me. We'll be married at Uncle Zack's after the foot-washin'."

He stood, his wet hat crushed in his hands, awaiting her answer. For all his strong words, he felt weak as a babe. And Averilla, for all her pretty hesitation, knew her power. She shredded a rose with her lips and fingers before replying. The rain had melted to a drizzling mist, a keen, clean damp that caressed even while it invigorated. The fog usual to wet weather in these altitudes stole upon them now, and shut them round with so close a curtain that they could barely make out the red square of the window. The ring and throb of the dance beat round and through them both. At last said Averilla, sulkily, vexed perhaps because he was not sufficiently jealous to be angry:

"No, there ain't no use talkin' about it. I ain't ready to be tied to any man, let alone a preacher."

It was a buffet in the face. He took it standing straight.

"Good-by, then," he said, keenly hurt.

Suddenly she leaned toward him, caught his face between her two hands, and kissed him on the mouth.

Could it be?— he thought he heard a tremolo of weeping in her "Good-by."

A week may be a fearful lapse of time under some circumstances. Seven days had passed— seven days of wandering with Brother Brock on circuit, of unavailing endeavor to devote his best strength to his chosen allegiance and the work in hand; of fits of bitter rebellion succeeded by bitter remorse; of failure— he knew well enough that the church people were saying he "never done no good sence the Puncheon Camp Bresh-meetin'. " Even Brock had not quite accepted the excuse he gave them for absenting himself from the foot-washing; but no one connected the boy's disappearance with Averilla Sargent, as they might have done if he had been seen with her afterward. Instead, all those to whom he was largely responsible for daily conduct decided merely, with sighs and shaking of grave heads, that he had been withheld from taking part in a peculiar and somewhat antiquated rite by the fear of ridicule.

In a primitive social organization like theirs, the stress of daily living is such that nothing may be spared for the pursuit of pleasure. Any surplus of spirit must be turned to religious exaltation; there is no room for the graces and caprices of idleness. And whatsoever is not for must be against the one symbol of unity, the church. Where law is lax, and the elaborately linked mail of convention is absent, the only moral protection of the community is its religion. Hence the line drawn between the belle and the wanton is but slight; both are wasters of men, though the waste be only of time needed at the plough and of mental purpose that should be devoted Bible study. A lad's opportunity is scant enough at best for getting together his meagre start of property, acquiring the rudimentary education necessary to his daily round, probably eking out some small knowledge of a particular trade or craft, and finally selecting and winning a partner for that domestic stability which is his one chance of life's happiness. He has no time to spend in catching butterflies. A man whose welfare depends on the crop of an acre is criminally foolish to sow any of it in wild oats.

But, in thus depriving beauty of excuse for being, the danger is not first and chiefly to those who undervalue loveliness and charm and so miss them out of life; the real peril is to these qualities themselves, lest, accepting the valuation, they disport themselves accordingly. Venus and Diana, when they could be no longer divine, metamorphosed into vampire and demon. Were the lilies of the field to become convinced that they were creatures of evil, they might not cease blooming, but it is certain that they would begin at once to secrete poisonous juices.

Averilla dressed herself most carefully on that midsummer Sunday morning; the shining hair was brushed to lustrous smoothness, and done in the way she knew to be most becoming: as for adornments, she waited till she could find them by Aunt Sa' Jane's gate. Any other mountain girl would have kept away from the Lowry cabin after what had happened, but no knight of old ever took more openly the path of conquest than this wearer of the dark rose. She sang as she walked, the ballad she had begun for Luther:

> " 'O Alizonde,' the stranger sang,
>   'The mortal sins are seven,
> And sweetest you of all sweet sin—
>   What hope have I of heaven?'
>   *If you love me as I love you,*
>   *O haste not into danger!*
>
> " 'For Christian knight, my fault is dire
>   As may not be forgiven,
> But lo, you, lady, of your rose
>   My soul shall pass unshriven.'
>   *If you love me as I love you,*
>   *What need have we of heaven?*"

She passed the groups of old men in the yard, noted that the boys were already pitching horseshoes about the barn, and appeared to Aunt Sa' Jane, where that matron sat shelling pease in her kitchen, still singing a little under her breath and looking about with an enigmatic expression. Aunt Sa' Jane glanced warily up. It would almost seem she was afraid of the girl. "Thank God, Luther ain't here to see her like that," crossed the old woman's mind as she got the full beauty of the glowing face and alert young figure against the light.

"Aunt Sa' Jane," began the newcomer, dropping lightly into a chair and beginning to help with the pease, "1 come over to ask could I stay with you while pap and the boys goes down to the Settlement and finds out that they don't like it. I ain't willin' to leave the mountains— not yet awhile, anyhow. Will ye keep me?"

Lord, these young girls, as wasteful of time and opportunity as they were of the hearts and lives of men! Who was going to pay for Averilla's keep if she left her father's roof? Yet, in an absolutely even, almost caressing tone, the elder woman answered her.

"Now, Averilly," she began, "I wouldn't feel that-a-way about hit, if I was you. Yo' pa needs ye. There's a heap o' good friendly folks lives in the Settlement, and you're more suited like to 'em in many a way than you air to the mountain. I reckon they have a dance mighty nigh every night down thar."

The girl pouted. "I don't know as I'll ever dance again," she murmured in a sulky tone that infinitely alarmed Aunt Sa' Jane. If she was going to carry her pursuit of Luther to the extent of playing saint for a while, the poor boy was certainly doomed.

"They's an association I've hearn tell of down there, whar the best kind of young folks get together," Aunt Sa' Jane pursued, eagerly. "I don't know as they dance, and I don't know *but* they dance; yet I've heard tell that the gals has a sewin'-meetin'— sorter like a quiltin'— about onct-every-so-often, and I reckon the boys comes—town boys, with town manners. That ort to be fine."

She was decoying the girl as craftily as ever a mother partridge lures the enemy from her nest. Averilla turned away her face, feeling rebuked, disappointed, and not a little angry. But Aunt Sa' Jane, having exhausted her resources of information concerning social opportunity in the Settlement, laid hastily hold of her next artifice.

"Now, here's a way ye can holp me," she broke off, reaching a folded paper from the high smoke-enamelled fireboard. "I got a letter yistidy, and all them men's been a-passin' hit from hand to hand. But Luther he don't write none too well, and we cayn't none of us read to do any good, so we ain't made out but part of hit."

The pease were forgotten. "From Luther!" cried Averilla, springing up so suddenly that she almost overturned the pan. But when the letter was put in her hand it proved disappointing. True, it said that he was coming—that he would be here this very morning— but it requested Aunt Sa' Jane to have his few books and other belongings collected and ready, since he expected to "leave." There was no explanation of where he was going, nor why; and the sheet rattled in the girl's trembling fingers.

"Well, there now!—I reckon he's a-goin' to take the far circuit. Wants his books—and I ain't got up a one 'em!" exclaimed Aunt Sa' Jane, determined to bring the lesson home to her hearer. "You wanted to holp me, Averilly; cayn't you jest step into the middle chamber and lay what you know t be Luther's on the big bed, ready for packin'? He's jest that-a-way, ef he's set his mind to go this mornin', only this mornin' will do him."

The spring was all out of the girl's step as she entered the middle room. There were his books on the shelf, but she stretched no hand to collect them. Instead, she sat down on the edge of the bed, leaned her cheek on her hand, and fell into a muse. Was Luther running away from her? She wondered if he was really going to take that far circuit which Aunt Sa' Jane suggested as his destination.

The inner chamber was closed against the sun glare, that it might not become heated through the summer day. A buzz of flies and the ticking of a clock sounded faintly from the main house. As her eyes became accustomed to the dim light, she made out the newspapered wall, the mirror on the old bureau, the boys clothes, of worn and faded home-spun, mostly, hung beneath the gun-racks, and their rough box-trunks ranged below. A stately cat was visible in the open loft, watching a mouse-hole, and lizards hunting flies flickered in and out of chinks in the sun-warmed roof. She looked at the four posters spread with counterpanes beautifully woven, wondering which of the pillows was to bear Luther's head this night. For ever since Aunt Sa' Jane had knit and washed his socks, and taught him the Bible she could barely read, and made his daily life for him, Luther had slept in this room with her other boys, and worked with them in the fields by day.

From without came faintly the chatter little ones building a play-house, the murmur under the trees, and now and again a brief and delicate warble of wrens from the nest beneath the eaves. Once there was an angry gobble, followed immediately by the yap of a scared puppy, and general laughter.

Then, abruptly, the heavy wooden shutter was pulled open and a dark rose flung smote her cheek and dropped softly her lap. After it a banjo was passed through the unglazed window and laid carefully on the counterpane. She caught her breath, for she thought she knew the hand

AVERILLA TURNED AWAY HER FACE, REBUKED AND DISAPPOINTED

holding the instrument. Leaning forward, she whispered only the name— "Luther!"

Instantly his face appeared in the window. There was a silent moment of hesitation. He half turned away; but Averilla was not to be so balked.

"Luther— wait, Luther," she began softly. "Aunt Sa' Jane give me your letter to read. Was you— did you aim to go away? I was tryin' to get a chance stay here."

He turned startled eyes upon her.

"To stay here?" he repeated, almost harshly. He studied her down-bent countenance intently, then put one hand on the window-sill and leaped in with a clear spring. Once where he could reach her, he turned her face up to his own, and, holding it thus between his palms, began his interrogatory.

"What did you want to stay here tor?

"You," responded Averilla, almost under her breath.

He laughed out suddenly. "And I was goin' to the Settlement after you," he told her, without reserve or modification. "I can't live without you, Averil. I can't forget you. I ain't no 'count for man nor preacher if I can't have you."

He dropped his arms down about her waist, and she laid her head on his breast. " Well," she said, softly, " you've got me, Luther. Does that make it right?"

"Yes— yes— yes! It's bound to. It makes everything right. I ain't no 'count for a preacher, anyhow. God knows I never meant to fail at . . . but this— this is stronger than I am. You can learn me to play cards and dance, Averil. I— we've got to be happy."

The beautiful head came up with a start. The girl stared at him with dilating dark eyes. She put a hand where her head had lain and pushed him away from her.

"No— no— no!" she cried, as if in answer to her lover's speech. "Oh, you haven't understood. You've got it all wrong, Luther. I'll go with you when you're to preach. I'll lead the singin'. Everybody shall see that here's one soul you've saved. Oh, Luther, I can be good— for you."

A moment they clung together, trembling. The room was very still. Summer sounds from outside wafted through its casement. Whatever had been of misunderstanding, whatever seemed foreign in this change that had entered their lives, melted away. This was the supreme moment. They were not mere man and woman— they were mates.

Published in
Harper's Monthly Magazine - February 1909

The Dulcimore

EMMA BELL MILES

ILLUSTRATIONS BY W. HERBERT DUNTON

THE MOUNTING SUMMER HAD AT LAST ESCAPED THE GRASP of the April chill, and the season's growth came on with a headlong rush. The forest was one rustling loom of life-stuff, everywhere thrilling to million-tinted glories of summer beauty and abundance. Between twin hills that lay against the sky, dark and softly rounded as the breasts of a slave-mother, the old smithy nestled. It was a log structure, low and windowless, and lighted like a grotto with blue and greenish reflections from the hot sunshine outside.

The young giant in the leather apron was clanking steadily on with his task, albeit he had a visitor. Straight from trysting with the wind among the blossoming laurel on the hill, she came into this place of grime and toil, with perfume yet on her garments, and her dreams in her eyes. Georgia Carden, daughter of old Jared Carden and his wife Selina, who lived on a good farm under which coal had been found in fairly profitable quantities, was a noted figure in her environment.

"She sha'n't go with the young folks around here," her mother said, half fiercely. "Let her roam as she will; the woods 'll be all lumber and tan-bark soon enough; let her enjoy them while she can."

In the twenty years of her wifehood, which began with galling poverty, Selina Garden's pride had never faltered, yet she had not been so foolish as to prefer utter failure to makeshift. She adapted herself in order not to die, and she had so managed that all her children were actually rich. For each babe that came were the clean changes, constantly forthcoming on demand, that she could not afford for herself. For the new babe's sake she forbore cruel toil a while. Later, she furbished her early knowledge to set them in the way of permanent riches, by teaching them what she knew of their immediate world, supplementing the crude schooling which was all they could have, to fit them to enjoy a life which had never been hers. But the Carden lads, as they grew, would have none of such impalpable possessions. Georgia alone, on the opening of the coal veins beneath the farm, asked the reason for the dainty fern-prints in the shale. Her brothers echoed only chance-caught information about freight rates and comparative values. Was it strange that the girl, her youngest, seemed of all Selina's children peculiarly her own— that the usual mother-dream of a relation to endure indefinitely was here intensified?

"Howdy, Return," the girl spoke from the doorway, her light lawn dress blowing about her, the sun at her back, facing the shadows. Her mother's indulgence had given her years of faerie wanderings and dreaming to remember; and now any day that dawned might hold ere sunset the hour of the Prince's coming, the morning of love, with music and white light. The consciousness of this imminence was aglow in her face as she flitted across the earthen floor and perched mothlike on the work-bench, where scraps and broken tools were piled in rusty confusion.

By way of welcome the young smith fetched her a drink of cool spring water in a dripping gourd. There was something about him that seemed near akin to the silent, incomprehensible, tireless earth itself. Toward her freshness and sweetness all his being drew with a yearning like that of the tides heaving moonward from unsounded depths; though one looking on would never have guessed it.

"I'll fix you a better place to sit," he said, and his voice had the sweetness of bees droning in honey-drunken meadows. It was an odd, murmuring speech, coming and lapsing like natural sounds, but very pleasant to hear.

"I can see better from here," Georgia argued, tucking one foot under her. "What's that you're making? I want to watch you work."

"Jist a cow-bell," replied Return Ritchie. "Man up the valley's got two heifers might' near alike, and it's his notion to bell 'em as near the same as he can; so I'm aimin' to match this here." He showed his model, and sounded it so that the clear tone filled the cavern of liquid-cool shadow. They smiled at each other, and he turned to blow the forge fire. A red flare shot up and illumined the smoky walls.

With the big pincers he drew out of the coals a thin sheet of iron cut into the required shape. She watched him bend it round the anvil's beak and deftly seam the sides before the metal darkened. Afterward he riveted the seams, fixed a staple rivet in the top to hold the clapper, and added a bar through which to run the collar strap.

"Now it's ready for brazing?" she inquired, with interest.

"Now it's ready; only brass has got so high that they mostly have to be brazed with copper; and copper's copper these days, let me tell ye. You never see one made afore, Georgie?"

"I never did. You're always making things; that's why I stopped in— that and to see Aunt Lucy." She looked on while he laid the bits of copper over the outer surface, wrapped them in place with a wet rag, and packed the whole bell inside and out with clay. Then he fired the mass, pulling regularly on the bellows.

"Now, when I take it out the fire," he told her, "the copper 'll be run in a thin coat clean over hit— all ready to put a clapper into and hang on the cow. This one here's been coppered— see?— and the copper's all wore and knocked off." He leaned that she might take the old bell from his hand.

"I expect it's travelled many a hundred miles through these woods, along of the cow, into wilder places than ever I've been," said the girl, holding it up. " Listen! Don't it ring sweet?— Do-re-me- faaaa! Return, can you read music?"

"Any Jack can read them songs they've been learning at the Blue Springs church," he allowed. "But without shaped notes I'm liable to git lost. I can't read the words any too well yit."

"I told poppa I was sure I could pick out tunes if he'd only buy me an organ; I'd love to have all-day singing at our house, and so would mother. But you know he calls all instruments 'inventions of idleness.' " She laughed deprecatingly. "If I even had a fiddle, like yours— Could I play that, Return, you reckon?

"You could learn. I'll learn you." If the words sounded gruff and ungracious, it was because he was taken unawares by the sudden opportunity. Here abruptly was the opening for which, all through the spring months, he had planned with such quiverings of hope and trepidation. Now the way was easy for presentation of his gift. Yet he found it necessary to make his approach obliquely, mountaineer fashion.

"D'you ever see a dulcimore?" he began, after a silence.

"One or two."

"How would one do, instead of a organ?"

"It would be music."

"I've— I've got one."

"You— What say, Return?"

"I've made ye one— a dulcimore." The new bell was imperilled while he groped into the recesses of his tool-box. Presently he held toward her a queerly shaped instrument of three strings, a little larger than a mandolin. It was whittled with innumerable patient touches out of dark-brown oak, unvarnished, the head resembling a fiddle's, but curiously carved in an attempt at ornamentation— a thing fitted only for the wild minors of native airs.

She took it and jumped to the ground; silent with surprise, she stood holding the dulcimore in both hands.

HE FIRED THE MASS, PULLING REGULARLY ON THE BELLOWS

"I sent back where Aunt Lucy was raised, in the other valley, for the pattern," he said, uneasily. "They've got lots of 'em there. . . ."

"Did you make this for me, Return?"

He pulled at the bellows, and made believe not to hear.

"You did make this for me?" she asked again, slowly; and at her tone a tremor of joy went over his averted face.

"I knowed you liked music," he muttered, as though offering an apology.

Still wondering and admiring her gift, she seated herself in the main doorway, on the sill white with road dust, and began to draw the strings into the weird and plaintive harmony of which they were capable.

Without letting go the bellows, he tossed into her lap a triangular plectrum of smoothed bone.

"You pick hit with that," said he; and, meeting the girl's eyes, was suddenly mastered by the laugh of utter delight that he had been trying to restrain.

A gray little figure appeared in the opposite doorway, which connected with his home cabin and truck-patch.

"I 'lowed I heared some music," quavered Return's only relative, the old aunt who had raised him. "Oh, hit's you, Georgie. Howdy, honey?" She came into the smithy, and the young man brought her a broken wagon-seat. She settled herself to look over a lapful of wild greens she had gathered.

"Eh, law!" she commented, when the dulcimore had been explained to her, "and that's what he's been a-whittlin' on all winter. Whar I come from the young gals used to sing to them things." She sat nodding and smiling, tapping the floor with her foot while Georgia coaxed a shadowy melody between false starts and fumbled fingerings. It was but a little time before impatience got the better of the air, and Barney McCoy fell away into faint monotonous chords.

"Well, I must be going," the girl said finally, rising. She cherished the little brown dulcimore in tender fingers, slipping her hands softly over its rough whittled sides as though she smoothed a child's tousled head. "Return," she said as she turned away, "if it's clear to-night, you come up to the house and bring your fiddle. We'll tune it with my dulcimore then. Maybe against that time I'll have learned how to play a little. If the moon shines, you and me and mother and the boys can all go down to the waterfall and sing there like we used to. Good-by, Aunt Lucy."

But the moon did not shine. That same evening a terrific storm, the tail of a hurricane beating up from the Gulf, swept over the valley. Throughout the half-hour of the storm's endurance the play of lightning was almost continuous. Between the twin hills, where it was caught and concentrated as if in the nose of the smithy's bellows, it went roaring like a battle. Day broke nearly cloudless over the wreckage that strewed the fields. Wherever a twist of the wind's erratic course had driven hardest, there was ruin. Return's chimney had crashed through his roof; and the old aunt's life had passed with the passing of the storm.

For weeks thereafter Return was a man lost in his own walls. He tried to go on as usual, but every hour of the day had its peculiar strangeness, upsetting all the habits of his life. The effort to eat in solitude a dish of his own contriving choked him. He had retained from his healthy childhood a sound, simple delight in the mere round of the day; but now, from the time of rising, when the early sunbeams shone on no little gray figure by the kitchen window, with deft hands moulding the morning's biscuit, to the sunset hour of rest on the deserted porch, nothing was as it should be.

"Poor Aunt Lucy! Jist looks like I cain't get over it," he muttered again and again. The presence of death seemed ever with him in its unsupportable majesty. "I reckon that's what sets people to thinkin' about ha'nts in houses," he reflected, forlornly. The unlighted lamp, the empty rooms, were terrible to him. The silence oppressed like a weight of dark waters. He mended the broken roof and rebuilt the chimney; then he resumed regular work in the blacksmith shop, and frequently prolonged his labors far into the night for sheer dread of the gaping doors.

In these days Georgia made the discovery that she had, while awaiting the Prince, unwittingly become bound to Return. She had a period of bewildered astonishment. How could this be her lover, this man of the stony soil?

One twilight, between mocking-bird and whippoorwill, sitting by the spring near her home, she told him, utterly trusting herself and him. In their great moment the habit of proud reserve cheapened suddenly to insignificance, and the shyness of youth fell from their hearts as the clay had shattered from around the perfected bell.

"I can't leave you, never, no more than if I was your mother," she said, with quaint frankness.

The dulcimore and the fiddle lay forgotten at their feet. But the gladness she looked for did not come at once into his face.

"I used to wonder sometimes, when we was little folks singin' by the falls, if you wouldn't come to me some day," he answered, gravely, with a deep tenderness. "I've always wanted you, but I had about give up. Have you thought, girl? . . . You must talk to your folks first."

"Whatever they say can't make any difference to me, Return," she promised. "I don't mind about the others; but mother— I'm afraid she's going to take it hard."

"I would do the very best I could for you, sister; you know that. But she'll think it's not good enough. . . . It's not good enough; but—"

Beyond the word there stood something too vague for expression, something great enough to face all opposing considerations with perfect calm. He wrinkled his big brows. "People have to put up with things sometimes," he brought out finally.

"And I couldn't see this coming," moaned Georgia's mother, as the two sat on the porch at twilight. "I could not see. I was afraid, too, for you to keep that dulcimore he made you; but music seemed to be your happiness— and your father wouldn't let you have the organ. Oh, I ought to have guarded you. But I never dreamed that such a man could have any attraction for a girl reared and taught as you have been. Why, Georgia, it can't be more than a passing fancy. Don't, don't think of it longer than you can help, dear, and it 'll go by. You can't mean to ruin your life!" And fear stood in her eyes.

To her, Return was little more than the freckled urchin with ready grin and a missing front tooth who had used to thank her for cookies. Georgia saw him transfigured by a light of dreams into something finer than he would ever appear to his fellows. He was still the barefoot playmate, but he was also in some way the Sungod. Which were the truer estimate, let him say who has dwelt longest in that unearthly radiance. Into the mother's mind flashed two conflicting urgencies— the need for prompt action if she would save her daughter, and the fear that one ill-considered word might fumble her slipping hold. Already she fell her grasp loosening, moment by moment, as Georgia before her eyes became a woman.

Her little girl!

Afraid to leave the subject where it had fallen, she hurried on: "Georgia, dear, you shall go down into the Valley— to the Academy— and have some music lessons. You've always wanted to; now you shall, honey; I'll manage it somehow. And time you come home I'll make your father buy you an organ. I can. I've never asked much of him; but I can make him do that."

"Music lessons— an organ!" echoed Georgia, piteously. "Why, that couldn't make any difference, mother— though I'd love to have them, to play for— him."

Her face expressed only wonder and pity. Poor mother! Did she believe the whole world of music would count for a minute against Return? There was no hesitation, no complexity, in the girl's mental processes. She had given herself to love— to her lover— she was wondering now how best to comfort her mother. It was as simple as a plant's attitude toward the sun.

The mother, leaning forward, clutched the slim wrists of the girl with both her dingy, toil-maimed hands. In her extremity she sought for help whence help had never come to her.

"Has he asked your father for you, then?" she inquired, huskily. "And you never spoke one word to me about it! Georgia, my poor child, this is worse than ever I thought. Oh, put it out of your mind. If you are too young to realize what is due to yourself, try to think, dear, is nothing due to me, your mother? I was nursing you and slaving for you when Return Ritchie was riding stick horses!"

"Yes, he asked father," the girl said, gently. "He says poppa told him I could do as I pleased. Poppa likes him." A little wistfully: "I'm sorry Return spoke to him before I named it to you."

"You're blinded," spoke Selina, heavily. "You can't see now; but when you wake up and find yourself dragged down to the level of his people, it will break your heart."

Looking into the young face, its roseate velvet all atremble with new emotions, the mother felt as though striving in a nightmare with bending, splintering weapons. She had reason to know that she was impotently dashing herself upon no human adversary, but one of those laws that seemed always arrayed against her, always defeating her heart's hopes, always crushing her pitilessly. Had she not fought this same losing fight once before? She had never forgotten the days and weeks before her own marriage; the struggling, resisting, calling to her aid all habit and tradition, all maidenly reserve and family pride— in vain. She had suffered in withstanding; she had suffered in yielding; and her suffering had not mattered in the least, would not matter now. Oh, the big blind forces, the dark brute powers! Why was it allowed, this stupendous cruelty? Who allowed it? She was near to arraigning the great laws of the universe.

Yet she gathered herself for the battle. Before, it had been to save herself from she knew not what; now, with experience behind her, she would fight to save her daughter from a fate all too bitterly certain. She would appeal to Return also, to the rude and genuine good heart of him. There, if nowhere else, might be a chance . . .

"Oh, listen to reason, Georgia, before it's too late. You don't know—" Her tongue ran into wild and futile repetitions. She became conscious of them and caught herself up. "Dear, you can't see what is ahead of you, or you would not think for a moment of doing this thing. Only let me tell you what it has been like with me. I never would let you know— I hoped I should never have to tell you. Just listen to me . . ."

She poured it all forth now, the story of the bitter years . . . "And they don't care," she whispered. "They don't know. Nobody knows but your own self. You never saw your uncles. My brothers wouldn't visit us. When things were at their worst they wrote and wrote, urging me to come back, to leave him; offering a home, offering work, offering to educate the children— anything, if I only would. Seemed like they couldn't give me up to lead such a life. They don't write any more now, of course— but then . . . One baby after another. Yet the babies were all that kept me alive. It's a miracle any of you got through; we hadn't any decent— arrangements. Oh, I suppose I was all that kept them alive, too— my body held between you-all and death. You look as though you thought that was something glorious! I tell you there's nothing romantic about cooking three meals a day with a teething baby on one arm and your face tied up with neuralgia. Nothing heroic about washing overalls, or following your man to the barn with a lantern at two o'clock on a February night to tend to young lambs, either. And look at me!" She stood up, a scarred and darkened ruin. "Look at me! It's what you'll be; it's the best you can hope to be. You that I slaved for— you that I nursed— the only one that is mine! Georgia, daughter, tell me you won't do it!"

"I won't, mother!" cried the girl, the heart wrung out of her by grief and compassion. "I'll stay with you. Return will understand. I'll take care of you—"

"No! I won't have you sacrifice your life for me any more than for him. Oh, you don't know. . . . It would be easy enough to die for a man; it's hard to live for him— to give him all your life just when you want it most yourself. And when you think you have given the last that is in you, comes a new demand. You can't back out; you've got to meet it. Why, I've done things I can't talk about even now— things any woman will tell you she can't do. I had to! Take care of me? Why, I'm easy now; I've reached the best life holds for me so far as rest and plenty are concerned. The hard work is over, and the long pain, and the cold. And the worry. But the disappointment will never be over."

She was striving for self-control now, overcoming by main strength an impulse toward the hysteric crying of despair.

"And it's no use! I see by your face that it's no use talking. Was it for this I have stood between you and the work and the hardships— have I carried the burden for years on my own shoulders only to see you take it up at last? Oh,

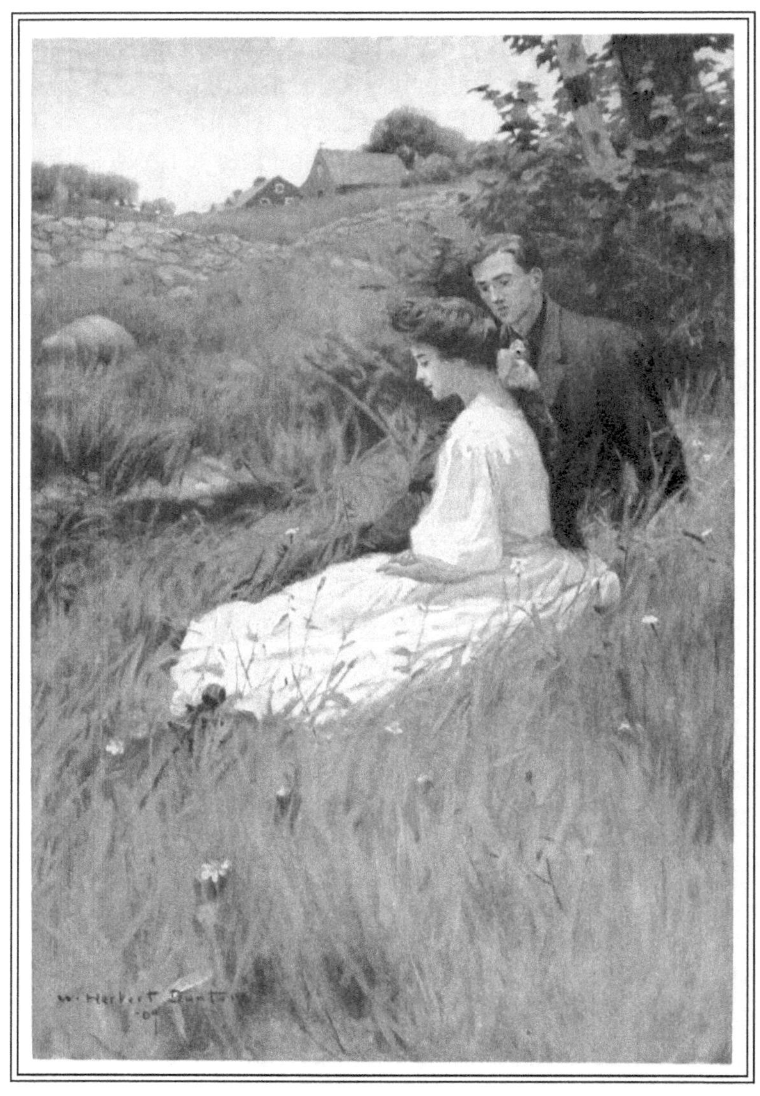

IN THEIR GREAT MOMENT THE SHYNESS OF YOUTH FELL FROM THEIR HEARTS

I've waited and watched, praying for a chance to send you away— to lift you out of such a life. I want you to have a chance . . ."

Poor woman! she had meant to be all in all to her child, at least until the coming of larger opportunity. And now here lay her treasure on the quicksands!

"But— Love?" whispered the girl, blushing exquisitely. "It was you, mother, taught me what love means. I— I used to wonder how you could bear— poppa's ways, until I came to see that you accepted them as parts of him, like his voice and hair; and you accepted him twenty years ago. People think their children don't notice; but— it's beautiful, beautiful, mother."

There was a wonderful light in the eyes she raised timidly, pleadingly, to the elder woman in the soft dusk.

"I taught you?" Selina's voice was hard. "Well, then, I can teach you the better, maybe, that this feeling you have now— won't last. It can't last. You believe it will, but it can't. Do you suppose I didn't have it? Ah! you think it lasted— for me?" She laughed bitterly. "Georgia, if you throw yourself away, I have lost all that made life bearable." Her face fell into lines of gloomy reverie as she looked away.

"She is remembering," thought the girl. "She had love once; she was young; she hardly knew what trouble was or pain. Now there is only heartache." She called up in her own memory as much as she had known or guessed of her mother's trials, and her eyes filled with tears. Yet it detracted nothing from the mysterious splendor of her own fate that its terror must be set over against its beauty. The glamour which invested her lover's figure would be no less bright if her crown promised to be one of thorns.

"Love," the woman's voice touched the word as though it were something hot which burned. The eyes of her spirit seemed to glance at it as though its brightness seared. "Love— Oh, Georgia, you don't know." Her tones sank, her head drooped forward; but she spoke again. "When I first came here, to teach the little school in the cove, I was as full of dreams as you are. I had money saved to finish my education; I wanted to be somebody. But I waked up and found myself married . . ."

The girl cried: "But you don't have to live so! What makes you?" Swift indignation at the man who had claimed all this possessed her. Less wise than her mother, she did not see past him to the eternal law, the Way of Things, of which he was but an expression.

"What makes me?" A dull interrogation showed through the blank and beaten face. "Why don't you go to your people?" pursued Georgia.

"Why haven't you gone long ago? Back to your own life!"

Selina stared for a second, and then threw out both hands with a motion as of casting something from her.

"Oh, I couldn't do that," she wailed. "Georgia, what would become of *him?*"

The girl's eyes, already wonder-filled, widened and widened as the full significance of these words went home.

"You see!" she breathed.

"See what?" queried the elder, tonelessly, detecting a low note of something akin to triumph in the cry. "Mother!" She clasped her warm young arms round the bent and quaking shoulders.

"Mother! Don't you see, now—" The rest was a whisper. "Now you have showed me— what love is, what it means to us women."

Selina sobbed on uncomforted for a time. At last she became quiet, and leaning her head on her hands, sighed wearily.

Dusk had deepened almost to night about them, sparkling with fireflies and throbbing to wilder songs than are heard by day. From the turn of the lane, where all the sweetness of the blossoming earth was being evoked by the dew, came suddenly the cooing of strings beneath a bow's caress. The girl's eyes lighted softly.

"I don't know," said Selina, without raising her head. "He's not fit for you. But. . . . he will always be a good man. And" — nervelessly— "it's the only way to live, I suppose. Maybe— by and by— I can be reconciled. But— My poor daughter!"

The strings sounded again, nearer, and as though at the touch of the unseen wapentake the girl rose. She looked long down the shadowy vista with that light upon her face that can shine but once in a lifetime; then turning, she reached from its shelf within the house door the little dulcimore that held all of music her life would ever attain.

Published in
Harper's Monthly Magazine - November 1909

The Home-Coming of Evelina

EMMA BELL MILES

SHE WAS AGHAST AT THIS LAST FAILURE OF HER long-nourished hope. As she plodded beside the pitiful stack of battered and rusty household gear—home-made for the most part, and the rest indescribably cheap and ugly—Evelina Kell, with her babe at her breast, found herself muttering and moaning over and over: "Oh, I'm sick of it—I want to go home. I'm sick, I want to go home—I want to go home." Tears at last blinded her eyes so that she stumbled. Her husband turned from his team with a kindly admonition.

"Now, mother, you 'd better hush that, or you 'll make yourself sick sure enough, goin' on so. Ride, honey; git up an' ride—the nags can stand it. Whatever air ye grievin' so about, anyhow? Look what a sightly evenin' it is—red— we 'll have a fine day to-morrow."

She listened with a bitter, discrediting half-smile. This year, what with Anselm's illness and a fire, the stack of household goods had dwindled until there was room for her to ride beside the children. The baby was now old enough to sit by her instead of being carried— "though there 'll be one in arms before the next movin', " she said bitterly, communing with herself under her shadowing sunbonnet. Moreover, the team and wagon, such as they were, were this time Anselm's own. "But there, we had to sell the cow to git it. Oh, I wish 't I could just go home . . ."

She climbed submissively up. Jolting, swaying, sweltering, powdered thick with dust, the forlorn little group moved along between the ridges, stopping now and again to rest the mules or to drink of the wayside water. It was to Samples' Mill they were going this time, and with every mile the country became wilder, more heavily wooded. Evelina scarcely spoke as they rode along; the little ones drowsed, or sat in apathetic silence, only at intervals pointing out a rock or a bird's nest amid the undergrowth. Anselm, seeing the general despondency, tried to cheer his woman as he ploughed through the dust, by assuring her of the tight shack and level truck-patch he had rented, and telling her how the mill men had offered him a chance to buy both. She murmured yes and yes, without interest. From having sojourned in many shacks she knew about what this one would be like—windowless, hot in summer and cold in winter as a paper shell, filled with fleas by the stray hogs that had slept under its floor, and impossible to render clean or attractive. As for the chance of buying—that, too, was an old story.

"Anyhow, I'm glad," said Anselm, fumbling for hold on his wonted cheerfulness, "that we decided to come out here instead of holin' up in Free-fight for the winter."

The wagon jolted and rattled over the stony road. Anselm was a sunburned, lithe fellow, with a good-humored, three-cornered face that held structurally a hint of mirth in it. His wife resented that look just now. Both the children were whimpering, and she addressed their father with a querulous tremor in her voice.

"I'm plumb wore out with this ridin', " she said.

He could make no headway against her disaffection; he could not warm or cheer her; he began to feel piqued, and became sulky. It was some time before he again spoke, glancing at the sun.

"Well, I reckon we'll make hit ag'in dark," he observed. "The little fellers must be gittin' tired, too."

Again, when the shadows were flung far across the road: "Hit ain't more 'n two mile furder. Our place is right on the p'int o' this ridge."

All drew a deep breath, and shifted position on the creaking, clattering load. Then, without warning, the off forewheel dropped into a chughole. There was a lurch, a strain, a crash of splintering wood; the children shrieked, the team plunged for a moment while their driver shouted and plied his whip. Then the calamity was quietly accepted, and all began to scramble into the road.

"Haf to take this wheel to the mill blacksmith's," said Anselm, tapping the smashed rim and tire with his whip-stock.

"And us camp here!" exclaimed the woman; but that was the extent of her outcry. Oh, well; it was of a piece with all the rest. Her lips were drawn as she went about unloading the needed bits of furniture, while her man unhitched and fed the mules.

"I'll go down into the breaks yonder," he proposed, surveying the land with an experienced eye, "and see if I can find us some water afore it's too dark. You know where them matches is at?"

She set the little ones to gathering brushwood, and presently on wayside bush and weed shone the shaken brightness, as ruddy a blaze as ever graced a hearth. But while the woman sliced the salt pork for their repast she was moaning softly, under the sound of crackling and bubbling, "I want to go back home"; and, though the children raced to her in delight over the find of a quaintly freaked box-terrapin no larger than a coin, and though Anselm appeared next moment with brimming buckets, having had the luck to stumble on a good spring not a hundred yards from the road, her heart lay like a stone.

All her life Evelina Kell had belonged to that portion of the mountain people who, sometimes through restlessness, sometimes driven by dire poverty, are continually shifting their habitations. Her father, Daniel Beaver, was not poor among his neighbors; he was only a type in which the instincts of the settler are forever conflicting with those of the rover. His way was to choose a piece of wild land, clear and fence a few acres, open a well-spring, build a cabin and a stable or smokehouse, raise his own cow-peas and truck for a season or two—and then, almost before Bess and Piedy were thoroughly assured of the whereabouts of the milk-pap, he would swap the whole for a larger piece of wilderness somewhere farther back, and begin the whole task anew. By this means he had owned, at one time or another, nearly every tract of arable ground on Sourwood Mountain, and, with the help of his strong sons and willing neighbors, built some twenty cabins. There is a tradition in the coves of Sourwood to-day that old man Beaver had a raisin' every fall and a barn-raisin' every other fall, his wife having a quiltin' on the off year. It used to be said that his dog, on seeing the wagon backed against the door, waited no commands, but ran at once to hustle in the chickens— all save one knowing old rooster whom some wag described as meekly holding up his legs to be tied.

So Beaver grew old in the full content of usefulness. In that land of pioneers he had been of inestimable service to his kind— like the historic Johnnie Appleseed of a more northern region. That the fruits of his husbandry must be plucked by others— that strange footsteps trod the puncheons of his hewing, and the laughter of babes unnamed by him echoed along the timbers he had mortised— this troubled him not at all. He made a good living and, with his five sons, enjoyed the almost nomadic life. But he wore out two wives in the process; and all his eight daughters had married pathetically young, hoping to escape, like Noah's dove, to the solid ground of a permanent home.

In Evelina's case the hope of haven proved a mirage. She had indeed married a man in whom the domestic instinct was dominant, but Anselm was no manager. He tried work in the mines "yon side the mount'n," and was at one time a hand on the valley railroad; he had tended the grist-mill on Caney's Creek, and there turned occasional pennies by fashioning bread-bowls of maple wood and baskets of oak splints. He had once set up a primitive jug-factory among the creek beds of pale-blue clay; and in season he helped with sorghum-grinding, cotton-picking, and fruit-packing on the valley farms. Shreds and ravellings these of any proper calling; yet Anselm was so hard and willing a worker that he always kept bread in their mouths and a roof over them. Evelina's sorrow was that the roof should be so frequently changed; for he never attained their common desire of a four-acre plot and cabin of their own. Something always happened just when they seemed about to settle— he lost his job, or learned of a better one elsewhere; the water failed, or they became convinced the place was unhealthy. Whatever the reason, the fact was that every year, sometimes oftener, they "shut the door and called the dog." To Evelina that proverb was a hateful mockery. Her part in the moving inevitably meant three or four days of hard work and exposure to the weather. The children seemed always fretful and ailing on moving day. Sometimes their scant bedding became damp with mountain mist. Often on the steeps they had to unpack the load and carry it piecemeal over a difficult pass. Once night overtook them stalled in midstream where Anselm had mistaken the ford. If they had a cow she was sure to break loose somewhere along the route and lead them a weary and anxious chase before they could start again. The children were all so nearly of a size that, until the last two or three moves, no one could be trusted to secure another on their precarious perch atop the bedding roll. And upon their heads was the summer sun and dust, or else the cruel frost, or a searching rain that might turn at any time into needles of snow. To-day's moving, in fine spring weather, was an exception.

The sun was gone behind the woods. Azalea fragrance floated in great waves from out of the hollow, and the whip-poorwills began calling. The road, white as if covered thick in meal, and printed over already with little bare feet, ran straight into the green tangle and was lost; butterfly-peas and centaury roses bloomed beside the way; fireflies sparkled in the shadow. Between the oaks was a glimpse of a blue hill like— well, she could not quite remember what blue vista, far in girlhood, was like to this one. But that blossoming chestnut tree, with its clear, vibrant hum of bees in the honeyed dusk, reminded her of the one at . . . no; again, she could not fix the memory.

"This place feels like hit used to at home," she sighed, when the supper was over and the children asleep on a pallet spread under the trees.

"Which home?" queried her husband, and awaited no reply. The moon glimmered through the boughs, and the camp-fire slowly faded to a skein of pungent smoke in the darkness. "We gotta get up early. I want to have that wheel mended at the mill forge afore breakfast, and git a soon start if we can."

So a second pallet was prepared, and on its hard, uneven length they stretched their weary limbs.

For a time she was wakeful, while the deep stillness and loneliness of the forest night took hold upon her heart. She lay breathing quietly, lapped like a lifeless thing in a sadness too great to be altogether of a personal quality; the weight of the world's pain was in it. Dark, still and chill with dew, swept by an unknown wind from the unshapen, empty homes of the air, the vast night hung over her— Night, older than Time.

She waited, not caring ever to rise to a new day, praying only for the passion of tears that should bring relief. Then she slept. It may have been about two o'clock when Evelina awoke from a beautiful dream. She tried not to wake; her spirit strove to grasp the golden thread and follow into the enchanted country it had quitted, but roused itself in striving. However, the charm remained like a perfume round her.

"I was back home," she whispered to herself in the darkness. "That was it. I was back home." Overhead the night-wind was swaying the treetops slowly against the stars. She heard the whispered counsel of the leaves. "I was back home."

She tried to piece together details of the dream picture. There was a blossoming orchard, of that she was sure. An orchard all light and bloom, aquiver in the sun— the one at the old Dease place, of course. Yet it could not have been springtime, for she was picking blackberries, and a cornfield rustled beyond the fence.

Also, by the absurdity of dreams, with the rustle was mingled a drumming undertone of rain as she had used to hear it on the dear low roof by Caney's Creek, and framed by the dark entry-vista above the purple-misted range she remembered from one of her first childhood dwellings. Through the house a shadowy, beloved presence— was it her mother, or sister Lib or Em?— had made itself gently felt; yet surely she glimpsed the sunny head of her little boy that died. Where was it, then?

Where and when was it, this home, the centre, the very core, of lifelong desire and remembrance?

Suddenly, with a soft, swift, tingling shock, as of a hand laid on her in the dark, Evelina knew. She became fully awake, and saw the truth as clearly as she saw the stars. This home for which she yearned was no place to be reached by any road of earth. What she seemed to remember was no single definite locality, but the ghost of fair, perished days in many dear places— a lovely composite of all the hours, perfumes, and pictures past,— essence of all she had known of love and youth and the joy of life.

Over her head a bird broke the deep silence with a brief and delicate nocturne keyed like the falling of drops into a lonely pool. On the instant, as if at a signal, the frogs' orchestra began. From the marshy little hollow below the spring a few piped severally at first; then followed a chorus of tinklings and flutings and trillings and tintinnabulations. All were bent on achieving rhythm and unison, and all, as usual among the frogs, gave up just when success seemed imminent. And then the awakened treetoads took up the strain, in long cool tones, half a dozen trilling at once in as many different minors. Occasionally a deeper note rang vibrant and heavy—the bass-viol of a bull-frog. Every littlest tinkle was given its full value, held separately afloat on the ocean of silence. Evelina, listening, felt the old bitterness fall from her like a broken chain. So the frogs' music had rippled, clear and merry, from so many marshes through the summer nights of her life; wherever she had lived— in the ridges, at the foot of Sourwood, or on the Side, by the river, or on the breaks of Caney— she had heard them without fail each year. And so the thrush foretold the dawn; so the chestnuts bloomed ever in the engulfing forest; so the treetops fanned the quiet stars. And all were hers, for she loved and remembered all. These, not one particular lintel, were her home and her children's home.

She turned, and drew a deep breath. Over the oaks a rim of gold began to widen toward the zenith; the thrush's harp-note rang from the creek below. She felt her soul adrift on an infinity of perfect peace and wholesomeness. The great secret had been whispered to her in the night. And though she might not put it into words, she felt that she should put it into life— a larger life than she had ever known. At home everywhere! It was given her to perceive, in a simple way, that this frame of mind was the greater gift, outweighing the ancestral acres, the broad hearths and strong-raftered roof-trees, of women she had envied. Here was her mansion, canopied by God's blue.

Day broke through the highland forest; and, with the pacific confidence in herself and trust in the blessed everyday world of men and things which is faith in God, Evelina arose among her sleeping household, for the first time in her life a woman at home.

Published in
Putnam's Magazine - May 1909

The Broken Urn

EMMA BELL MILES

ILLUSTRATIONS BY ALDEN DAWSON

Above the cabin, in the edge of the clearing, stood a great irregular block of sandstone. Gaunt and barren it may have been, as first fallen from the cliffs that towered behind the forest; but centuries of weather had made it a thing of friendliness and comfort. Succulent grasses, rooted in the loam accumulated by the yearly drift of fallen leaves, sprouted from every crevice; ferns trembled over its edge; the fence led only to the rock on either side, so that its bulk interposed to spare the mauling of several dozen rails; a hollow scooped under it on the woodland exposure afforded shelter in winter to any number of pigs; and beneath the overhang facing the valley two little girls had built a playhouse. Here signs of frequent occupancy were not lacking: the ground was lightly printed all over by slim bare feet, and the rock was smudged with wood-smoke above a tiny furnace of stones. No real playthings were visible, but the rock shelves were stocked with potsherds

[76]

and broken crockery, and there were tin pails and even little skillets and cookers, cleverly fashioned from old tin cans, for the making and serving of real bear-grass salad.

It was, however, too late in the season for bear-grass. The tide of young summer had brimmed the valleys, and came rushing up the slopes to burst along the bluffs in a high-flung surf of laurel bloom. The two small friends were seated now on the grassy top of the rock, shaded by a great arching tupelo; they were piecing quilt patterns. They had laid out for comparison on their knees and about on the grass, the Eagle, the Dream, the Texas and Kentucky Stars, the Crazy Ann, the Tree of Paradise, and three or four varieties of brick-work and log-cabin. The pattern under immediate consideration was the Broken Urn.

"I been a-studyin', " said Nigarie, the sprightly, dark one, "whether hit would n't be the prettiest to piece the urn out whole."

"Let 's try hit that-a-way," agreed Sarepta, a child with an angel's face.

Against nature, the beauty was also the worker, and Sarepta's small skilled fingers swiftly cut and laid out in pink and brown calico the design they had mentioned, her big gray eyes shaded by sumptuous lashes, brooding full of tender dreams above a tangle of flaxy-gold curls falling about the down-bent, intent face, pure in outline and tint as a pearl.

Even loquacious Nigarie sat acutely observant, scarcely speaking, her three-cornered kitten countenance with its hard, round little cheeks under the beryl-green eyes puckered to disproportionate anxiety, till the urn was an accomplished fact, so absorbed were they both in this, their one avenue of artistic expression.

"Hit's some like grandma's Vase of Friendship," commented Nigarie, drawing a long breath when it was done.

"We could call this the Friendship's Urn," suggested Sarepta, timidly. Nigarie usually did the suggesting for the pair.

That small person now ran a reckless hand to the bottom of her basket and plowed up her collection of scraps. "This rosebud sprig's the prettiest I've got. Hit's a piece of Easter's weddin' dress," she volunteered.

"I've got one block all pieced outen scraps Easter an' Ellender given me," Sarepta showed it.

"*I've* got one made all outen the boys' shirts, and some over," Nigarie tossed her braids. "Harmon's and At's, and this pink stripe's Macon's, and this 'n's Joel's, and here's Mart's; and hit's set together with Sam Stetson's."

"Sam Stetson's!"

"Cert'n'y; I reckon Sam Stetson ain't none too good to have a piece of his shirt in my quilt if his pappy does keep the hotel, an' he is goin' to school in the settlement. I wish't I could swap you out of that blue gingham, Sarepta. I want hit to go with this sprig weddin' dress."

"I'll— I'll let ye have it all for— for that one." The gray eyes glowed as she indicated the pink striped scrap from Macon Kinsale's shirt— and she cherished it tenderly, tucking it jealously deep in the bottom of an orderly basket when Nigarie willingly exchanged it for the blue gingham.

The trade effected, they sewed busily.

"That's goin' to be plumb pretty," commented Sarepta at last, leaning to look at her friend's work. "Do you reckon you 'n 'me 'll ever— make us a weddin' dress?"

The sweetest imaginable color crept over both little faces, and shining eyes were bent swiftly to their needlework.

Sarepta's fingers stole toward the pink striped scrap in her basket.

"Mine 'll be silk," said Nigarie confidently.

It was even so. . . . All through the years, Nigarie was shielded, favored. As an only child, she went to school while Sarepta was fulfilling at home the duties of the eldest girl in a large family. Work was found for Nigarie at Stetson's summer hotel, and when she came home it was to make ready for her marriage to the proprietor's son, Sam Stetson. Sam was in business now in a flourishing little city, and doing well. Nigarie promised to write often to Sarepta; but soon the letters became fewer, and after a time they ceased.

Even while there was communication, Sarepta had slight understanding of Nigarie's social evolutions, as described in occasional newspaper clippings enclosed. Statements about refreshments, decorations and costumes conveyed little meaning to a mind accustomed to clothe its thoughts in the antique dialect of the mountains. But she made out that the wedding dress and several others were indeed of silk.

She was not disturbed by that, for she could dwell on her own wedding, when she came down-stairs, shining with a mysterious happiness, in her lawn and cheap ribbons, to find the big log sitting-room filled to overflowing with her kin. She had tremblingly given her promise to love, honor and obey, and had kept it, with a willing spirit if not always to the letter. But Macon's "protect and cherish"— well, as a true wife she never permitted herself to form any conclusion as to whether it had been forgotten five minutes afterward. Macon had done the best he could; as time went on she reiterated that to herself almost fiercely. He had done the best he could!

After the first infare with their meagre furnishing to a cabin on his uncle's land, they had moved, in seven years, nine times, from shack to cabin and from cabin to shack, hounded by poverty and circling like stags as close to home as possible. Macon had indeed done his best; but Sarepta, whose wants were so few, had to pinch in ways she considered hardly decent. She had always lived on little; she learned now to live on next to nothing. She ate food which she had always regarded as fit only for pigs or chickens. Her mind was occupied, not occasionally but constantly, with problems that were like gravel in a shoe, as insistent as they were contemptible: "If I divide this inch of pork, will it season Macon's potatoes for supper and again at breakfast? If I pick a mess of services to-day, have I got sugar in the house to make a cobbler for Sunday dinner? Can I, by piecing Macon's shirt sleeves, and lining the yoke with flour-sacking, get enough out of this gingham to make me a sunbonnet?"

Women always get the worst of poverty. And Sarepta was no miser by nature. Some wives eat the biscuit end of the pone and the skin of the meat because they are afraid no one else will; she chose them because she could not bear that any one else should have to.

Again and again they strained every nerve and sinew to win a shack and clearing of their own, only to be disappointed. Every time, just as the signing of the deed seemed a probability of next week, something happened— a drought on the garden, a murrain on the cow, or another baby. Three of these had come—and gone— leaving no more visible impress than a little less elasticity of Sarepta's figure, a little deepening of the shadow behind her beautiful eyes; for each, after a few weeks of ineffectual striving to digest the cows' milk which the poor mother was obliged to give it, had quietly straightened out in her arms and died.

The fourth was three weeks old and already ailing, on the day of Nigarie's return.

Sarepta heard the news from a neighbor woman who shared her tubs and huge pot and did washing for the hotel people. Nigarie's fat baby, her airs and her summer wash frocks were subjects of an intermittent conversation that went on all morning below the spring in the hollow. The mountain woman's beauty one might almost say was undiminished by her hard life. In the limp unlovely frock it shone out a luminous, incongruous fact. No one seeing her, pounding away at the bat-block and replying with mild monosyllables to the rhapsodies of the other, would have guessed that she was almost sick with terror lest this last puny life slip also out of her grasp. A woman must learn to chatter of other things, lest the gods take notice and in pity slay.

It was the first of April— beautiful weather, but the hard time of year, when the hungry winter has gnawed the last scraps of pork rind from the smoke-houses of well-to-do farms, and the small fruit and truck-garden have not yet begun to relieve the poor. Sarepta was dreading the approach of hot weather on the baby's account; yet she was wondering how to round out a good dinner for Macon from bulk pork and meal. As she carried the last of the wash up to hang it out on the fence, she saw the flicker of a white dress moving along a woods-path. Some one was coming to see her— some one fashionably attired, yet carrying a baby on her hip like any mountain woman! Then she recognized Nigarie.

She stood and trembled, without a word to say, abashed not at all by Nigarie's finery, but because she did not know on what ground the visitor would meet her.

Transgressing all mountain custom the new-comer flew at her with a little laughing cry and kissed her on the cheek.

"My, ain't you pretty yet!" she said half enviously as she entered the cabin. "I've been to the bear-grass rock—remember, Sarepta?" Nigarie's bright eyes were full of misty recollection as she untied the baby's cap. "It's just like it used to be," she said thoughtfully. "Funny how things stay, and we change. I filled Sammy's apron full of bear-grass; shall we have a sallet for dinner? Where's your baby, honey?"

With a catching of the breath that was almost a sob, Sarepta brought out the thin little occupant of her cradle. Without a word she laid it across Nigarie's knees.

The little creature began to wail feebly, and before his mother could take him and hush him, Nigarie, moved by what impulse of immortal compassion who can say, lifted him to her breast.

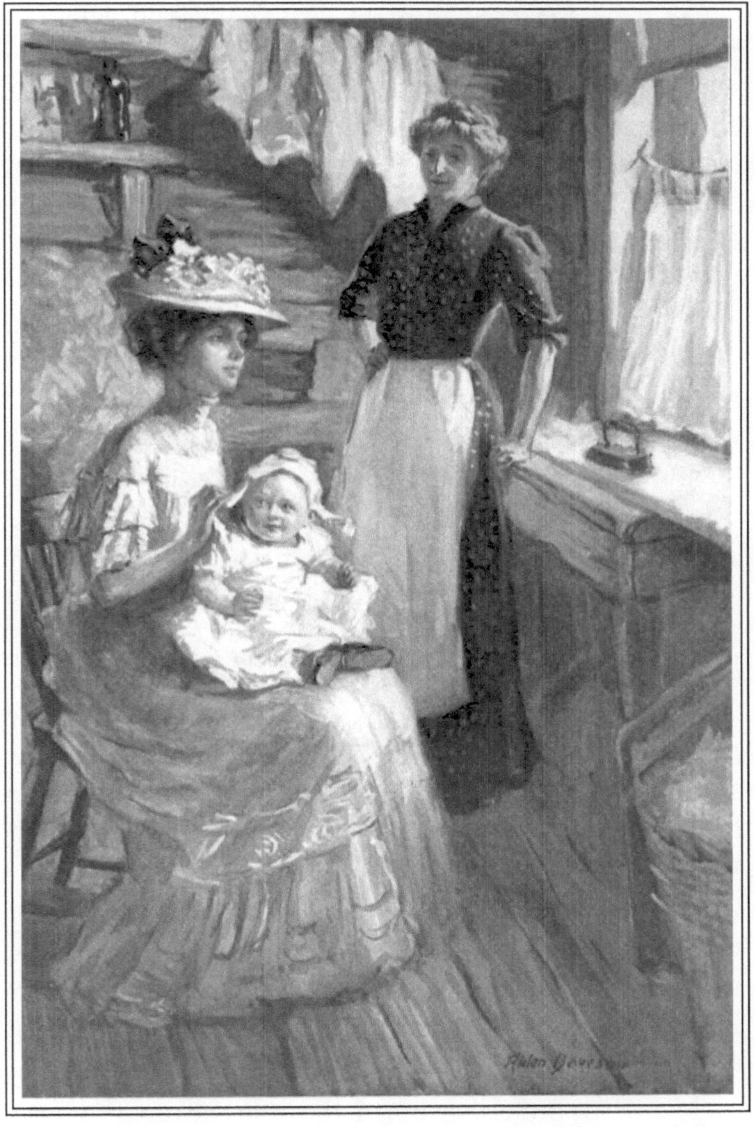

NIGARIE'S BRIGHT EYES WERE FULL OF MISTY RECOLLECTION AS SHE
UNTIED THE BABY'S CAP

"Why, he's starved most to death," she said gently. "I reckon you ain't been able to nurse him. I wish I could— why couldn't I?" She broke off and laughed in her usual elfish inconsistent fashion. "Sammy pesters me most to death," she said with apparent irrelevance. "There ain't any fun stayin' at a hotel with a baby. I'll bet I'll never try it again. As soon as he's old enough I'm going to leave him with Mother Stetson. He's so spoiled he would n't do anything but holler if you put him down."

But skilled Sarepta had taken the fat little new-comer with his royal airs of kinghood and disposed him on a quilt upon the floor. Smilingly, silently, she furnished him with a green switch, and attracted the cat's attention.

"Well, you are a wonder," Nigarie said— "but then, you always were. I'm sick of the hotel—do you reckon you could board me for the rest of the time I want to stay? It would be like the old days—and you could take care of Sammy when I wanted to go somewhere."

Sarepta on her knees looked up at the ruling spirit, sitting above her, nursing her baby, and a mighty gratitude, a wordless emotion which she could not for the life of her have expressed, shook her from head to foot. Here, then, was the answer to her prayers.

"I'll make you as comfortable as I kin," she managed finally to say. "We're mighty poor folks— but you know that—you heard it over at the hotel before you ever put foot in this house. Oh, Nigarie, if you would only stay with me a while!"

And so the butterfly woman, the little cuckoo who never wanted a nest of her own, folded her wings for a season in this humble place. She nursed Sarepta's baby as she nursed her own. The envious eyes of the mother were on her as the little fellow's thin body rounded, and the puny limbs grew stronger. To Sarepta it seemed almost a miracle from heaven, and the little cabin a holy place.

The days were filled with a deep peace and vital joy. Nigarie was happy in having some useful work, or rather in being herself actually necessary to the daily welfare of others; Sarepta, in watching her child grow, in the presence of a dear and merry companion, and in seeing Macon take that long-looked-for "start.." For he, profiting by Nigarie's presence, secured work with a valley farmer, and began working out the purchase of some two acres of land. He came home every Saturday night, carrying on his back provisions for the coming week, and left before day on Monday morning. Hence Sunday was the white milestone of the week to both women; for Macon was gifted with temperament and charm.

Sarepta's kitchen outfit was hardly less crude than that of the playhouse had been, yet she always contrived a little feast for his day at home. Talent he had, too. All the long still afternoon and after the moon had climbed above the mountain he sat on the porch, his chair tilted back against the house-logs, and played upon the banjo. He played, and set the whole fragrant night throbbing, until their only neighbors, among the pines far up the height, sat listening too, in another cabin door; played until the two mothers, the long-continued rhythm going to their heads, sprang up, took hold of hands and danced together like two girls over the shaking puncheons; played until the spiders peeped out from the roofboards to hear, and the whippo-wills came right up to the fence and thrilled the night with their wild jodeling. And in truth his music was hardly less eerie than theirs; a barbaric jangle, interspersed with strange rocking whoops and calls, and elaborated with curious fingerings— snaps and slides and twangs unknown to banjo-players outside the mountains.

There were in it tone-pictured incidents of cabin life, and echoes of the larger enfolding life of nature— murmuring undertones as of drumming rain, ghostly half-whispered minors, and long chuckling meditations mellowed as if by the product of hidden stills. He sang too in the excellent baritone of the mountaineer— not the elder ballads which girls delight in and mothers croon, but man-songs— real folk-song of raid and foray, rollicking drinking-songs, with boast and challenge, and peculiar baying rhythms that reached a climax in the long-drawn hunting-yell.

Some of this music was known to his hearers; some, unacknowledged, was his own composition or improvisation. Nigarie had heard better in theatres, of course, but this was knit in with her earlier recollections. To this every fibre of her being responded as to the dramatic element— breath of sweet keen frost or exultant storm.

She had not known such contentment since she left the mountains.

"We've been everywhere, Sam and me," she remarked one evening as the three sat together in the dark. "I've lived at the sea-shore, in the West, and we had a winter in New York; but I always wanted, I think, to come back here— on a visit," she added the concluding words hastily, for she knew that no place on earth could hold her long.

THE TWO MOTHERS JOINED HANDS AND DANCED TOGETHER

In the fall Nigarie Stetson returned to her own life. Those restless, wayward, eager feet went back to seek new paths— and yet new ones. Sarepta watching her departure through tears that were not all bitter, a round, rosy baby on her shoulder, knew somehow that the visitor would never return. And she wondered at herself meekly. Where was the bitterness of loss, where the canker of envy she had once thought to endure when this moment arrived?

She turned a thoughtful face and kissed her child. She entered her small dun dwelling and looked about at smoke-browned beam and rooftree with new eyes. She began to realize that in the unhurried, intimate conversations of those long summer days she had come into an understanding of the quiet, unassailable dignity of her own position, and learnt the intrinsic worth of usefulness as contrasted with the false value of unearned riches. She felt dimly and half unwillingly, as she contemplated Nigarie's lot, that there was something almost disgraceful about being "kept" in soft and delicious idleness. Even the remembrance of the three starved babies was no longer a bitterness. Surely it were better to have borne and loved and lost them, every terrible, precious memory of them, than to bear the burden of feverish apprehension which Nigarie evinced toward motherhood itself; to speak continually and openly of the baby as an unearned burden.

She established her boy in his cradle, preparatory to taking up her work. She was suddenly full of a zest for life to which her days had long been stranger.

Macon, having completed his purchase of land, was now busied near home, hewing logs for a cabin of their own. By way of doing his best he had come into the house, ostensibly for a drink, but really to try a new tune on his banjo. At some political meeting the phrase about "dipping the pen in gall" had caught his fancy and suggested to him a new couplet to which he was tentatively fitting an air:

> "I dip my pen in golden ink, to
> write my love a letter,
> And tell her that most every
> day I love her a little better."

The nearly perfect monogamy of the region renders it unlikely that a mountaineer compose verses in honor of any but the one woman. As his wife came in Macon tossed the new song at her with a half humorous, but wholly gallant bow.

She laughed, as it seemed to her, immoderately— there was so much to laugh at! She turned once more to the babe in the cradle; how rosy he was, and how he laughed, too. She went, on feet that love made light, to prepare her dinner of herbs.

Later, she might lose sight of the vision somewhat, for we are all as incapable of holding constantly to great thoughts as of putting such definitely into words; but when the trailing glories paled, here was a child, gloriously alive, to remind her that she had once been inspired with the profoundly rational courage of seeing things as they are.

And on the cradle, pieced by Nigarie in the summer mornings while both babies slept, lay a little quilt of the pattern they had named the Friendship's Urn.

Published in
Putnam's Magazine - February 1909

Mallard Plumage

EMMA BELL MILES

ILLUSTRATIONS BY F. De Forrest Schook

I.

WAKED IN THE NIGHT BY THE FIRST THUNDERSTORM OF the year, Roma sat up, suddenly restless. The rain sounded hollowly, with a noise as of drums on the roof of the big log house, and she could hear how the wind exulted through the tossing forest. Slipping out of bed, she opened the window and leaned across the sill. The drops whipped her sharply in occasional gusts. She stood breathing deeply the lightning-sweetened air, almost ready to yield to the spell of the storm— to run out into the downpour with mad laughter, to shout with the wind.

To run out into the storm and be part of it! Behind her there was the even breathing of a sleeper on the bed. She was like a thing with a leg chain, she might run but so far, then the clog she dragged would catch in some barrier and throw her on her face in the dust.

"To fly away, like Atlas," she murmured.

She was thinking of one wild as herself, with whom she had once taken shelter from such a storm under the Hanging Rocks. While the lightnings flared pale green and blue and rose, he had piped for her on his hickory whistle; they sang together, "Oh Brother Green;" and once after a tremendous peal he made her laugh out by shouting, "Whoop-ee! Blow again, Gabriel; there's some of 'em ye'll have to dig out!"

And the bitter aftermath of that escapade; how the gossips' tongues had wagged, and her own people talked and talked till she felt herself a thing disgraced. Atlas Cleaverage went West to escape their petty persecution; and she had been persuaded into marrying the gray haired preacher, Boaz Guthrie. They had no reason to watch her now; she was hedged about with righteousness— and hated it.

She was not unaware of the comfort and distinction of her position. In a locality where most women, especially those newly married, still prepared their meals on the fireplace, it was something to own a cook-stove, a reading-lamp, a sewing-machine, and any number of ducks and chickens. That these had been the property of a former Mrs. Guthrie did not lessen their value. There was, besides, something newly bought which counted more in Roma's estimation than all other possessions; her organ, whose twenty stops and square of mirror now gleamed dimly through the dark.

Yes, the organ would have been worth giving up much for if she could have been left to enjoy it in her own way; but in the preacher's house no music was permitted except that of the church. Roma was forbidden the dance tunes and ballads learned at home, and provided with a number of books containing the religious rag-time her husband admired. Having learned these, she became passive hostess of a series of "all day singin's" at which the neighbors spread a basket-dinner on the grass of the big front yard, and sang with fervor till evenfall. On these occasions Guthrie, throned in a rocking-chair and beaming on the guests, had flattered himself that he knew better than most how to treat a wife so as to keep her contented and happy.

And after such days there were apt to come nights when Roma sat, as now, gazing sometimes at the dim bulk of her organ and sometimes at the world outside. Once, among her Pekins— fat, milk-white creatures who demanded not even swimming water— she had reared a mallard. She loved its dark plumage, the very turn of its alert head, the sweep of its powerful wings. But the wild one joined the first flock of its kind that flew north in the spring, and she never saw it again.

If a door were open to her like that! If it were only to join a flight of her kind— and away!

She sat, until the storm blew over, and the pallor of coming dawn outlined the rifted clouds. Then she dressed herself and went to get breakfast.

It was a Sunday morning. Attired in a new print, with a ribbon at her throat, Roma fared to church on a blanket-square spread on Buckeye's croup behind Guthrie's saddle. She sat through the hours of meeting, distrait and rebellious. More than once she caught herself "faulting" the want of sense in her husband's argument. She knew by heart his round of phrases. References to "the cold-bleak-and-icy mountain of sin!" or "the teeming millions

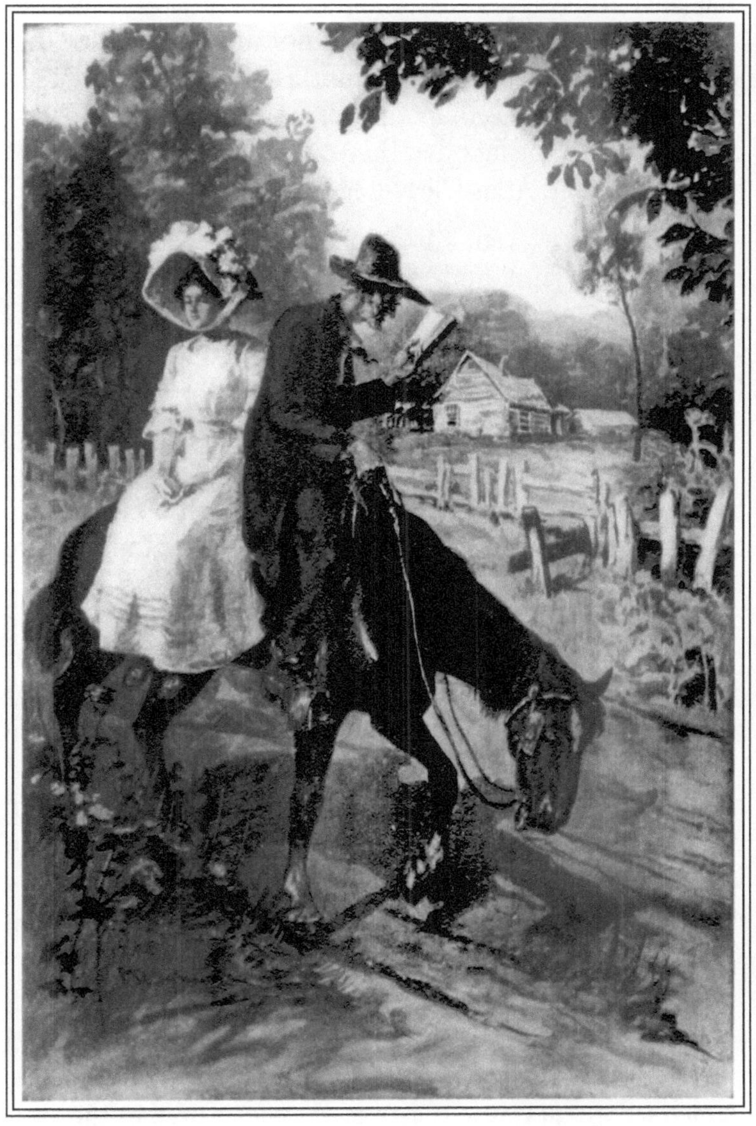

ROMA ON A BLANKET-SQUARE BEHIND GUTHRIE'S SADDLE

that have outstripped us," rang as familiar on her ears as the cracked church bell. This was not the first Sunday that she had preferred to recall memories of unregenerate days rather than give heed to the sermon; there was no real coincidence in the fact that there sounded from the woods, at that moment, Atlas Cleaverage's own peculiar yodel.

A patent stir went through the congregation, though the call was faint and musical and far away. Guthrie, recognizing the note, took it evidently as a direct personal challenge from the powers of darkness. He plainly began to gather his forces for he knew-not-what conflict with Apollyon.

When, after a few minutes, Atlas' figure filled the doorway and then slipped into the nearest seat, the rambling sermon concentrated its fire upon him. All eyes but Roma's were turned, more or less openly, for a glance at the prodigal come back so tanned and muscular; and curiosity having prompted a first look, his mallard beauty, with its color of unguessed romance, was sure to draw a second. He sat quietly attentive and very straight in his place, showing no resentment at the preacher's personalities. The same old neighborhood, he was probably thinking, the same group of inextricably intermarried double-cousins, fenced in with no mental occupation but the gossip which inevitably runs into backbiting; forever brooding trifles and hatching mischief!

Atlas Cleaverage come back, and sitting in the church with her husband! Roma's inconsequent girl's mind had never conceived this conjunction. She strove only to bear herself as one unconscious of anything strange in the situation. When, after the service, she with Guthrie passed the newcomer in the yard, her cheeks were burning, her eyes down-bent, and her limbs trembled. He gravely took off his hat to the preacher's wife, which innovation caused the lads around the threshold to catch their breath.

"Reckon you come back to the mountings to get ye a wife?"

The leading question was put to him curiously as the young fellow lingered among his former cronies after service.

"I— well, there's no denyin' I did start with that notion," Cleaverage hesitated. "But some things back here has turned out different from what I expected, and I reckon I'll take my money and buy me a loggin' team, and stay around here for a spell."

Yet the next week, and the next and the next, Atlas did not come to church. Finally the preacher, unmindful of that portion of Solomon's wisdom, which in effect bids a man let well enough alone, rode Buckeye down the creek to the sawmill, where Cleaverage was at work, and flung him a bidding that was a challenge to attend next Sunday's service. Atlas had laughed at the news that he had been made the subject of a special intercession at a recent prayer-meeting; but at this summons to show why he should not be utterly condemned for contempt of church, he straightened himself, looked the elder man in the eye, and answered:

"Very well, sir, if you say so, I'll be there."

Guthrie's main reason for calling the interloper out to church was that during these weeks he had thought of many more effective things which might be hurled at him, and the sermon was pretty well devoted to the shortcomings of a certain fool who had flouted the faith of his fathers and gone west into heathen lands. Atlas received the charge almost smiling, with that look under his eyelashes of an inner light or knowledge which fascinated and daunted the duller witted. Roma, shivering in her seat, dreaded the collision which she thought must follow. But young Cleaverage had learned better ways of fighting for his own. At the close of the sermon, he asked and received permission to make a few remarks. Instead of rising in his place to address the congregation, he walked the length of the room and took his stand on the low platform that served for pulpit. Guthrie sullenly stepped down and seated himself in the amen corner, unwilling to endure the withering comparison of standing beside the younger man, yet quite unconscious of that fact.

"Friends, kinsmen, and neighbors," Atlas opened in unknowing plagiarism of a greater speech. At the first word the houseful felt the thrill of the unexpected. That he should begin, unhurried, unabashed, without singsong or gesticulation, to address them as he might if they had met him on the open road, riveted their attention; the stature, strength, and beauty of the man, and first and last the deep, bell-like *timbre* of his voice, held and swayed them.

"I aint here to defend myself against old charges or new," he said, half smilingly. "Time has cleared my name of mighty near all I was blamed with. You all know who poked Brother Guthrie with a stick through a crack durin' the big meetin' in this church two years ago. I reckon you can guess, yet nobody says much about it, seein' the man's dead, who it was that shot through the churchhouse door at Shiloh. As for the story of my playin' cards all night in the loggin' camp, that's neither here nor there; I was run out from this neighborhood by tales that seemed to be hurtin' somebody else worse than they could ever hurt me— an' I was a fool to go. Nor I'm not goin' to apologize to you for never havin' been baptized, neither. I've lived out yon where there's room for men of my religion, and a free life for all, and if I hadn't got to honin' for something I'd left behind me, I reckon I'd been livin' there yet."

Roma bent low her head over the hands close-gripped in her lap. The color ebbed swiftly from cheek and lip and abruptly returned when Guthrie rose, put forth a shaking hand, and interrupted the discourse.

"Oh, no," objected Atlas, coolly "You've had your say, Brother Guthrie. Leave it to the folks now. If they want me to hush and set down, I will."

The easy confidence of this proposition won the instant suffrages of a people who prize courage above everything. Of the entire assembly, Roma only could follow the speaker's thought, and she less by reasoning than by the answering leap and thrill of kindred instinct. At no point did the round of their contracted lives touch the greater circle, which he now tried to make real to them; yet they were eager to hear. It was not his statements which charmed and carried them with him, for they were incapable of logical thought and set no value upon it. It was not the interest of a novel point of view, for novelty is anathema throughout the region. It was the sense of sweeping, elemental occurrence— of winged life— of wind and rain, and snow and hail in the hothouse, which startled and enthralled them.

"Go on, Brother!" cried three or four men at once; and Guthrie sank back in his place silenced: whipped out in his own kennel, ashamed for his congregation, and jealous of the figure he cut before his young wife.

Atlas spoke at length of his life in the West, his longing for the mountains (one heart beating with guilty rapture guessed what that longing meant); and finally asked his old friends to come forward and shake hands with him. They were moving up by twos and threes, all singing, Cleaverage's clear baritone leading the tune, while the little windows shook to the clang, when the preacher came to an understanding that his meeting had been fairly taken away from him.

It was Roma herself who had to remind him with a soft touch on his shoulder that it was time for the formal dismissal of church.

His bearing at home during the ensuing weeks was hard for a wild young creature like Roma to endure. All day he sat brooding in his big chair on the porch and allowed the farm work to lie. The mantle of dignity seemed to fall from him, leaving him a sulky, irritable, old man. Once when the girl could endure it no longer, she flung out at him in reply to some bitter taunt of his own.

"Is that yo' religion?" she asked. "Atlas Cleaverage has mo' good will in his little finger than you have in yo' whole body. Is that yo' religion?"

He turned upon her with a sort of snarl. "You mad at me because I don't fellowship with that there— that—" The fit epithet was wanting in his vocabulary, and he went on: "I shake hands with no man that's got neither beliefs nor principles— that's not even a member of any church!" But after a heart-sick pause he added, staring down at the floor,

"I may be a mighty ill somebody to live with, but I think a heap o' you, girl."

"I know hit," she answered scarcely above her breath.

She did know it, and to her cost, for every day it was coming more bitterly home to her that she had sold her birthright of young love and a mate of her own feather; bartered it for ignoble peace, for a cook-stove, a lamp-shade, an organ with a square of mirror let into the top. And from this time on Atlas inevitably strode into her dreams and her waking thoughts, strong and vivid, a creature of sun and earth and air, the embodiment of the life from which she was shut out.

II.

So passed the summer; and the season drew nigh when the great migratory instinct should again send the wild birds South across half a world. It chanced that Boaz Guthrie was much from home about this time; the young wife was idle, thrown upon her own resources, and this perhaps was not well. Returning from an appointment at the head of Sequatchie Valley one day, the preacher found his cabin shut and locked, and Roma gone. There was no message nor writing left for him, but inquiry among the neighbors soon showed that she had fled with Atlas Cleaverage in his wagon, the pair striking out across country.

Guthrie lost no time in determining his course of action. Was he, after all, so greatly surprised at the outcome of things? Had he not, from the first, looked for just this? He had married a wife less than half his age, on impulse, as most men marry; yet with him the impulse ripened to a passionate attachment— that almost embittered devotion of the old for what is young, and full of life, and beautiful. Now his faith taught him no scruples against vengeance, nor did his church "think strange" of his armed pursuit. Atlas and Roma had a week's start; but at first he did not grudge them a day of it, deeming the cumbrous wagon easily traced.

Where love and tenderness must carry a little home of comfort with them, naked and single vengeance could follow swiftly unincumbered. Taking only his gun, a shirt or two, and what ready money he could get together, from camp to camp, by creek and gap and break and ford, across Sequatchie County and up through the Cumberlands into Kentucky, Guthrie followed. But he was delayed by one mischance and another— a rumor of change in the wagon's course, a strain of Buckeye's withers, a flood where Atlas had forded safely the day before, an invitation hardly to be refused, to preach in return for hospitality; and the sixth week found him still on the trail.

Whither were the fugitives heading? To the coast? Was it their plan to sell the team and wagon there and take passage on a ship? The thought staggered Guthrie, for to the mountaineer's consciousness the world beyond the water looms almost as dim and unreal a shadow as it was to the aboriginal inhabitants of his land. No; more likely Atlas was tending toward the place of his childhood near the Carolina border. There might be some fastness of the ranges known to him alone, some little valley enclosed by walls of rock, some "jug" cave defensible by one against an army. That the pair he pursued might be in mere, aimless, mallard flight, wing and wing, snatching each day's delight from under the sword, did not occur to Guthrie.

The strain told on his years; but he lessened the distance between himself and the team by a little almost every day. At the same hour when he camped miserably in Kell's Cove on what he began to fear was a blind trail, Atlas, only five miles away across the range, was purchasing a coop of a dozen chickens from a huckster, because Roma said she must have better food.

That huckster met Guthrie next morning, and replied to the haggard stranger's question:

"Why, yo' man mout a-been in with a gang o' traders that come thro' here with a string o' mules three-fo' days back. You mout ast some o' these-yere folks livin' along the road 'at seed 'em go by. I did meet a feller 'n 'is wife yen side the ridge, but they was settlers here. They wasn't gwine to'ds the coast. He 'lowed he aimed to put 'em up a shack some'ers hereabout. Couldn't a-been yo' man, I don't reckon?"

"No," said the preacher, never guessing how Atlas could have altered his plan overnight. He thought it not unlikely that the pair should have joined the traders' camp for better protection, the more as they must be nearly penniless by this time, and Atlas' skill of horseflesh might in such case stand him in good stead. He made inquiries as the huckster had suggested, and was told that there had indeed been a couple among the "gypsies" answering the description he gave.

He overtook the traders at Nashville. There, in the jockey-lot, sick with disappointment at having wasted weeks on this false scent, he collapsed with "the winter fever.'"

"I AINT HERE TO DEFEND MYSELF AGAINST OLD CHARGES OR NEW." HE SAID.

His mind, fiery with the lust of vengeance, was wearing out his body; and through the long weeks when he lay "tended on" with rough kindness in the gypsy camp, it haled him back upon the track and showed him pitilessly where he had played the fool in passing by the squatters of whom the huckster had told him. It was mid-winter when, disregarding all remonstrance, he again took the road.

Back into the Cumberlands he headed, clamoring upon the only God he knew for that wild and blundering justice which was his sole notion of Right; but every mile and every moment put behind him set his revenge further away. Although his heart was still hot, it began to be that he was pursuing a phantom. The constant endeavor to reach an understanding, in order to forecast the fugitive's probable course, unwittingly bred something like sympathy with his enemy's mind. For weeks he had continually asked himself, "Now, if I was Atlas, what would I do, and where would I go?" That this persistent question must result in some harmony and consequent final agreement between pursuer and pursued he had not the insight to foresee. He could not realize that under his anger, day by day, his purpose was ebbing from him.

After all, were they not kin by birthplace and tradition? Had Atlas been quite incapable of religious passion, he could not have so overpowered and humiliated the preacher that day in church. And had Guthrie felt no stirrings of an untamed nature, he would never have been so determined to marry a madcap girl.

III.

Title-deeds in the mountain-country read "from the bluff" and "to the bluff;" but the bluff itself is, like roads and rivers, Public Domain. Atlas had, in common with many mountaineers, an indistinct and limited knowledge of law, but an unbounded faith in the Government's good will towards men; it was perhaps with some idea of placing himself and Roma under Government protection that, when she could go no farther, he chose their habitation, like an eyrie, half way up the mountain-wall. The great cave at Wolf-Pen Gap had hidden many a refugee aforetime: the red man, or those who fled from him, scouts and spies of older wars; now it became shelter of this wild pair during the first frosts and storms of the year. But ere winter locked the Gap, Atlas sold the team and wagon, and managed to erect a tiny cabin on the wide-arched ledge at the cave's mouth. He worked now and then, when the weather permitted, for a farmer in the valley, walking to his toil before day, and carrying provisions home on his back at night. At other times he fished and hunted and trapped. Their walls were half covered with drying pelts. Roma broiled venison and trout and pheasant over four stones in the middle of the hut, since there was neither floor nor chimney to their dwelling. The smoke-escape was an opening in the roof.

It was the life of their dreams— of their dreams. And yet, dreams have a cynical trick of coming true, clipped, shorn, presenting the semblance and denying the substance. Roma had said to her companion in the first day's ride:

"I do love you, Atlas; but if ever you tech me ag'in my will, I'll leave ye; I b'lieve I could kill ye for hit; I'd never look on your face again."

And now, at the end of their wanderings, she was farther from him than ever.

A flaming autumn had swept the mighty slopes, and the long rains followed, extinguishing the last sparks of the splendid conflagration. November handed them over, along with the woodland creatures, to the hungry winter; but unlike their lesser brothers in fur and feathers, this pair was cut off from even a diminished natural food-supply. Then one blow after another was dealt them by the weather: it turned warm to rain, turned cold to snow, and cleared with a sunshine that only mocked their eyes through the glittering air. They ate food that neither had ever before tasted, things they had dreamed unfit for human consumption. The mountains towered about them pitiless as if built of white metal; the valleys might be open, but at that altitude the snow lay thick. All day, in the frozen forest, stripes of blinding silver changed places with shadows of steel.

And yet from this strange companionship, the love that was in them, the wild free zest for happiness that was common to both, wrung a taste of joy. The home in the cave's throat was a nest of kindly human warmth. In the long evenings, by the torches and the red hickory blaze, they achieved a dear comradeship in spite of the sword Roma had laid between them. They sang together, all the songs they knew— old ballads handed down by word of mouth for centuries, and new ones, quite as wild, of their own composition and rhyming. And they talked, like Indians, in voices low and even as the rain upon their roof, with long intervals of meditation. Roma, at least was happy. The dull emptiness of her other life was a thing of the past. Atlas could always interest her with tales of hunting, herding, or trading. His keen humor, and the swift, strong, level action of his mind, even more than his grand build and strength, made him seem bigger and freer than other men. She felt she could have gone with him to any fate.

The man, taught a little in life's school, kept wondering how it would all end, hearkening ever for the footstep of that change which would put a stop to the strange, impossible situation. But even so it was unexpectedly that the avenger came upon them.

Guthrie, circling where he lost the trail months ago, heard of the couple keeping house in the cave, and in the face of a sleet-storm walked, from the valley farm, up a path which Buckeye could not travel. He knew better than to attempt such a journey at such a time; everything was against him: failing strength, bad footing, wind and weather; the paths obliterated, and at best a way he did not know; but there was that in him that drove him forward.

The rain, freezing as it fell, thickened on every twig until the trees hung heavy with their burden, groaning aloud as the strain neared the breaking-point. Now and then a sapling bowed slowly to earth, or a big branch snapped like a shot in the tense stillness. He wandered, stumbling and sliding, along the talus of the bluff, where hand-hold and foothold were varnished with ice. It was too late to turn back even had he wished, and he would not relinquish the gun that hampered him dangerously. The low sun broke through the clouds as he scrambled, and for a moment the forest flamed with more jewels than Aladdin's garden. In the fading light he saw the clouds run scattering, driven by the whistling scourge of the wind that now began to search his vitals. The preacher was wet, sick, and disheartened. But at last he descried, on the heights above him, a moving light as of a pine torch carried in some one's hand.

Relieved that he had not passed the Gap in the dark, he began to climb heavily, this way and that, over the rocks. Almost impossible, he knew, was the ascent as he had attempted it. There was only one pass here, and how was he to find it in this black-diamond night? Still he climbed. It was his intent to burst open the door and cover the hut's interior with his gun.

But he was not destined to enter so. Quite near the cabin a young tree, loosely rooted in a crevice overhead, heavy now with the storm's burden of icy despair, let go and crashed down upon him, breaking what bones he could not tell, and burying his gun. Because his knife still remained to him he ground the suffering between his teeth. Slowly he freed himself, and dragged his broken and nearly exhausted body to the cabin door. Here, lying in the withering cold, he raised himself at cost of torture to a chink from which the firelight issued; and he could see.

Roma, thinner and yet more lovely than he remembered her, sat by the fire with something in her lap. The heart of the watcher leapt at sight of the tenderness in her face, and leapt again, as she bent to the little bundled thing she held.

For the first time he wished that he had not come.

He could not see Atlas Cleaverage from where he lay; the bit of warm, smoky brightness held only mother and child, like a madonna in a niche; but the man's voice came out to him shaken with strong feeling.

"I can't stand this no longer," Atlas was saying, evidently in continuance of a conversation. "I tried to leave you oncet before, honey—the time I was out huntin' for so long you 'lowed I was killed. I said to myself hit was nothing but a torment to live with you this way; but I found hit was a worse torment to think you might be sufferin' an' me not here to do my part. I had to come back. I can't leave ye; I can't live on with ye this way. I don't know what to do. If there was any neighbors, or if I was fixed to provide ahead for you and the little feller until such time as Boaz Guthrie could git here, I'd go back and give myself up. I've studied a heap about it, an' that seems to me the only way."

"I don't want to go back," said Roma gently, glancing across the fire to some point out of Guthrie's view.

"I don't believe," the man continued, in a voice that shivered with feeling, "that people ever get what they want in this world."

"*I* believe that if they be patient and do the best they know, they're liable to get something better in place of it," she answered half musingly.

"I never wanted anything on earth but you, Roma," burst out the man's deep tones; "you know that; and you're not mine— you never have been. I see now you never will be. And nothing could ever take your place."

The listener outside sank down unconscious. When he came to himself he was lying in the hut on a bed of pine boughs and blankets, and Roma was chafing his hands while the baby miaowed faintly from another couch.

"Let me see hit," were the preacher's first feeble words. "Mine," he whispered to the top of the downy head. "Pore little soul— mine!"

They gave him whisky and an atrocious liquor of boiled pork rinds as the best they had. All the next four days, while the pass was chained with sleet, he lay with eyes closed or watching Roma and his child. Atlas was out of ammunition; but coming on Guthrie's gun tangled in the branches of the fallen tree, he dug it out and with it killed some rabbits, that the injured man might have broth. Yet as he lay, tended upon faithfully by these two whom he had come to destroy, tasting the nature of their life and beliefs as would never have been otherwise possible, Boaz Guthrie felt his end draw near on steady foot.

"Sing something," he whispered once; and Roma sang a favorite of his, "One Day Nearer Home;" but at its close he only said, "No— some o' yore kind o' songs— somethin' you like."

So she sang to him of the "Ladye Bright" and of "Wearie's Well," and the ballad of "Roma" for which she was named. When he lay quietly listening, she ventured on love-songs quaint and foolish with wild minors of refrain. Whether they carried aught of meaning to the dying man she could not tell. Tears gathered in her eyes as she sang.

Near the end Atlas, in answer to the reflection of a wish on the graying face, put out his hand. Guthrie took it and held it.

"Yo' fo'give me?" asked Cleaverage, choking.

SHE SANG TO HIM OF "THE LADYE BRIGHT" AND OF "WEARIE'S WELL."

Guthrie's quiet eyes went from one vivid young face to the other; they traveled about the smoke blackened interior of the rude nest Atlas had built for her.

"I wont say I forgive you two," he whispered at length, "beca'se I see some things different now. I don't consider that you done far wrong; an' I'm a goin' whar a man travels lighter if he casts out hate. Send for a preacher whenever the ice melts, and have me buried right; and if you will, best have him say yo' ceremony after mine."

He spoke no more.

By and by a puff of wind shook open the rude door and sent the smoke and white ashes whirling about the hut. It was turning warmer; and the new day shone in upon them.

Published in
The Red Book Magazine - August 1909

Flyaway Flittermouse

EMMA BELL MILES

ILLUSTRATIONS BY W. HERBERT DUNTON

Ever since the first of the week, when the elder children started for school, with a basket of biscuits and fried pork and a First Reader among them, Flittermouse had been lonely. Today it was worse than ever; for not only had Pappy left to work before she waked in the morning, but even Mother was almost inaccessible through the malignance of a headache. As for little Man-alive, the only playmates that interested him were his own sea-shell feet and hands.

Aunt Libby, having "drowned the miller" in making up her bread, came to borrow flour, and stayed to help with the churning; but now she was gone back home across the field, and Mother lay with tight-closed eyes on the bed. Flittermouse tried for a while to keep store, in imitation of her brothers, on the plank shelves they had arranged in the fence corner; but after pouring out the cans of water which represented barrels of oil and sorghum, and dismantling the rows of patiently moulded mud loaves and red-velvet oak tips, galls, and acorns which made up the rest of their stock, there did not seem to be much to do here; besides, she had an uncomfortable conviction that the boys would not approve her activities when they came home.

Across the fence, in a great airy cavern of shade beneath an oak, was a playhouse of more domestic character, all aglitter with broken china and upholstered in plushy moss. She had so often slipped between the rails to play here with sister that the fascination of forbidden fruit was absent from its neat and pretty house-wifery, and the two little bare feet did not linger, but only printed the ground lightly as they pattered past.

Along the dew-damp sand broad shadows lay invitingly, though the day was not yet too warm. A cardinal flashed between the trees as she looked, and, "Birdy," she greeted him, with an indescribable circumflex; adding immediately and regretfully, "Flyed away: gone wa-ay off-in-woods." She heard the *Song of the Open Road* as plainly as it was ever sung. The iridescence of wings in the azure air, the happy z-z-z-ing of gnats and honey-lovers— it was all a siren lure. She was drawn down the road's green, sun-shot vista irresistibly even before her Great Idea took shape; but once having glimmered into consciousness, it speedily became evident to her mind that Pappy was coming, somewhere yonder, probably just round the turn.

"Go'n' meet him," said Flittermouse, firmly.

Forthwith her toddle quickened to a trot. The little checked cotton frock she wore would have been for a time distinctly visible, flickering in and out of the bands of sunshine that lay across the road; but the eyes of the housemother were so dimmed with headache that even had she roused herself to look from the window she could hardly have seen. Besides, had not Libby said that she might take the child home with her for the day?

So, all unchallenged, unhindered, a little gipsy went dancing down the green-arched lane like a butterfly drifting on the breeze. The road as it ran away seemed to laugh back at her over its shoulder; she followed it on and on. From time to time she was tempted aside by a shining cluster of berries; she stopped to gather her hands full of flowers, and to splash and wade in a rivulet rutted by passing wagons; she poked in an interesting hole, and was startled by the appearance of an exasperated toad; she squealed in delight at a jewelled dragon-fly; and once, absorbed in a phenomenon which she afterward described as "two bum'lebees rollin' a mobble," she came near forgetting her purpose. But after the minute of wonder, she got to her feet and went on, looking eagerly down the road where she expected, every moment, to see Pappy appear.

Ah— there he was! She ran forward with a shout; then her footsteps lagged and faltered as she saw that it was not Pappy, but a stranger. Out of sheer interest she came to a halt and stared. The newcomer was so bristly gray, and had such fierce eyebrows!

She kept her soft dark gaze steadily and gravely on him. That he was grim and surly she did not know, any more than she knew that she herself was the most enchanting bit of human perfection the old fellow had beheld in many a day. This was a Man, and her experience of men had not been at all disconcerting; the whole race was typified, of course, by Pappy.

But such a funny man! He was about to pass her, when she giggled, showing all her little teeth like grains of rice. The man stopped and stared in his turn, as if he had not seen her until that moment.

"Huh!" said he. Then, "Whose little gal air you?" he asked, in a queer husky old voice that matched his bristly gray hair.

She knew the answer to that question. "Pappy's."

"Huh! Where you think you're a-goin'?" came the next query.

"Go'n' meet Pappy."

He looked at her a moment, made as if to laugh, and went striding on. But his face had perforce relaxed a bit; and as he went he muttered: "Little dickens — watch them feet o' hern! Jest like Cinthi' said, young critters sca'cely knows whether they dancin' or walkin'. Eh— law— Cinthi'. "

She had scarcely watched him out of sight when a murmur of voices caused her to look the other way. The two now approaching were deep in some altercation; they were, indeed, quarrelling, not with loud words or angry bluster, but in the mountaineer's way, with a growing tension of distrust. Behind their immobile faces thoughts were gathering that might separate them for life. But at sight of the little girl they dropped, for the time, whatever they had been talking about.

"D'you reckon she's lost, Jeff?" said one, using his companion's name in a kinder tone than he had employed since the question of that misplaced fence came up.

"I'll see," the other answered, peering at her from under a green corduroy cap. He bent upon Flittermouse a pair of very pleasant gray eyes. "Want to come?" He held out his hands, broad, brown, flexible, the palms calloused with field work. "Lemme tote ye home, pretty. Where is hit you live? Where's Pappy?"

"Down road. Go'n' meet Pappy," exclaimed Flittermouse, confidentially, liking the man's voice and manner. "Uh-huh; go'n' tell him— dot— szschicken for zupper."

"Oh," the man smiled, drawing back a little, "is Pappy down the road? You waitin' for him?"

She nodded. "Go'n' eat a szschicken bum' tick."

"Come on, Jeff," urged the truck-grower. "The baby's all right— ain't ye, sweetness? She knows what's she's headed fer."

Flittermouse accepted this with dignity. Here was a man who recognized ability when he met it.

The man in the green cap hesitated "Well— I guess it's all right, and I— I ain't got much time." He appeared to be apologizing to the little stray before him. "But I declar' you do look like Clay's kid; and if that's so, you're a right smart piece from home."

But as Flittermouse continued to back away, step by step, not suspiciously, but as one who is sure of the course of duty, he decided that the child's father could not be far distant.

"If she *is* lost, we'll be apt to hear of hit a ways on." And returning to contemplation of his own thrice-vexed affairs he made haste to overtake his companion.

They did not take up the quarrel exactly where they had left it. Instead, each cast about for something to say which

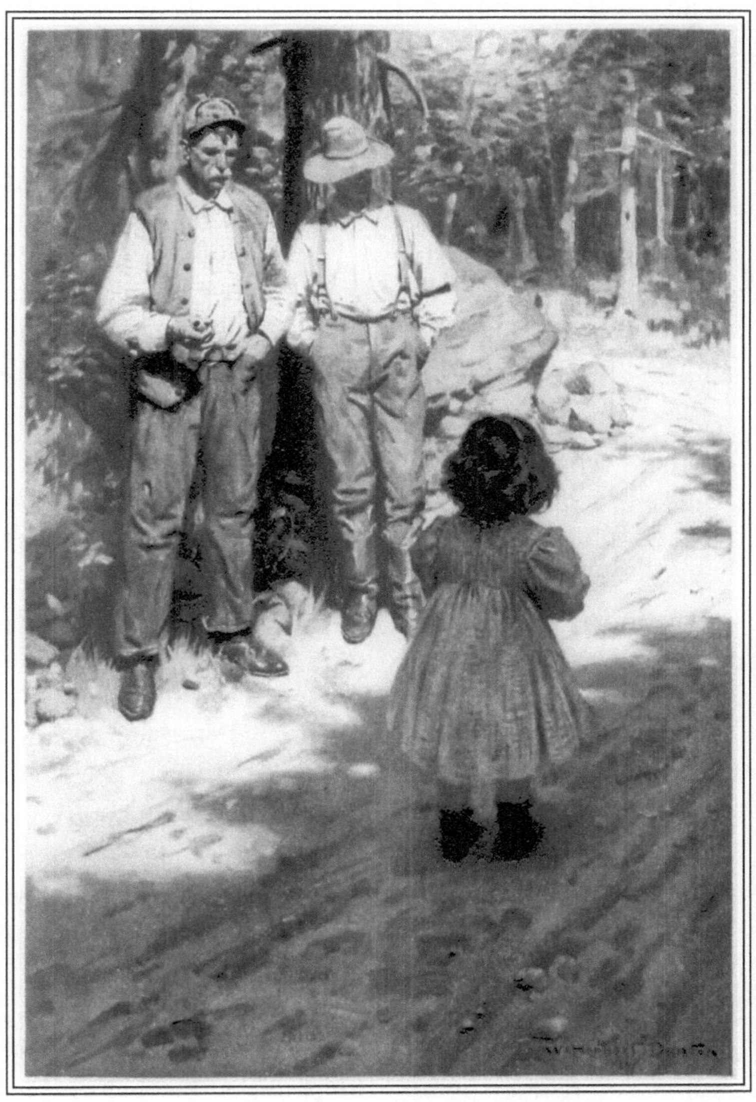

"D'YOU RECKON SHE'S LOST, JEFF?"

would conceal from the other the fact that he was thinking deeply.

"Who was that went on in front of us?" inquired the man in the green cap.

"Old Provine, goin' down the creek to see after his sawmill," replied the truck-grower. "I looked for him to say somethin' to me, but he took it out in glowerin'. Old man's got it in for ever'body since him and Aint Cynthi' Macklin had their last set-to over her granddaughter's church trial. That was masterest argu-mint I ever heard."

"She whupped him out, though."

"That's what she done. 'Lowed the Good Book says there's a time to dance, and Orphy should choose her own time about hit. They let the trial go over for decision, didn't they?"

"Yes; but I look for 'em to turn the pore gal out next month." He spoke with his mind centred on something else, which sharpened into utterance in the next few steps. "Look a-here, Jeff; tell ye what I'll do. Let your fence stand, and I'll sell you the ground as fur as the mistake occurred, and take the cow in part payment. Now, that's fair, ain't it?"

"Why, yaas, that's— why, that's fair enough; and I'd be willin' if hit was any other cow, but— Well, tell ye, Riley! I've got a heifer in the woods, fraish in Feb'wary; how about her and, say, five dollars cash?"

The tension had disappeared. A play of emotion almost boyish came back into both bronzed faces; their speech was once more interspersed with chuckles. Just before they passed out of sight one glanced backward to where a little checked cotton dress gleamed against the dusty briers.

Flittermouse had forgotten them. She was intent upon a streak of black ants, hurrying to and fro on a narrow trail of their own pioneering, on mysterious, alien business. "Free, four, five-six-seb'm- eight- nine-ten-leb'm-eight-nine-ten-leb'm- eight- nine-ten," she counted. At this point she was, by the similarity in sound between seven and eleven, invariably betrayed into a circle of four numbers. When she tired of it she began building a wall of sand, and placing chips inside it. "Pigs in a pen; a-a-all fensh op. Sooey, pig! Soo-o-ey!"

She tucked one foot under her, and grasping the other, rocked herself to and fro to the rhythm of a tuneless song: "Bat, bat, come un'er mine hat, an'— when I bake—" She forgot the rest, but the idea of baking reminded her of a certain promise of chicken for supper. She about to rise and resume her quest for Pappy, when a shadow fell on the ground beside her, and she looked up with a start that ran all the way from her top braid, the size of an ear of wheat, to her brown toes.

A shock-headed boy of twelve stood there, grinning. He carried a pole and line in one hand, and in the other a string of four perch. He was clad in a pair of homespun breeches and a man's shirt that, through various rents and a buttonless front, let the sweet wind flow all over his sunburnt body.

"What you think you're doin'?" he inquired.

In a country where two or three youngsters count for no more than a nest-egg, and a man's mother is likely to be only fourteen or fifteen years older than he is, children lack the opportunity, among the everlapping generations, for acquiring self-consciousness. Flittermouse was accustomed to take herself very much for granted as the next-to-youngest in a considerable family— neither the trusted eldest nor the petted baby, but just an extremely small girl whose duty was to keep out from underfoot and not meddle with hatching weedies. Her world was a child's world; she was used to being fed, played with, scolded, kissed, occasionally upset and run and run over by Joe and Orrion and Susy. It was only by accident that she stumbled to-day into the grown-up's country.

So, angry at being startled, she spoke to the boy as she felt, somewhat belligerently. "I'm zingin' zong," she announced. "You funny at me?" And as the freckled grin flashed broader, "No funny at me," she cried, and scrambled to her feet for a charge. But she came to a stop a few feet from the enemy, who had himself retreated in haste, snickering.

"I'm ain't go'n' kill 'oo," she reassured him, with more than a touch of magnanimity; "I was des a-p'ayin.'"

"Got a chip on your shoulder, though, ain't ye?" suggested the boy.

She followed herself round and round in her tracks, like a kitten, in the endeavor to ascertain whether indeed that portion of her anatomy bore such a decoration.

"You sure have; jist look!" he encouraged her, enjoying the manœuvre. "Well, if you ain't the funniest young 'un I might' near ever seed! What's you' name? Whar's you' paw? Want some May-apples?" he asked, with a motion toward his pocket.

But she shook her head, growing sulky with his increasing merriment, and stood pouting, her hands behind her back.

The spontaneous generosity of boyhood was on him, however; it was positively necessary that he give somebody something. As he went whistling on his way, he decided that it would be a capital joke to drop a mess of fish into his grandmother's water-bucket when she was not looking.

Alone once more, Flittermouse reseated herself on the sand. The shadows shortened as she played, and began to creep from the opposite side of the road. After a time she heard a patter of hurrying footsteps, and turned to stare at a girl who seemed to glitter as she came through the sunshine, so vivid was her hair, so brilliantly clean her apron.

Here again were approaching the thoughts that had power to divide like blades. "I can't live with her no longer," the girl was saying to herself. "It's her contrary ways, her weecked old tongue— they ain't to be endyored. I'd do better to run away to the Settlemint; I could make out to git me a new dress there oncet in a while, anyways. The idy of her a-havin' me pick berries all th'oo the season, and not lettin' me buy so much as a yard o' lawn! 'Be shore ye git the change right, Orphy,' she says. And now I've got to pick some more again' supper . . . . I can git away, and I jist will."

Then out of the wayside bushes blossomed a living rose— a child's face, wide-eyed and wondering, but with lips curved, ready to break into laughter.

For all her haste this girl, too, paused to go through the same sequence of questions as had the other people. It was a colloquy of which Flittermouse was beginning to tire. But this time it terminated charmingly. From her pocket the

[121]

girl produced a fat cooky, wide as a saucer, and gave it into a ready little hand.

" 'Oo nelcome," said the baby, with such gracious promptness that Orphy was moved to reply merrily, "Well— thank you!" She scurried along the road, tittering still; but she had ceased to scowl, and she went more and more slowly. At last she almost stopped, and counted over a few coins in her palm.

"I could keep this, and git to the Settlemint all right— git a dress, and find me some work," the girl muttered. "But she worked for hit as hard as I did— and the half I leave won't be near enough for her. Maybe I can stand to stay with her a while longer. She won't have nobody if I leave. She is my granny— I mustn't forgit that. And she was good to take me when maw died. And the time I had the mumps— an' then the way she stood up for me to the church folks—" Orphy laughed, and shook her shoulders. "If she'd only make up with Uncle Zeke's folks, and go visitin' oncet and again— Well, I vow, I'll stay with her a while, anyhow."

The bright figure was no bigger than a flower down the green vista now. Flittermouse, having eaten her cooky, sat happy as a lizard in the broad glare of afternoon light. Overhead shone the blue day; the rustle of the woods was all about. She laughed and cooed, patting sand-cakes with her chubby fingers; she rolled over like a puppy, and sat up shaking the sand from her plaits. Her hands were scratched and stained, her frock dabbled with mud through which she had waded.

What was there to be happy about? Nothing and everything. She might as easily have reflected that she was far from home, and found ample excuse for disturbing the peace with desolate cries. But she had, in baby fashion, the deep sense of reality that comes with joy; she felt the ocean of life beating, soft and warm as summer, strong as fate and salt as blood, all round and through her little being. Life everywhere! In the woods, the sky, the ground, it crept and swarmed burrowed and flew; life eyeless, helpless, dumb; life of a woodland grace, or elfin-quaint as Chinese carving; life winged and swift like a soul; life, the red gift of the sun! She heard its murmur, a summer sound, as of running water for and sweet. And oh, listen!— her features became rapt; she caught her breath and sat winking in intensity of attention— the Birdy was singing! Singing to Flittermouse as if she were the world and all. He must have known that she listened, there under the rustling trees. She uttered a gurgle of happiness; he sang again. In her heart the tide of feeling swelled; it rose and rose, till it was ready to brim over into tears or ripple out into laughter, she couldn't quite tell which. She loved things so!

Something seemed to take her by the throat, as if she were about to crow, or else to cry; it just trembled in the balance—

All at once she spied on the ground a short, thick stick or root, with an irregular knob on one end, like a head. It much the same as any other stick, and it had lain there all the time; but the little girl had had no need of it until now. From "head" to "baby" was made the instant connection of she scrambled eagerly to catch it up.

"Howdy, doll! What you be dere for?" " 'Ish is doll. I'm rockin' little doll; rocky-bye—" and before she knew it, Flittermouse had, like the bird, turned the almost unendurable tension of the moment into song. A queer song, bubbling tuneless but sweet from her plump throat, its words mixed up of two Mother Goose jingles learned from the older children:

> "Rocky-bye— wind blow,
>   We sha' have 'now,
>   C'adle rock: po-o-oh shing,"

over and over. She wrapped the doll in as much of her short apron as she could well get hold of, and rocked and crooned, her round knees showing like two eggs beneath the hem of the scarlet garment she always spoke of as her peckitoat. She sang to the bit of wood in her arms, but it was her own body that responded to the lullaby. It became increasingly difficult to hold the doll in its cradle. The firm earth bore her up so strongly; the sky watched her with measureless kindliness. It was as though she for once usurped the place claimed of late by little Man-alive, and lay clasped in her mother's arms. A good spot for a nap. But this reminded her that she was sleepy, and sleep, she knew, was what ended each of her beautiful days. She struggled to her feet, resolved to fight, this time with all her strength. She would not tamely submit to see this delicious hour snatched into oblivion!

But it was already drawing to a close. The touch of antagonism, as soon as she said to herself "I won't," shattered the whole lovely structure, like the fairy palace of frosted grasses that brother Joe had once brought in and set beside the fire. She found the same old weariness and disillusion that made sleepy-eye time coming upon her, eclipsing her happiness as usual. And she had supposed it would last forever, this beautiful runaway day!

She began to cry, heartily, as she did everything else, with a view to rousing succor from somewhere. Her way in trouble was to appeal vigorously to the cosmos: it had never failed her yet.

It did not now. From a hitherto unperceived by-path came stepping a quaint little old figure carrying a huge pail of blackberries and clad in a sunbonnet, neckerchief, and straight-gathered calico dress. A face with twinkling blue eyes peered out between gray curls— a face like a Limbertwig apple that has hung into November and shriv-elled with all its keen flavor retained inside. Flittermouse ceased her wailing, and gave the new-comer a glance of recognition, not of the individual, but of the type. Through tears she even smiled, with a little gasping cry of relief, as if at sight of some one she loved. This was a Grandma.

"Why, what's the matter with a little gal, out here all by herself?" asked the old woman, in a true grandma tone. "Air you lost from home?"

"Want a d'ink!" Flittermouse offered that as the most expressible and instant of her woes.

"All right; we'll jist go and find one," comforted the Grandma. "What's yore name, honey? Whose little poppee-doll air you? Tell Aint Cynthi' yore name!"

She set down her pail, and the mite, with a confidence born of long petting, instantly attacked its contents.

"Flittermouse," the redlips replied, juicily, between berries.

"And whar's yore Pappy?"

She gave the same vague answer she had given several times already. It did not, however, deceive Aunt Cynthi' in the least.

"Well, is that all the name you got? Don't Mammy call you something different when she scolds ye?"

Now it so happened that this little maid who fared forth so bravely into unknown lands that summer day was afraid of her real name. She wouldn't for any thing have attempted it. Her tongue had a trick of transposing sounds that some-times got her into difficulties; and at best this making people understand was the most serious and complicated business she had encountered in her life. So she remained silent, helping herself industriously, contentedly, from the berrybucket.

"And how'd you git here?' marvelled old Cynthi' Macklin, half to herself.

With a momentary return of the morning's exuberant spirits, Flittermouse threw her arms up and down and laughed out. "Des flyed away!" she said.

"Uh-huh! An' air you aimin' to fly back? You 'des' better fly along home with me, till I can find out who wants ye the wust," cooed the old woman, deep in her throat, fond blue eyes on the baby.

But this it appeared the tired child was unable or unwilling to do. They made two or three starts, but each time Flittermouse lagged and came to a whimpering stop.

Cynthi' was in a quandary. Neither the child nor the berries might safely be deserted, and she could not carry both. "If that triflin' Orphy was with me," she thought. "But thar! the gal's but a gal. I mind when she looked so much like this 'n' nobody could 'a' told 'em apart."

She was on the point of hanging the bucket in a tree, to be out of harm's way until she could come back for it, when she had an inspiration. At a wet-weather spring that trickled from a bank she dipped a corner-of her apron and washed the dusty, berry-stained little face ("Ain't go'n' ky," said Flittermouse, heroically, mindful of past struggles), and, taking advantage of the refreshment temporarily afforded by this process and by a drink from a leaf cup, she mounted the two tired legs astride a goodsized stick-horse, which pranced over the remaining distance without a sign of fatigue.

They turned in at a wooden gate half buried under honeysuckles. A house peeped at them through a screen of cherry trees beyond. For all her light-heartedness in wandering, Flittermouse went suddenly limp all over at the thought of getting somewhere at last. There were other houses in the neighborhood, of course, but they sat aloof to right and left of the road along which she had come, wher-ever was a sheltered lap of the hills or a spring hollow. The little girl yawned, her mouth opening like a hollowed rose, the tongue curling up as it were a single interior petal; and "I'm zo-o-o zeepy!" she complained, toddling after Cynthi' up the path.

She was hardly able to make away with the bread and butter she presently found in her hand. Sitting on the porch, she drooped and nodded over it, only half aware that a cheery old voice was recounting a story for her benefit: "And the fire began to burn the stick, the stick began to beat the dog, the dog began bite the pig, and the pig began to go-o!" After a while, in the big log room, Cynthi' Macklin stood looking down at a dimpled brown body relaxed in the depths of her feather bed. So heavy with sleep, so rosy and fragrant! She had almost forgotten what a bit of sweetness and tenderness a baby could be. She noticed how the long lashes swept the cheeks, how the under lip pushed the other slightly out of place, like a twisted azalea bud.

"She does favor Orphy when she's a baby; an' then agin, she's jist about the age o' Sam's Dythie," the old lips murmured, as Cynthi' bent to lay a cloth over the slumber-flushed face. "Jist about her size. Eh— law! I'll ventur' Dythie's forgot me— wouldn't reco'nize her granny a-tall. I'm e'en-about minded to go over and see Zeke's folks a-Sunday, me and Orphy. Ef hit wasn't for that no-'count boy o' his'n— they ort to put him to hoein' corn. I seed him go on this morning with a pole and a canful o' red worms."

She tiptoed away, turning to dip a gourd of water from the shelf by the kitchen door.

"Well!" she exclaimed, in astonishment. The gourd remained poised as she stared into the bucket. There, in the clear water, swam at some inconvenience a couple of shining perch.

"Well!" she said again. "That boy! . . . I will go over thar, come Sunday." A smile spread slowly across her features twinkling from her eyes in a sapphire gleam, seaming her pink cheeks into kindlier wrinkles than Orphy, just coming in with her afternoon harvest of berries, had ever suspected there.

"H'sh, Orphy," was the grandmother's greeting. "I got me a baby in here asleep."

"I'll bet hit's the little gal that was playin' in the road," the girl whispered, tiptoeing in to look. "Whose is she?"

"That's what we've got to find out, I reckon," the elder returned. "But see here what some one fetched us for supper! Now, Orphy, you blow up the fire, and I'll be in therectly to holp ye fix 'em."

She left the house, to lean over the front gate. Chestnut flowers were falling noiselessly through the dusk beneath the trees; old memories came to her on the perfume of these and the honeysuckles, now heavy with the approach of evening. She heard the deep brass of cow-bells, sounded from winding paths that led up out of the creek; fireflies began to sparkle in the shadowed grass. She might have been a maid harkening for her lover's footfalls, so youthful a brightness shone in her eyes.

By and by the old man whom Flittermouse had first met was seen returning at the same plodding gait. Cynthi' hailed with a question— an inquiry that made both forget the occasion of their last meeting. John Provine responded with grave interest. No, he couldn't say whose little gal had run away; he had seen one up yon a piece this morning, but had heard no stir of searching. No, couldn't come in, he was belated already, settling with a feller that owed him for some lumber— been around and let him have a ixtension of his note, like a old fool. N-no, he'd be late to supper— "and then like as not Sis' Betty she'd take 'n' set hit off the table; you know she's kind o'— No, thank y'. Well, I don't know jist—"

He found himself edging through the vine-bound gate, setting himself erect, and getting hold of his most stately manner. The gray curls that topped Aunt Cynthi's alert head quivered as their wearer fluttered to the house; she seated her guest in the place of honor on the porch, and took advantage of a half audible sigh from the sleeping child to run in and slip on— a bit of youth, of tender sentiment, of wistful remembrance, made visible— the lace collar that she had worn when a girl.

"And, Orphy, honey— if you'll hurry and make up some o' your best biscuits, and set on a jar of cherry preserves, I'll— I'll git ye a new dress in time for us to go to your Unc' Zeke's a-Sunday," she whispered, through the half-open door.

"Good gal to work, ain't she?" commented Provine, as the spirited old belle settled herself in the rocker opposite him. "She's shore goin' it lively at that supper-gittin'. Her feet sounds like she was a-dancin' again."

"I'm afeared you 'n' me 'll git into a argu-mint if we set here *too* long, so I told her to hurry up a bite for us," Cynthi' answered, twinkling. "Do you ricollect, John Awthur, the first quarrel we ever had?" Her cheeks were even pinker as she put the question. "We've been quar'lin' ever sence."

But there was no answering gleam of fun in his face. He made one or two efforts to speak, failed, and finally brought out: "I been sorry a thousan' times about that. You was half promised to marry me, Cynthi'— and then you went and took Macklin."

"Air you sorry you called me a witch?"

"I wish't somebody'd a-whupped me right thar when I done it. I do, I do, shore. Might 'a' learnt me some sense. Cynthi'," he stole a glance at her half-averted face, "you— you're the only—"

"Thar— thar's— I do b'lieve thar's Clay Sanders a-comin' home from work," she cried, jumping up nervously as a girl, "Let's us ask him about this here baby."

So it came about that Flittermouse, feeling herself swung into a well-known resting-place, was not put to the trouble of opening her eyes. She had followed the beckoning of fate that day, and traversed a wider circuit than she would ever know, carrying, all unconscious, her lamp of love and joy and innocence to light sundry dark places.

Flittermouse snuggled closer on the big shoulder, and murmured drowsily:

"Oh, Pappy, I'm des been a-coming— tell 'oo— dot sz-z-schick'n for zupper."

And Aunt Cynthi', hearing the gate close behind the pair, turned to the man beside her and asked coyly, "Do you ricollect ever seein' me wear this here collar before, John Awthur?"

Published in
Harper's Monthly Magazine - July 1910

The Breaks of Caney

EMMA BELL MILES

ILLUSTRATIONS BY HERMANN C. WALL

ZARALDIE

THE HOUSE SMELT LIKE A TAR-KILN from the billet of pitch-pine that blazed on a rack of two iron strips driven into the wall. The log next above was half charred away from having many times caught fire. The whole bare wall was richly darkened with smoke; goblin tags of soot depended from a ridgepole inaccessible to the sedge-grass broom. A freezing rain drummed on the cabin roof; the sword-song of the wind over the chimney was mocked by the joyous roar of the fire. Drops falling made little explosions in the embers and tinkled on the lid of the bubbling pot.

Dad Farris, for once perfectly sober, was basking in the warmth and radiance, and Orphy turned to him her steady eyes and good brown face all alight with eagerness. She had chosen this evening to discuss with him and Zaraldie and Man her project of seeking work in town.

The younger sister was seated on an oaken block directly in the rich light, a creature small and lovely like a bird, with dark curls falling on the rose-velvet of oval cheeks. Orphy, coming to stand behind the block, drew Zaraldie's hands back and held them so in a half-unconscious clasp.

"Looks to me," she said, "hit's the only way. We've tried our best to all stay together and at home, but ever' year gits harder."

"Hit's a long ways to the Settlemint," objected Man, from the shadowed corner where he had curled himself on a sheepskin. He was entering his teens, but was still "Little Man," having been christened "Jesse Edward" too late to oust his milk-name.

"Hit is so," agreed Orphy, swinging gently the hands she held. "But when there's only one thing to be done, why, there aint but one thing *toe* be done, and no multiplyin' words— "

"Why, howdy!"

They turned as the door swung wide, letting in a great gust of chill and storm. It was only Bud, the elder brother, come home for over Sunday; the plashing of the eaves had covered his approach. He walked in without greeting, threw a sack of provisions into a corner, and spread his hands to the blaze. When he became warm he drew a plug of tobacco from his pocket.

"Here, dad— and there's shorts and potaters, and a middlin' o' meat, in the sack. But that'll hafto do you'ns, now, until next week," he warned them, glancing round.

" 'Taint nigh as easy livin' somehow as hit used to be here," complained the old man.

"That's why I feel obleeged to make a new shift," Orphy reopened the subject for Bud's benefit. "We got to look furder away for a livin'. "

"I don't see how us folks 'll git on without ye here, Orphy— let alone Prentice Roark," said Bud, covering a deal of affection with a jest.

For the first time a quick shade of impatience crossed the face of the older girl.

"I don't care for vou-all knowin' here and now," she cried, "that Prentice Roark's one main reason why I aim to leave here the first day I can git ready to go."

They looked at her, standing proud and sweet in her warm youth and womanhood, daring the known and the unknown together, and they turned their gaze to the fire again, helplessly.

Orphy began to set the table for supper.

"Hit's strange she never has liked Prent Roark like the rest of us do," said Zaraldie, a week from that evening, after all farewells were said and their sister had adventured forth. "But ne'er a one of our folks ever wanted to leave home, either, did they, Dad?"

"Your Uncle Ed," the old man reminded her. "He's West somer's."

"Prent he jist bothers her; he's bound'-determined for her to have him," explained Bud. "Well, hit a-gain' to be hard a-gittin' along without her, but I don't believe she'll stay no longer'n the water gits hot."

He took the trail to the valley farm, where he worked for a weekly portion of provisions and his board, and Zaraldie bravely assumed her sister's duties at home.

After a few days of it she cried to her father, sitting futile though sympathetic in his place:

"Well, dad, if Orphy had sech a time as this— "

"She did; ye nee'n'to think otherwise," he replied. "You know, she had you two chaps besides, at first; your mother left Jess'-Ed'ard a baby in arms."

He bent forward, trying to assist in the rescue of the dinner, which the pot had turned out on the hearth.

"Why, here comes Prentice to fill up ol' Tiger!"

Old Tiger sat in state on the fireboard, a sleek and shining presence, and young Roark was wont to see to his plenishing. Prentice's clear and merry gray eyes recommended him to the lads, and this week he won a welcome by saying, as he helped to set up the pot:

"Well, I seed Orphy when I was in the Settlement yesterday. She's workin' for Dr. Lewis' wife— housework and cookin'. She hoped you-uns was well, and aims to come out and see ye whenever she can git away."

Zaraldie took the apparent message at face value, though she might have guessed that whatever Orphy had to send them of help or cheer would come through the far off mountain postoffice. But it was quite true that Prentice had not permitted the girl of his choice to escape him by merely going to town.

"I've got business thar pretty frequently," said he.

His confidence in the discretion of these friends was such that he did not mind their unavoidable suspicion that his business was in the interests of a still concealed under the breaks of Caney.

He continued a frequent visitor at the cabin, but what with bad weather, manifold duties, and the heavy winter roads, it was near New Year before her household saw Orphy again.

She came to them at last like a mother bird, bringing in a basket the substance of a holiday feast.

"But what makes ye look so worried, Orphy?" demanded Bud.

"I'm a-studyin' about you-uns," she answered. "Man looks peakid to me."

"Why, he's been well all along," said Dad. And the boy supplemented gruffly, "Aw, I aint sick."

"Well, another thing's worse, and that's Prentice Roark. He's been a-comin' too often."

"Not often enough," cried the owner of Tiger in sheer bravado.

Orphy, not wishing to spoil anybody's appetite, said no more at the time, but once abed the sisters talked it over.

"Bud spoke to Prentice," admitted Zaraldie, "and he laughed and 'lowed that so long as Dad's got obleeged to have liquor, hit mought as well be from his hand as anybody's. I think myself that's about the rights of hit.

He— he— brung me a right pretty pin from the store a-Christmas, and I didn't want to take hit. He told me that he was aimin' to be a brother to me as soon as he could, so hit was all right."

"He knows good and well there aint a true word in his mouth when he says that," Orphy assured her. "I aint able to think well of him, Raldie; and I do wish he'd stay away from here."

"You don't have no idy, Orphy, how lonesome we git with you and Bud both gone, and Prentice is good company," pleaded the little maid, loth to lose at once a hope and an ideal.

"I'm old enough to know my own mind, sister. There never was but one boy in the world for me, and I don't never expect to see him no more."

"Well, I'll give Prent back his pin if you say to."

"You better—and have no more to do with him."

Next morning, Orphy, more than ever uneasy, cornered Bud.

"Why'n't you notify Prentice to stop hangin' round our house?" she began valiantly.

"He don't hang round enough to bother me. Good Lord, sis! what have you got agin Prent? I'd have a fight on my hands right now if I was to send him a word like that," countered Bud.

"You'll have wors'n a fight if you don't look out. I'm afeared for Raldie; she talks as if he was much to her. Our little sister! I don't like hit."

"Shpppp! That all? She's only a little switch of a gal. Now don't you worry; me and Dad's enough to look out for her. If you feel anyways bothered, you'd best think better of what you've said, and take him yourself."

After parting with Raldie, who had "walked a piece" of the way with her, Orphy left Bud's well worn trail to the valley and turned into a fainter one that led across the creek.

By the dark sheen of frozen pools, past filigrees of the spray and drip of little cataracts woven over night, through the shivering trackless woods she descended, mile after mile, following the waters of Caney.

Prentice, in the rock-house that sheltered the still, had just got his fire going in the primitive furnace. Two other men, joint-owners with him of this industry, had left him in charge for the morning, and had gone to haul a sled of corn. From time to time a noise of squealing and trampling came from the thick brush down-hill, where his hogs in a pen were awaiting their share of the waste after boiling.

"Condamn your thick hides," he sent good-naturedly to their address between tasks. "Want to call up ever' revenuer in Tennessee?"

Suddenly, with an access of squealing, was mingled a clear young treble, singing an air that he and Zaraldie and her brothers had sung together round the cabin hearth not a week ago. He straightened himself and stood, gun in hand, with puzzled eyes on the trail.

As the girl's blue-clad figure came gradually into view through the semi-transparent maple brush, he drew a

THE GIRL'S BLUE CLAD FIGURE CAME INTO VIEW

breath of relief, although his face still expressed consider-able anxiety.

"Well!" he greeted her blithely, striding forward with lowered weapon. "I make you welcome, Orphy; but you've took a good deal on yourself a-comin' here! If ye hadn't a-sung that song, I'd a-took a shot at ye. Git to the fire and warm. We set on that boulder." He threw his coat over it for a cushion. "I been tellin' 'em this here place wasn't well hid."

"Tellin' who?"

"Oh, my shotes down yonder!" he laughed. "Why, you aint clumb all the way down Caney to find that out, have ye?"

"No, nor to look at shotes, neither."

She had laughed with him, but had not accepted the proffered seat, and now faced him with hands clasped before her.

"Prentice," she said, "wont you please stop a-goin' to our house?"

"Why, Orphy! whatever's got ye now?"

"Well, I've got a special reason for axin' sech a thing, or I wouldn't. Hit would please me mightily for you to promise me you'd never go there no more."

"Now, Orphy, s'fur's the old man's concerned, you know he's nachally got to— "

"Oh, don't say that to me!" she cried sharply. "That's what they all told me at home. Hit's something else I mean."

"I aint, honestly, doin' you-uns any harm that I know of."

"You know—"

She began in a low voice, halted, and then rushed on:

"You know I never have thought so much of you as my folks do; and I don't want Raldie to think too much of ye, neither."

She had chafed so against the necessity of asking anything of Prentice that now her impatience and confusion betrayed her into unguarded speech.

The young man stood looking at her flushed face, and thinking of what she had said.

"Oh," he said, quietly. "Why, I reckon the little trick likes me as well as I like her— for a sister. And I bid her to look at hit that way, too, because I'm always a-hopin' hit'll come to that yit."

"Well, *I* let her know hit'll never be!" cried Orphy, exasperated.

"Whatever made you do that, Orphy? Couldn't you see that only made bad worse? She ain't been studyin' about me noways but as a likely brother, and now you've fixed things so hit may change."

"But if you was to never go about her any more," urged the girl.

"There's an easier way, you know," he suggested, coming closer. "Jist change your mind, Orphy. Make me her brother. Oh, now, don't fly off. This is the first time the woman I want has ever sat by my fire. Jist think of hit. I wont stay away from yourns' house— not for sech a reason. Don't— don't send me away. Whilst I'm in this business there's but few I can trust, and I've got no folks of my own. I'd fur ruther give up distillin' if that 'll move ye," he begged.

Her face softened as she thought upon his plea. It was true, there were few houses he could enter with confidence. Yet she had waked the weary night thinking of Zaraldie; she must not weaken now. Even should Prentice sever his connection with the blockade still, she would have but little to offer him.

Sadly she propounded the immemorial triangle:

"But if she was to care for you and you for me, and I care for— "

The incompleted sentence maddened him.

"Finish that sayin', " he demanded harshly, pouncing on her and catching her by the shoulders. "Finish hit! Who do you mean?"

"Nobody," she answered doggedly.

"Tell me!" he insisted.

"It was a long time ago," she at last confessed. "I aint seen him for years."

"I knowed there was some reason I couldn't make no headway with you, but I never had thought of that. Mart, wasn't hit— the boy your uncle raised? Shucks! we was all chaps-like when they went West, and he's likely enough dead or married long ago."

They stood silent, gazing out across the wintry gulch. At last she despaired of attaining any adjustment in this way, and turned to go. Her errand had failed.

"Aint ye goin' to give me a answer?" he asked softly, turning with her into the woods.

"You've had your answer long ago. What you can want of a gal that deespises you, I can't see!"

HE FOUND ORPHY MORE THAN EVER DEFIANT

"Maybe because I've followed ye so long; maybe because I've told folks hit was to be; maybe because I'm jist that kind of a feller, but want ye I do, and have ye I will." He spoke earnestly and without bravado. "I'll let ye know how Raldie is, when I come to town next week."

"You'd do well to go slow!" she retorted. "I give Bud what I thought about it, and he promised to look after her."

Prentice would not let her see how deeply he was hurt by this; but under the lash of her defiance and suspicion he struck without taking thought:

"Oh, Bud's all right. He's a-learnin' to take his liquor like a man."

As he turned back to stoke the rude furnace, and indeed all the rest of the week, he was haunted by the white shocked face she turned on him before vanishing round the rock.

When he again visited the cabin Bud showed him a letter from Orphy. It's cry went straight through Prentice's armor:

"Bud, will you tell me, for God's sake, is it true that you are drinking? I can't sleep since I heard that. Let me know what could have started such talk.."

"I wonder who told her that tale," was the boy's comment.

"You write a answer and I'll take hit down with me," Roark advised, a little uneasily. He had not meant to be cruel.

He found Orphy, as he had feared, more than ever defiant, flung a little off her usual self-possession.

"I jist come to see if you'd changed your mind," he began. "And to tell you that Raldie aims to keep that pin for a while, anyway. You don't never know for certain."

"Oh, Prentice, I'm might' near sick. What makes you do me so? Didn't Bud git my letter? Oh, of course you'd not know. I ask ye oncet again, wont you stay away from our house?"

She laid down the knife with which she was scraping vegetables, and looked steadily at him over the big pan in her lap.

Prentice folded and refolded his soft hat between his hands.

"Orphy, I can't see for my life what makes you take on so. I've got a letter for ye from Bud; you can read hit right here. I was mean to tell ye what I did, but you'd riled me till I wasn't fairly at myself."

She reached for the letter, but he held it back.

"Tell me first," he begged, "that you'll give me a note to Raldie takin' back what you've told her. Orphy, I aint sech a bad one as you believe. I jist want your word that you'll marry me or nobody else," he insisted.

"Oh, I'll give ye that."

"And you'll write to the folks to say so?"

"Yes, yes; give me my letter!"

He came close to her, keeping the letter in his hand, looking in her face.

Orphy had risen, and now sprang back crying:

"Don't you touch me, Prent Roark— give me my letter!" and he obeyed.

Eagerly Orphy scanned the lines in which Bud assured her that the only liquor he had taken was when he caught a chill from being out in the raw winter rain. He could tell her, he would never love liquor; he "knowed too much about it now for his own peace." This was quite enough to set her at ease about Bud.

"If hit does you any good to know it, Prent, I hate you worse than ever for that lie," she declared, folding the paper slowly.

"Don't say that. Give me the writin' to the folks, now, and I'll go. I'm satisfied for the present to know that no man gits you if I don't."

So word went to the cabin home that sister had changed her mind and would some day "have" Prentice. But when the young, wild-catter explained to Zaraldie that she might now wear his pin, she answered that she did not care for it any more— he could have it back.

It required resolution of a high order to remain away from home under the circumstances, but the wages that supplemented Bud's earnings were not to be lightly fore-gone, and the woods were dark with summer ere Orphy came again. Dr. Lewis had planned for a few months' vaca-tion in Colorado and this allowed her a considerable stay.

July days are doubly long in the silent, beautiful lone-liness that broods over Caney. All the blue, drowsy after-noon the girls sat on the porch and the boys sprawled in the shade in the clean swept yard. They held little speech, satisfied to be together under the home roof.

But here was a grown-up Zaraldie, quiet and reserved for all the old impulsive affection. Orphy thought she perceived a shadow on the young face beyond what a few months of responsibility should cast.

"Have you been worried about Man, honey?" she inquired.

"Why, I never noticed he was poorly till you spoke of hit," replied the girl with some compunction.

"I reckon what you need's a tonic, Man; but they tell me might' near all of them's got liquor in 'em, and I don't want to commence givin' ye that."

"Prentice might have let me have some o' his'n," said Man, "but when I named it to him he 'lowed he wouldn't hardly dast to with you promised to marry him. He told me he aims to quit makin' liquor this month, anyway."

"He's 'lowancin' mine," was Dad's contribution.

"Would you go to see Dr. Lewis before he goes West, Man?" she asked.

"Aw—I don't know."

The doctor's office was no dragon's den to Orphy, who had often put it to rights in the morning; and she was able to partly overcome the boy's trepidation. It was decided that Bud should accompany his brother to the Settlement next day.

But Zaraldie's trouble was beyond medical aid. That night, while the whippoorwills wailed in the edge of the woods and the garden sparkled with fireflies, Orphy was aware of her sister's wakefulness; she could not be sure whether there was a tremor of inaudible sobbing.

At last she could no longer keep silent.

"Honey, what ails you? I can't stand it not to know. Tell sister!"

She crouched beside the girl, on the patch work wrought by patient hands long dead, and speaking as to the child who a few years ago had been content, on waking from some terrifying dream, to find that sister's breath still stirred her hair.

But she knew it was a woman who answered:

"I want to go away. I'm tired, tired of· hit."

"Where you want to go to?"

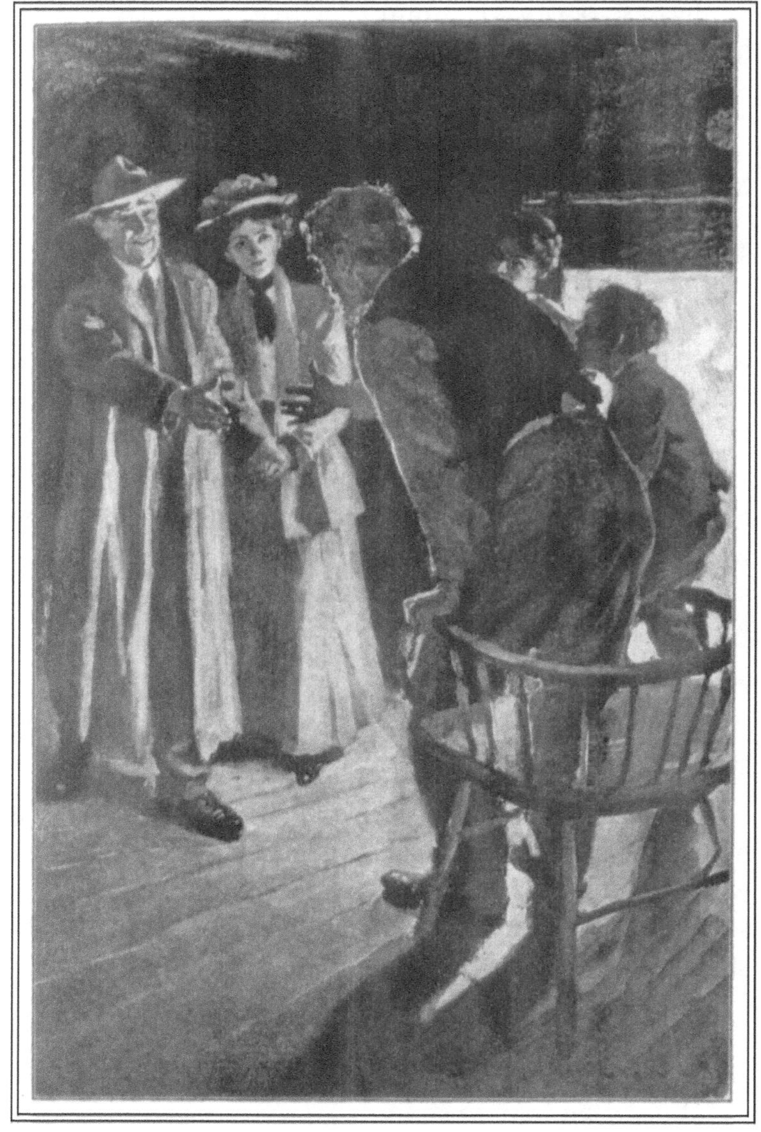

"WHY, HOW'RE YE, JESSE?" HE RUMBLED, GENIALLY

"I'd like to git me something to do, like you did. I can cook good now. Why can't you and me jist change places?"

"I don't see how we could do that, Raldie," said the maid-mother, knowing how different was the work in town from everything learned in the cabin, and sure that Zaraldie among strangers would wither like transplanted mountain-laurel. "You see, when you said you wasn't goin' to school, I promised Miss' Lewis I'd go back and stay with them another winter. But I wont promise for no longer, so you can get away next year."

"Next year. Oh!" and Raldie's voice broke.

"The boys and Dad couldn't make out without us, or I'd jist take you with me."

"Aint ye goin' to git married and settle down?"

"Not this year," temporized Orphy, weakly.

The days drew forward, slipping one by one, beads of a golden rosary, but threaded on a triple strand of pain.

One night as they dressed for a play-party in a neighboring cove, Orphy inquired, as she was about to fasten Zaraldie's collar:

"Where's your pin?"

"What you axin' me that for?" flashed Zaraldie. "You still mad cause Prentice give hit to me?"

"Why, I jist thought hit would look pretty on you. I wasn't never mad about it," said Orphy, in surprise at the outburst.

"I done lost hit long ago."

And Raldie fell to brooding.

That evening, in the course of a game, Prentice chose Zaraldie for a partner— Zaraldie in a white dress, curls, and string of beads, sweet and warm as a velvet rose. "Fire on the mountain, fun, boys, fun," he sang, dancing all over with the mountaineer swing, his head just clearing the rafters,

As he took the girl's hand to lead her through their part, suddenly Orphy knew. That flushed, sweet face, with a dark-eyelashed twilight of modesty veiling its starry happiness, could mean but one thing.

It was Prentice who, on the way home, let her know how he and Zaraldie had been together at a number of frolics during the past winter.

"She's good company oncet she gits a-goin'. And I think, seein' she's to be my sister, you nee'n'to object. I do think you treat me scandalous."

Orphy was baffled, wordless. Prentice never presumed on the promise she had given him, but she felt bound by it to a semblance of friendliness. There seemed nothing she could do.

As the summer went on, her knowledge of Raldie's poor, little, unconfessed love became a wall between the sisters. Neither was able to speak of it; neither could think of anything else. Prentice's appearance in the low doorway at any hour sufficed to set both girls acutely on the defensive.

And he caught himself more than once watching Zaraldie, or doing small services and offering small services for the glance of warm thanks she could not forbear giving him. Zaraldie was being happy while she could. Orphy had promised that she should go to town when Prent was married; but "I needn't go; it will be the end of life to me," thought the young girl; and meantime, "Nobody need know that I care." Yet sometimes, when she and Prentice were alone together, a current of emotion flashed from one to the other; their speech fell away into silence, and they smiled at each other with trembling lips.

"If Orphy would only look at me like that!" was his longing.

One day, when the blue and gold of September was inclining toward the richer purple and scarlet of autumn, Prentice hauled a load of apples to town. As Orphy was now ready to return to her place there, he offered her a seat in his wagon.

"If Man'll help me load 'em he can ride over the mountain with me, too, and see that doctor again. My Limbertwigs is all honest produce this time," he added, laughing. "I'm out of the liquor business oncet for all."

Almost the look he craved rewarded him.

When Man came home he sat till far in the night recounting what the doctor had told him of the West.

"He seed our uncle Ed out there. Says you can ketch feesh with your hands in Uncle Ed's errigation ditches. And he raises, I don't recollect what all; you ride over his land a hour before you git to the house. And when he heared the doctor was from this part of the country, he axed about us, and Doctor Lewis he told about me, and— and he 'lowed he aimed to send for me to come out there."

"What did the doctor say about that?" asked Bud.

"He judged hit might do me a power o' good, and he hoped how soon I'd go."

November spilled the year's wealth upon the land in wild frost-sweetened fruits and mast and chestnuts, and Bud's hearth-fires grew in glory, fed with fat knots and roots of pine-flowing over logs, licking round 'the kettle, whirling against the soot-mossed back of the fireplace, displaying rainbows of strange colors: and pouring finally into the black throat of the chimney as a waterfall disappears into a sunless gorge. No stranger can ever know the real beauty of this red heart of home, which mocks the old north with its low, cheery music— with soft roar of burning, with laughing sparkle, with flicker and blue flutter, with the fusillade of hickories, and the "treading snow" of brands half-consumed, and the last clink of the falling ash at sleeping-time.

Into this radiance came Prentice one evening, his lungs and his garments filled with the breath of the keen dear night.

"Hit'll frost to-night," he said, nodding all round. "Like a young snow."

"I make ye no less welcome, Prent," complained Dad Farris, "but hit's a ondisputed fac' that I aint had a drap o' good whiskey sence the last you give me. This here boughten stuff's a sin to the lizards. I cayn't drink hit."

"Sorry," laughed the young man. "I'll show Raldie how to make persimmon beer, and we can all drink some. But I got shut of that business in a good time," he continued, seating himself in one of Orphy's new chairs. "You'ns aint heared about the raid?"

"We never hear anything 'thout you or Bud tells us," Dad's tone was still aggrieved.

"Well, they sure made one today. That marshal must be a devil-yarker! Went right down Caney alone, and slipped up on 'em in the still— ketched 'em makin' a run, and slipped between them and their guns and covered 'em. They got rattled and run spang into his arms. Got 'em both."

"Oh, I'm proud you was out of hit long ago," breathed Zaraldie.

"I am, myself. Orphy she'll be glad to hear about hit. You can write her."

They told the thing over and over, and discussed all its aspects again and again, fixing it well in mind. Afterward the conversation turned to Orphy; where was she, and when would they see her again? Was she growing too fond of staying in town? Or was she, on the contrary, unhappy with homesickness?

Bud and Prentice were upholding one balance of probability, and Raldie and Dad another, when again the door swung open, and Orphy herself appeared.

"I was hopin' you'd all be settin' up together!" she cried joyously, before any of the startled occupants of the room could frame a question. "Dad, here's Uncle Ed come to see you. We walked out from town together."

A tall man stooped through the doorway behind her— a man browned with many summers and grizzled with many snows, yet in appearance younger than Dad.

"Why, how're ye, Jesse?" he rumbled, genially. "You're gray as a rat. What y'been a-doin' to yerself?"

"Are you Uncle Ed? Are you Dad's brother?" screeched Man in delight, dancing on one leg all round the hastily quitted circle of chairs.

The two men shook and shook both each other's hands; then the Westerner caught the mountaineer by the shoulders and shook him; then they fell to shaking hands again, Dad reiterating all the while that he was indeed "powerful weak, powerful weak, Ed, but hit does me a world o' good to see you."

"Well, I aint so surprised," said the newcomer, standing back at last, "not when I look at your family, and think Ann's been dead this many years. This Bud? Howdy! Man ever' eench. Orphy's been a-tellin' about him as her and me come on. Raldie, honey, come and give your ol' uncle a kiss. They been skase things in my time. Like sis Betty, aint she, Jesse? Here's the boy that's goin' home with me? Looks to me you must have growed too fast, Man. They ortn't to have give ye sech a name to live up to, and then ye might have took your own time to hit. You can read and write, can't ye? That's right. I always 'lowed there ought to be a few scribes in amongst sech a bunch o' Farrisees."

Dad slipped his word edgewise. "This here's Prentice Roark— old Arch's boy, Ed. He's e'en-aboyut one o' the family," with a nod toward the fireside where the two sisters stood.

"Howdy, boy. I'd a-knowed you was Arch's by your looks. So you and Orphy's promised? Well, well— she never named you to me, and I was jist a-fixin' to tell her what Mart said. You recommember him, do ye? He 'lowed if she wasn't married he'd be glad to hear from her. He's in with me on the sheers."

"Mart!" breathed Orphy. "Is he— how is he?"

"He's all right. He's turned out well, honest and stiddy, and smart with hit; jist the man for any gal, be she free.

Good thing for Mart he don't know ye like you air now, or he'd be powerful disappointed."

They fell to planning for Man's going away; then Uncle Ed must hear the news of old neighbors, and the others must be told of the wonderland West. But Prentice sat silent, drawn back into the corner. He looked from one sad girl face to the other, and bethought himself of a way to lighten the shadow on both.

But like the Indian who inhabited his forests aforetime, the mountaineer moves with caution until the moment to strike. The hickory log had burnt to a bed of coals ere he finally spoke the word that freed them all from a false position.

"You're mighty right I aim to be one o' the family," he stated abruptly, "the first chanst I git, but you're mistaken in the gal."

Uncle Ed, unaware of the sensation aroused by this seemingly innocent explanation of a very natural mistake, talked on.

"I had good luck takin' one boy to raise; I feel considerable encouraged to try another. And if so be you aint promised to nobody, Orphy— well, I wouldn't let Raldie put me to dance in the kettle if I was you."

But all the young people, at least, knew what Orphy meant by her murmur as Prentice took his leave:

"I might have treated you better, Prent."

"That's all done and forgot about," he answered.

The light of the embers reddened moment by moment on the group of happy faces, and the brave housegear that

Orphy's service had introduced. A hoarsely jubilant chorus of cock-crow arose from the chimney shelter outside.

It was Zaraldie who flung open the door for Prentice; and they two stepped forth to say good-night beneath the black-diamond stars.

Published in
The Red Book Magazine - March 1910

Three Roads and a River

EMMA BELL MILES

ILLUSTRATED BY HOWARD E. SMITH

Before the cabin ran the wild mountain stream, its dark-green water, wonderfully clear, sliding under steep banks overhung with thickets of laurel. Just here, after fretting for miles against the bluff, its current swung wide over the shallows and rippled quietly up the shore; up to where the rude raft that was Hutson's Ferry lay idle under a leaning service-tree tasselled now with silvery bloom. The warm sweet tide of spring was rising in the valley, its line of advance visible far up the mountainside in the shapely gold-green tops of tulip trees. But for the first time in fifty springs no quickening of travel was perceptible at this centre of the fan-like network of trails that threaded the ravines and ridges. The government had last year flung a bridge across at the Narrows, where four pines stood black against the tender opalescent mists of the April sunset. And the government's new highway, unmindful of the fate of Hutson's log house and its inmates as of an unfortunately placed ant-hill, cut diagonally across the old road which

Hutson's grandfather had built before the war. It short-ened the distance between town and settlement by several miles; and even if it had not, what countryman laden with game or produce but would ride out of his way if need be to escape the payment of ferriage and toll?

So, instead of hailing his acquaintance from the toll-shack— which had latterly been put to use as a chick-en-shed— old Zion Hutson brooded in his doorway and smoked all through the long spring mornings. The road which his son, Shell, had been wont for a livelihood to keep in tolerable order was rapidly becoming impassable. Thus seated, the old man could pretend to forget the woful ruin, since it was out of sight; but from the field spring it showed for a long way up the mountain, a mangy scar, worn more rutty and sidling by every rain. And farther up, he knew, the "corduroys" were rotting, and overhanging stones were being let down one by one in frost and thaw.

The winter had been a hard one for a valley in this lati-tude. Grandmother Hutson, unable to endure it, died of "winter fever" and lack of proper nourishment, and the old man, lost without his mate, was daily becoming feebler. "Every change o' the moon takes something out o' him," said Ona. He muttered to himself continually as he smoked and drowsed in the sunshine; sometimes he broke into curious fragmentary prayers, he was being shredded of his wits by the dragging days.

There was little to eat in the house. To old Zion, who used to kill from five to ten hogs every Thanksgiving, the fact of being without meat was incomprehensible. His mind reverted again and again to the subject, trying to account for the omission of killing-day from the winter's calendar.

He seemed to believe that it was in some way Shell's or Ona's fault.

"I don't see what ever could a-went with that big barrer," he would begin, fretfully. "Last time I seed that hog was—" and he would recount time and place with circumstantial detail.

"Why, pap, I'm satisfied the pigs all died up in that bad spell in Jiniwary, same as the bees did," Shell would explain.

"Ef there'd a-been any mast last fall, they'd a-lived through." The old man always accepted Shell's view until next time.

"Yes, ef there'd a-been any mast."

"Anyhow, y'uns missed hit by sellin' ol' Piedy."

Here Ona, who on her children's account needed the cow sorely, turned consoler: "We couldn't a-kep' her through, pap."

"Well," he grumbled, "ye might a-made hit th'oo Jiniwary with her on what crab-grass ye've got stuffed in them two straw-ticks. We-uns could a-slep' on saidge-grass or leaves."

They forbore to argue, and old Zion relapsed into silence.

The orchard came out bravely in its spring array, and Ona helped her husband dig up a truck-patch and plant it with the seed saved from last year's garden— beans, beets, and okra, pumpkins and cucumbers, and a larger patch of cow-peas and field corn; but seed potatoes or onion sets were not to be thought of. The meal was low in the barrel; the coffee was out. There was only a little sorghum, a little lard— salt in the piggin, and vinegar in the keg. Ona felt more frightened at this state of affairs than either of the men.

The two children alone remained outside the shadow that rested on the house. Behind the kitchen was an old Limbertwig whose branches swept the new grass in a circle round the body of the tree; and within this flowery screen they made a playhouse with piled stones and broken crockery, and moss from the spring branch, and early flowers— Sunday-shirts, fish-blossoms, rooster-fights, and wild honeysuckles, stuck into a rusty baking-powder tin. Here they frolicked as though the crumbling smokehouse contained all the plenty of former years. One rainy day they fretted at being housed, till their mother threatened to shut them in the toll-house with the chickens. She put them to bed an hour early, and sat with folded hands before the fire. The darkness was turbulent with rushes of rain, alternating with whooping gusts. Early in the evening had been far-away gleams of lightning and half-heard thunder; but now it was turning cold.

Presently Shell entered, and drawing the loose brands and the forestick forward, threw a thick log on behind.

"Now, Shell, you haul them chunks out," remonstrated old Zion from the shadows of his corner. "You know the sayin', 'A house built over stumps never stands, and a faar built over chunks never burns.' "

"Turned a right smart colder, ain't it?" asked the woman, anxiously.

Shell nodded. "Gwine to be a freeze, I'm afeared."

"Blackberry winter!" muttered old Zion.

"That frost last week only peenched the peaches some. But this here—" Shell's gaze went out the little storm-beaten window, and returned to the bed where his children lay. The danger was too grave for many words. So much depended on the orchard's yield.

Ona, in the firelight, crouching, looked up at her husband. Woman-like she took little count of her own plight; but the sight of her man ragged and hunger-bitten filled her with pity and dismay.

"I wrote to Nettie a-Tuesday," she said, abruptly, breaking a silence. "I 'lowed she'd maybe holp us out some— till the gyarden truck begins to come in."

"Well, shorely 'n' ondoubtedly she will," put in the old man. "Did ye tell her I ain't got no tobacker?"

"Why, she'll know in reason you ain't," said Ona, smiling.

"Ne'er a chaw!" said old Zion, plaintively.

"A-Tuesday— then she ort to git the letter afore this time, I reckon," said the younger man, kicking the fore-stick and sending up a crackle of sparks. He was ashamed to show the relief he felt at this slender hope.

"She may holp us out till the gyarden comes in."

"Yes, till the gyarden truck comes in."

"I heared Steve Miller was a-doin' well."

"Lord! thirty dollars a month, and nobody to keep but them two."

"Well, he does send some home to his mother," said Ona. "But I hope he can make out to spar' us a little."

She got up and went into the dark inner room to get a drink. Something crackled ever so faintly under the gourd as she dipped it. Was it a leaf? A dry leaf that had fallen into the bucket on its way from the spring? Forgetting to drink, she felt over the surface of the water with trembling fingers. Even then she refused to be convinced; she obtained a sliver of fat pine and lit it at the hearth.

"What you lookin' for ?" asked her husband.

"I— drapped the gourd." she replied.

By her miniature torch she examined the thin crystals fast forming round the sides of the bucket. There was no mistake.

"Hit's a-freezin'," she whispered through dry lips. "Hit's a-freezin'. " Extinguishing the little flame, she stood staring into the darkness. Their only hope lay now in Nettie's generosity.

"But she cain't, she couldn't keep us that long. We'll have obleeged to— move. Shell can maybe git work in town, where her man is. . . "

A knock, sounding above the drumming rain, brought her hastily into the main room. Shell flung the door wide; and, pushed by the storm, a woman staggered across their threshold. She reached the fire and crouched over its red warmth with a little moaning cry before throwing back the shawl from her haggard young face and dripping hair.

"Nettie! Lord, if hit ain't Nettie!" cried Ona.

"Why, we-uns was jist a-talkin' about ye!" quavered Nettie's father.

"You sick?" inquired Shell, briefly.

"Well, up-on my soul! what you out in this rain fur? Ain't ye might' near dead?" Ona advanced toward the newcomer, trembling, incredulous.

"I rode as fur as the nigh cut in a huckster's wagon," answered Nettie, spreading her shaking hands almost in the flame, avoiding the gaze of all. "But I got wet walkin' the rest of the way. Hit's a-sleetin' now— freezin' up everything." She folded her arms on her knees and bowed her head upon them. "I don't know what y'uns 'll think o' me comin' home like this, pap; but I didn't have no place else to go."

"Why, Nettie! what's the matter?" Ona crouched beside the shivering form and touched her sister-in-law gently. "Come, honey, git up and set in a chair."

"Steve, he's gone," explained Nettie, without raising her face. "Nobody don't seem to know where. He couldn't make nothin' after the mill shet down, and he got out o' heart. I reckon he may have went to look for work som'er's. But people there got to makin' a mock o' me, and I couldn't let on no longer to know where he was at, so I come home for a while, till I hear from him. Oh, my Lord, how I suffer! . . . I didn't have no other way to turn."

"There now! there now!" Ona patted the heaving shoulders, but her own heart sank. The wind, as always before a cold wave, made nightmare sounds over the chimney, hooting like the great ghost-owl of Cherokee myth: the sleet in a fiercer gust leaped and clawed beast-like at roof and door.

"You better fix her a bed, Ona, and a hot drink," said Shell.

"There ain't no coffee," his wife reminded him, going to her store of quilts.

There was a new sound in the cabin before the close of another day— a pinpoint wail stabbing the vast mountain silence, a cry of unnameable desolation, a protest, bitter and piteously thin, against the untried task of living. Ona, alone tended on the helpless two. Ere the lean years had gnawed away their substance, the Hutsons had fronted their world with a gay independence, a cheery arrogance which neither asked nor gave; they would not now cry for help. And since latterly Zion had relinquished his post as autocrat of affairs religious, the three or four neighbors, a few miles up river and down, had more than ever got into the way of letting them alone. So Ona and Nettie won through the terrible hour unaided.

The sun on the evening of the birth set golden fair, but it was on a blighted garden. The orchard was a spectacle of marvellous beauty—bough after bough sheathed in clear ice ere a bud could shrivel or a petal fade; fairy gold, sure to melt with dawn. Shell broke a glittering spray and fetched it in for the women to look at.

That week saw the last of Ona's chickens, each of which tided the family over another day and furnished Nettie a bowl of broth. Old Zion almost forgot his longing for tobacco in his joy at seeing his daughter at home; but Shell and his woman, needing every bite for their own little ones, could give scant welcome to another mouth. The situation was managed, however, with the adroitness usual to the mountaineers, and it was not until she was up and about

[164]

SECRETLY ADDING THE CONTENTS OF THE BOTTLE

again that, in helping with the housework, Nettie discovered their extreme necessity.

She felt bound to speak of it. The two women were sewing, having found some old things that could be cut into little garments. The light from the doorway fell upon their glinting needles; the air came in softly, as if no blade of frost had mowed the land.

"Yes— two days more, and there won't be even pones and white gravy," Ona confessed.

Nettie swayed gently the little bundle in her lap beneath the sewing. "Nor no more white beans like we had yesterday?"

"I borrowed that mess from Mis' Nicklin; I've done borrowed of her till I'm pine-blank 'shamed to show my face there any more. Howsomever, I got obleeged to go som'er's to borrow some for seed."

"You got nothin' to plant again?"

"Little okra, and some beet seed, that's all. Shell, why'n't ye kill some rabbits?"

The man addressed lifted his head and stared sombrely out upon the barren field next the river. "I ain't got more'n three charges o' powder."

"Well, ketch a mess o' them little bony pyerch, then. Lord! we cain't give up."

"Used to be," piped old Zion, suddenly, "that a man here could go out and kill him a deer or a turkey afore breakfast,"

Shell took down his gun from the rack over the fireboard and fared forth. All that day he was gone. When he returned, after dark, he flung down something heavy, slamming it on the kitchen table without a word. It was a shoat he had killed. It looked to Zion much like one of the Nicklins'; but the head, which might or might not have borne the Nicklins' earmark, was missing.

"Shot all to pieces," the hunter explained to the womenfolk.

There were pots full of pork and strong gravy now; but this was not the food needed by the young ones, who soon began to look puny and downcast. So Nettie, leaving her baby in Ona's care, went far and wide, foraging in all fence corners and under sunny banks for frost-nipped shoots which the sun had coaxed out afresh. These salads, deliciously contrived with salt, vinegar, and dripping eked out their fare for many days; meantime, as Nettie was fond of pointing out, the bean vines came apace. Only in the young mother's sea-colored eyes was a radiance of hope; her spirit was as bright against the others' moping as her hair against the smoky interior of the cabin.

Ona was frying the last of the meal (they had traded a quarter to some camping hunters for meal), when the little boy ran to her crying, "Mammy, I'm find somep'n." He showed a handful of crumpled green tips. "In gyarden."

His mother could not restrain a cry of delight. "Them white multipliers o' ma's— and pa'snips! Oh, I do hope there's enough for a mess— "

The child, elated at having produced a sensation, went to point out his trove among the dry stalks and kecksies of the unploughed field; and that day Ona surprised the family with vegetables for dinner. "Hit ain't a mess— jist a bite around," said she. But Nettie slipped her portion on to the children's plates.

It was two or three days after this that her own baby began the continuous moaning fret of hunger. She looked upon him in despair.

"I'd take 'nd wash that baby in the deeshwater if he was mine," said Ona. "That was my mammy's rimidy. I couldn't count ye the peakid babies she fattened that way. Hit's greasy, you know, and they git the strength of hit."

"There cain't be a great deal o' stren'th in our deeshwater," said Nettie, walking the floor with her child. She had maintained that same unavailing pace for hours.

"Eh-law!" said the other mother, watching her. "Childern never pays for their raisin'. "

"They do!" flashed Nettie, lifting the downy head to her cheek. "Mine evens up hits little account with me every day of hits innocent life."

That same evening Shell returned from a three days' quest for work.

"Nobody wouldn't talk to me about hit," he said. "Where I wasn't knowed at sight they taken me for a tramp. I heared the's men now a-walkin' the streets in the Settlemint, so I never went there. But a feller told me of a womern furder on that lived by herself and wanted a man to take charge of her place. Well. I went plumb on out there, and she— she— sicked the dawg on me."

He fell silent, but the two children burst into sobbing.

"Pappy— never— brought us nothin'!" cried the little girl, burying her head in her mother's lap.

Shell Hutson stood up. His face became terrible. Ona shrank away from him affrighted for a moment; but all he said was: "Oh, baby! Honey!"

Then he went out. The children cried themselves into a restless sleep. Though the two women sat beside the hearth till daybreak, Shell did not come in again.

There was meal gruel for breakfast, and in the cloudy dawn old Zion set forth with knife and basket, having bethought himself of a burnt cabin down the river where might be found yet another mess of poke salad. It was a dark morning, the sheet of cloud drawn smoothly over from the west; for all daylight a low pale illumination streamed from beneath its fringes that swept the eastward forest. Sounds came far through the heavy atmosphere; he delayed his plodding more than once to hear, with a deep despondency, the wheels of laden wagons crossing the government's bridge, like the very car of progress leaving him and his in its desolate wake.

He was not disappointed; round the cinder-strewn area stood plant after lusty plant, fresh and succulent as anything ever forced under frames for a city market. As he sat resting on the door sill of an outhouse which the flames had spared, the glint of a bottle, thrust in a high chink and forgotten, caught his eye. Old Zion reached for it in hope of finding whiskey; but the contents turned out to be a dark fluid of sinister strength, some unknown chemical, at which he sniffed gingerly, till the skull and cross-bones on the label apprised him of its dangerous nature.

"Wow! Hit's a good thing I didn't take a swaller 'thout lookin', " he exclaimed. But after he had gathered his basket full of greens he tucked the bottle carefully under the broad, glossy leaves. He had no idea what use he could ever make of it; he acted only from the ancient, half-superstitious reverence for virtues and drugs, and from an inborn reluctance to throw away anything.

"Y'ain't seed Shell yit?" he inquired, as soon as he reached home.

No one had.

"Have ye got ary bit o' meat-grease left? Poke's liable to make people sick if hit ain't cooked up good and greasy. Now, Ona, don't you go and th'ow out them stalks, You'ns have got lots o' vinegar. I'm a-gwine to make us some pickles; they'll be good again' supper-time." The greens were bubbling in the pot and the sun lay some hours beyond the noon-mark, when Shell came in. Then from every one of the little assemblage broke a cry of astonishment and joy; for he carried a bag of meal and a salt pork middling.

"Bought 'em," he informed the company, shortly. His face had not relaxed since last night. Into the hand of his woman he poured a jingle of silver coins; then he dropped heavily across the foot of the bed as though he had been drinking.

"Now, by Jackson!" exulted the old man, "I want you gals to cook like ye was feedin' a rigimint. I wonder— how do you reckon Shell got—" He broke off, and his face changed slowly as he looked at the figure prone there, defeat, in this moment of seeming victory, showing in its every line. In the eager preparation for a supper feast no one heeded old Zion's staring at his son, sinking lower and lower in his chair. Finally he rose unnoticed and hobbled out-of-doors.

Nettie meantime came to the voicing of a matter which had occupied her thoughts all day.

"Ona, you think if you'ns had a cow ye could feed my baby, without me, so he'd thrive?"

"On a bottle ? Why, I reckon so. Why, yes. You ain't studyin'—"

"I'm a-studyin' about goin' back to the Settlemint. I can git work there, and holp to keep us all."

"Why! you said ye tried and couldn't!"

"Oh, that was before the baby was born. I can, though, now I cain't hide here with you'ns; this little bit o' grub won't do us no time." Nettie knew that there was work in town at which a woman could always earn enough to feed several mouths. It seemed now the only way.

"Well," cried her sister-in-law, an edge put on her tone by her insistent misery, "I wisht ye'd a-said so a good while back!"

Nettie laughed and went to put the baby's small belongings in order. She must send Shell to bargain for Nicklin's fresh cow tonight, and go before the child should awake in the morning; there was no time to be lost. "Pore little man-boy! I'll come home every week, to see that they take good care of ye," she whispered to the wee shirts and frocks. All at once she lifted the blue silk cap that the baby's father had bought only a few days before his disappearance. Something else was folded inside, as being, like the cap, too dainty for actual service—the lace handkerchief Steve had given her on Christmas morning. Heart-wrung, she laid her head on the window-sill and cried her slender strength away.

It was near sundown when she again looked out of the narrow panes; and as she gazed her face brightened unaccountably, as if by some spiritual dawn invisible to the other woman at the hearth.

"I reckon I won't go yit awhile— not tomorrow," she said. "Wait a day or two. . . "

On the bank of the river old Hutson walked up and down, wringing his thin hands, swaying his head, and muttering, muttering, muttering. He was praying for a sign. He had in mind the starved wife he had buried; his daughter deserted and helpless through poverty; his son, he suspected, driven to crime. The vision of destruction clutched his failing heart like the talons of those fiends that abounded in his theology. He could not endure the thoughts that came to him. But there must be some way out, if he could but find it; and he prayed, prayed desperately, that his God would show him the way.

Overhead the clouds were breaking with the close of day. Under their flying lights and shadows the river changed, and changed again, with indescribable pale hues, colors of strange metals molten, alloys of copper and silver; now sheeted gray as aluminum without a gleam, again taking lights as of dusty gems, amethyst and emerald and beryl, with riffles of blinding silver spreading below the shoals. With eyes closed, still crying out with all his soul, he turned round and round slowly, in the midst of his unsown field, seven times. . . Now for the sign.

He looked upon the cold, rain-swollen stream. Here beside him met the crooked ways of all the world. Behind him his mother-mountain had cloaked herself in the majesty and mystery of Sinai. To him those smooth-worn phrases, names, and metaphors coined in the vanished fervors of a people's lyric passion were glorious with deathless values. The meanings he read into them, however different these might be from the intention of originators in the ports of the Levant, had through a lifetime's brooding worn, not grooves, but sunless gorges in the fabric of his mind. To one who habitually sought the imagery of the Apocalypse everywhere, cherishing even homely plants by such fantastic names as Balm of Gilead or Tree of Heaven, it was inevitable that the mountain stream should long have symbolized the River of Death. And across there, as he looked, the sudden glory of a sunset clearing after rain turned the spring-empurpled hills to rose and gold. The water flamed into glass mingled with fire; for a few moments his world lay steeped in a jewel-light. It seemed a covenant and a promise.

"Jist over, jist over Jordan," he muttered. "Hit must be so. Death 'ud be better for all of us. The Good Master never intended for anybody to live sech a life, anyhow. . . Hit's onchristian. Hit makes women like pore Nettie and her mother; and thar's Shell's boy— ef he don't learn to rob and steal, he'll end up jist like— me. Provideth not fur his own— too old." He joined his hands and shut his eyes once more; and shaking his white hair in the soft damp wind, he concluded very softly:

"Lord, I thank Thee for the Sign; send me now the grace and stren'th to do Thy will, and receive us all in the kingdom. Amen."

The water faded swiftly to a pallid jacinth in the gray matrix of twilight.

He went slowly back into the house, and forthwith prepared his poke-stalk pickles, secretly adding to the vinegar the contents of the bottle he had brought from the burnt cabin shed. They were presently set on the table with a great steaming bowl of white gravy, and the greens, and the pones and fried meat. How delicious it all looked and smelled! The two children wriggled on their chairs while the old man asked an unusually long blessing on the food he believed to have been stolen; but he would not eat anything except the relish he knew to be poisoned, partaking with the air of one receiving sacrament. Then all ate of it but Nettie.

"I'm afeared to resk givin' the baby a colic by the sour," she objected, when urged.

Her father turned upon her, his face working. "You're a fool not to eat 'em, gal," ho cried, in an uneven, febrile voice; then, as she shrank, he muttered, "God's will— God's will be done," and said no more, evidently deeming that the matter might be safest left in the hands of his Lord. But Nettie wondered, not for the first time, if her father were mad. Shell and his family presently staggered away to bed, curiously drowsy, leaving the dishes unwashed, the hearth unswept, and no wood brought for the breakfast fire.

"A heavy supper does make a body so-o sleepy!" smiled Ona. "What air you a-singin' for, Nettie? You ac' like ye had all the money in the bank to draw on."

"I have," answered Nettie, with the mountaineer's inconsequent defiance. It was truer than she knew. Had she not from the first drawn upon the living strength whose source is inexhaustible?. Ona lay down without removing her clothes, and drew the coverlet up to her chin. It was Nettie who straightened the house for the night, brought chips in her apron, and went to the spring for water, singing still, with that strange mingling of content and hope imperishable in her sea-gray eyes. Night had fallen, with the blind clouds again riding swift and low; now and then one swooped to blot out every vestige of the landscape; she could not see her way, but her feet found their path a step at a time—and she could sing.

Afterward she sat before the few embers that remained of the cooking fire, nursing her babe. The rain again set in, and she closed the door lest the damp blow on the little head. Old Zion was still nodding; his voice quavered faintly from the corner shadows, and she made out that he was trying to repeat a hymn— "Will the waters be chilly?" But the rhythm faltered and sank into muttering. "Death in the pot," she caught; and then, "The will o' God, the will o' God."

They were his last words. She laid the baby to sleep, and turned to persuade her father to go to bed. It was close upon midnight now. Something in the huddled posture of the figure in the chair struck cold to her heart. She was suddenly aware that she no longer heard the breathing of the sleepers, which had been loud when they first lay down.

On trembling knees she halted forward, her hand outstretched. "Pappy?" she whispered. "Pappy! Pappy!"

Her fingers touched the withered cheek. It was already cold. With a scream, she crouched back, staring; then turned and ran to the bed where Shell and Ona lay side by side, their children at their feet.

Still crying out, she grasped and shook them. "They cain't be dead! Oh, pappy— Shell— Ona— cain't you hear me callin' ye!" she sobbed, over and over. "Why, hit's only a little while sence we was all settin' at supper!"

She turned once more to the hearth, only to find the old man's body slipped sideways from the chair. The blades of Fate's shears had swung together, dividing Nettie and her child from that doomed family. As she clamored, beside herself with the sudden horror, the little creature waked and added its shrill wail to her outcry— and the others were all still and mute as stone. Catching up the babe, she started, with an unformulated intention of going for help; she did not know that she had already twice shrieked her husband's name.

As if in answer to that cry, the door burst open; fragments of its rude latch flew spinning across the room, and a man halted a moment on the threshold, bewildered by the firelight, unable at first to see what lay before him.

"Oh, Steve! Oh, Steve!" she cried, running to him, clutching the arm he put out, clinging to it, the child between them, and dragging him so into the room. In the terror of that moment she found nothing strange in his presence there.

"Nettie!" his deep voice reassured her; his big arm went around her with a sturdy support which brought comfort, even facing the stark tragedy to which they now turned.

The next day, while Mother Nicklin and the neighbors who had been summoned put everything in order for the dignity of death, Nettie lay on her bed as one half stunned. After all was over and the poor bodies laid to rest in the burying-ground on the hill, she rose and went with Steve and their child down to the river, to sit, pale and weak, on the old raft in the quiet sunshine. She had passed worthily through her great trial, and gained the peace that lies on the other side. Little waves lisped and patted upon the black half-sodden timbers; small perch leaped now and again with a happy flash; overhead the ripening service-berries hung against the new-rinsed sky. The hills were wonderfully blue, swept with a besom of rain; and up and down stream was a miracle of purple rhododendron.

She smiled at her husband over the baby's rosy sleep. He softly stroked her shoulder, though he wondered at her smiling.

"Hit was pore pappy— caused— what happened back yon," she answered his look. "I've seed for some time his mind was failin'. "

The young husband agreed soberly. "Some o' the folks found a bottle," he told her. "Aconite, they called it. Your pappy must have been out of his mind."

"Yes," Nettie murmured. "Nobody would want to die. We seed a awful hard time, Steve," she added, simply. "But look like where the' was little 'uns— nobody would aim to die."

The man's brown cheek crimsoned. "Oh, Nettie," he cried, "I was comin'! I come as soon as I had anything to fetch ye. I've been seekin' for ye, up and down and all about, for two-three days, honey. I'd never been here, you know, and look like nobody couldn't tell me so I could locate the place. I was right nigh here a-yesterday, with money in my hand for ye— and them that's gone, pore souls— when a quare thing happened; some scoun'l set on me— knocked me down from behind, and robbed me of several dollars in silver before I come to."

Nettie caught her breath and looked at him stealthily. But Steve had not recognized in the shrouded and shaven

"SOME SCOUNDREL KNOCKED ME DOWN FROM BEHIND"

Shell his assailant of yesterday, and his wife did not tell him of her suspicions.

"I never heard of a robbery in these parts before," Steve said. "But the feller didn't take my roll o' bills! Never found it, I reckon, as it chanced." He showed her the precious little hoard lying in his hand. "Now, Nettie," he glanced toward the house, then to that one of the three ill-mended roads that wound away toward the burying-ground, bent his head a moment with the air of one who makes his devoir to the dead, and went on, "you 'n' me 'll go back to Pyriton, where I've been. I can have steady work there; and we'll send this chap to school when he's older."

The wife nodded above her child's head, the wisdom of the mother-creature alight in her sea-blue eyes. "I knowed you was a-comin' back to us, Steve. I just knowed that," she murmured. "I said so to myself when I was a-singin' the baby to sleep last night."

"Last night." The awe and wonder of it grew upon the man's face. " Why, girl, do ye know, I'd 'a' turned back last night, I was that tired and discouraged, but I heard you singin'— and then you called me."

"Yes," she answered, with simple confidence, "I jist expected ye, from the time I looked out yestidy and seed the sun shinin' on the hills across the river."

Published in
Harper's Monthly Magazine - November 1910

[179]

In the Track of the Storm

EMMA BELL MILES

ILLUSTRATED BY HARRY TOWNSEND

THE CABIN WAS SET ON A STREAM'S BANK AND BELOW A pond at the foot of the cove; upon its broad hearthstone the fire, as it sank, shone redder and redder on the faces of the two who sat beside it: hale old faces, seamed with wrinkles got of outdoor living. Aaron and Verona Brymer had picked over their nightly stent of cotton and read the usual chapter. They were reading the Bible through together for the fourth time. The accomplishment was too rare to be squandered; so they never spent it on any but the Good Book.

Now it was bedtime. Taking off his shoes, old Aaron rose stiffly from his chair, laid by the faded coat and vest that seemed to have grown with him, like the bark of a tree, a mere response to the weather and the woods, and then wound the clock on the fireboard. His wife loosened her shoes, coarse and mudstained as his own, and slipped her feet out before the coals. Of a sudden the embers began to sputter with raindrops.

"Ever'body I seed in town to-day," remarked old Aaron, " 'lowed there's been sich a sight o' bad weather that they'd got no crops in sca'cely." He breathed once before he added, "Harvey rode out with me this evenin'. "

A silence. Then, "Did he name me?" asked the old woman, her eyes on the coals.

"He sure did, Mother, jist like he's always done. I know in reason hit makes him think long o' the time, not to come to see you nor have you go about them. Folks is noticin' hit, specially sence the little chap come."

"Harvey can visit me any day he's a mind to, s'long as he comes by hisself. He knows that 'thout my sendin' him word of hit." She did not raise her voice, but her fine eyes flashed, her mouth straightened as she spoke.

"But, Mother, you jist natchally can't help admirin' his spunk in not goin' where his woman ain't welcome, and her a good wife to him-now can ye?" urged Aaron.

"I don't know how good a wife she may be," Verona Brymer spoke evenly and slowly. "He's made his ch'ice betwixt her and me; let him bide by hit. Jensy Lusk'll never pass in by my door with welcome o' mine. Her nor hers will never be friends to me. That Harvey should 'a' picked her, of all the gals he knowed—"

She sat a moment shaking her head. There came a far muttering of thunder to fill the silence.

"When he was courtin' her," she went on, "he was so afeared, one while, that thar town cousin of hers would git her. He told me oncet that he might stand to see her well married, but to see one he thought so much of given to a man he jist deespised, he could not endyore. 'Well,' I says, 'Harvey, son,' I says, 'ef you marry Jensy Lusk, I'll haf to stand by and see the one I think the most of given to a womern I deespise.' But he, boy-like, never thinks of that now."

A chill breath drifted shudderingly between the two, stirring their scan gray hair to the roots. Instinctively he bent to poke the fire, first drawing the bed of embers, and then selling the coals from the half-burned logs like kernels rattling off a cob.

"Hit'll be apt to come a rain in the night, and then turn off cold," said the old man, his tone an admission that the more personal subject might safest be let fall. "I reckon we'd as well kiver the fire. Coals'll be a sight of help with damp wood."

While he plied the shovel, the wife rose from her chair, laid aside her skirt, waist, and neckerchief, tied her gingham apron over her head, and stood ready for her hard-earned night's rest.

Aaron sat on a box by the bed looking at the smooth-scoured puncheons as though he had lost something down a crack there. At last he said, raising his mild, bright blue eyes to her face: "Mother— ye know what we read this evenin' in The Book: 'Let not the sun go down on your wrath.' I'm always a-hopin' you'll come to that mind about Jensy some day."

"Some day," repeated the old mother bitterly. "Ye needn't look for it. The day won't never dawn that'll see me in Jensy Lusk's house. This place is mine, ain't it?" She looked somberly at rafter and wall, threshold and lintel. "I can keep my home, ef I couldn't keep my son— she shan't never come here."

The old husband shook his head. "Well, well," he said at length, with what was for him unwonted spirit, "you can use yo' pleasure, Varony; but ef I was you I'd put away sech feelin's, an' go up thar to-morrow mornin', 'Twas to bid you to Sunday dinner to-morrow that Harvey spoke to me, an' I said I'd name it to ye— name it to ye."

Verona turned and looked her mate over broodingly. How long did one live with a man before he knew one's real mind? She gave him no answer, and the light was blown out in silence.

II

The two cabins stood in one gulch, down which Nameless Creek took its capricious way. As the woods had not yet thickened to their summer capacity, the two roofs were even in sight of each other.

The round shoulders of Chilhowee were almost bowed over Harvey's new cabin, whose clearing was spread like an apron, green with spring against the gray woods, on the mountain's knees. It was a peaceful place, too lonely to be quite homelike except to a mountaineer. But the wild trout-stream, that here laughed into white ecstasies of foam, widened to a meditative pond in the cove a half-mile below, and brightened the meadows round Aaron's older home— a cabin dark with century's wood-smoke and set about with gnarled apple-trees.

[183]

Mid-April should, according to the mountaineer's calendar, see the send of the "borrowed days," but here it was a week past, and yet there were no signs of a satisfactory settlement between March and April. Perhaps the year, still in arrears for an unusually splendid autumn pageant, had borrowed the major portion of the month. Certainly there lingered, round the pond's brim, frosts of a wintry woolliness.

To-day, however, had turned suddenly warm. The fall of dusk had brought with it an apparition of singular beauty- a perfectly pink moon, blooming full like a rose over the smoky horizon, looking across the low fields, and changing as it mounted to a disk of copper— to an orange— to a deep golden bowl; a faery presence, but soon overwhelmed by a rolling and billowing of heavy clouds.

Jensy had watched it as she crooned her baby to sleep; she now lay beside him with a guarding arm thrown clear of the pillow. A young mother whose ears are quickened with constant listening for the small cry wakes more readily than does the open-air toiler. She was roused toward midnight by the rattling crash of something falling. Lying in the bewilderment of sudden arousing, she heard the wind as it leapt upon their roof, shaking it by the four corners, tearing like a wild beast at the stoutly mortised timbers. For a moment she remained hearkening to the rising gusts, then summoned Harvey to wakefulness.

"Must be the whippoorwill storm!" he cried, sitting up in bed, listening. "I believe in my soul I never did hear such a racket."

Round the house the tempest roared like a battle; the loins of Chilhowee shivered to an appalling resonance of thunders.

"Looks like somethin' must go," the new householder debated. "Reckon I better try to get them shutters shut."

He was out of bed and at the window when Jensy turned up the flame in the little lamp. This was at once blown out, Harvey could not hold the thick oak shutter; it was wrenched from his grasp and banged against the house. A gust of rain dashed upon the two. In the play of colored lightnings they saw dry leaves and twigs, whirled high, passing the window like flights of arrows. The mother turned from the sign and groped toward the bed where her child lay. They heard a clattering of kitchen things as the back door gave way. When there was a momentary lull about them, sound came up of the gusts rending the forest below; and now and then a crashing and splintering as a tree went down. From over the valley the wind swept in, fierce as from open sea. With every fresh impulse of the gale, a stupendous uproar raged on the sandstone bluffs above; its reverberations boomed as though the whole mountain were hollow, beaten like a drum by wild fighting hands. . . .

Then as abruptly the shutter was flung shut, cutting off the glare, though not the roaring of the storm. Panting, Harvey fastened the latch, and groping forward, found Jensy with the baby in her arms cowering at his feet.

He knelt beside her and put his arm around the two. The house rocked and shook. They could not hear each other speak. The roof crackled and snapped as nail after nail gave to the terrific strain. They crouched on the floor together, listening to the wind's trumpeting loud and louder on the dreadful dark. The baby boy, roused a bit, turned in his mother's arms and slept on. . . .

So tiny a cup of warmth and human kindness is the cabin home, nestled on the floor of the haunted Vast! So short a way its windows let their light into the Black! Our utmost achievement weighs so little; our highest ascensions but prick the lower strata of the air; our loudest cannonade reverberates scarcely higher. If men could realize how alone they are, would they not let go of old spites and vanities— would they not make haste to clasp each other's hands? . . . If all that earth contains of hate for man were loosed at once— what then? . . .

Below in the gulch, where the stream widened to its pond, now brimmed bankfull and churned to foam against the barriers by the sudden down-rush of waters, the elder cabin slept, black and silent. The old folks slumbered within; resentment like a coal at the core of the mother's heart failed to disturb her repose; patient sorrow seemed to smooth Aaron's pillow and lull him the faster asleep. It was just as the creek-pond leaped its bank and came swirling down on the dooryard that the fiercest lunge of that night's storm pounced upon the cabin itself, the old house that had weathered so many wild nights, that had crouched to the beating of so many mountain tempests. And at last, the sleepers wakened to a world of chaos, to terrifying blows from unseen sources and the lash of the storm itself breaking through their habitation.

In that region the vagaries of the swift, boulder-checked mountain streams make land boundaries uncertain. Sometimes a creek in spring flood will change its course, scour off a field and deposit it on some stretch of barren land half a mile away. To-night, Nameless Creek was to christen itself, and thereafter to be known as Harricane, namesake of the tempest which set it wrecking Verona Brymer's homestead and strewing the wreckage of logs and puncheons, hand-rived boards and shingles for miles along its course.

The old man was spared by log and rafter; gasping, whirled against this and that by the force of the wind, he freed himself at last and looked upon the ruin of his home, a blur of blackness against the steel gray of the storm. By the fantastic illumination of the lightning he saw he was alone, and began calling, "Verony! Mother! Oh, Verony!"

There was no reply, only the whip of icy rain upon his aching flesh, the multitudinous wild voices of the tempest, the goblin laugh of the water as it sucked hollowly away down the gorge. Battered and bleeding, he groped about until at last he found his old mate, pinned down by timers against whose rude bulk his frantic efforts were futile. He found a shred of what had been their bedding, with which he hid her poor face from the sky; and working by inter-mittent flashes of the electric blade, he managed to shelter the unconscious woman from the storm's full strength— a fury now abating. Then he was off, making what headway he could up the mountain to their son's house.

The cove was strewn with woods-wreck. All the sky resounded like one huge war-gong. At first the wind, like a current of fluid blackness, cut the breath from his nostrils. The rain was driven in his face, lifted and waved up and down in sheeted squalls. For a long time he feared each step would be his last. But imperceptibly the hammering of

[188]

HE FREED HIMSELF AT LAST, AND LOOKED UPON THE RUIN OF HIS HOME

the thunders gave way; the swelling uproar slowly sank and changed, like an orchestral combination, from the strife of the wind to a drowning, steady pour of rain.

It was growing colder every minute. He won each foot of ground by a separate effort; he slipped on the winter-sodden leaves, fell sprawling on rocks, stumbled over logs all fallen one way, and upwrenched roots straddling hight where the path had run the day before. Through it all he toiled painfully, seeking help to bring his wife under shelter. Strange fancies drifted through his dizzied brain. Would Verona be willing to receive help from her son? Would she be carried to the house of that daughter-in-law against whom she held herself implacable?

When father and son returned, stumbling down the cove together, they thought at first that a dead body lay pinned under the wreckage of the old home. So it was with unseeing eyes and a stilled voice which could not be raised in protest that Verona Brymer came into her son's house. And thus for days she lay there barely conscious, glad, in a numb, animal fashion, of her daughter-in-law's tender ministrations and nursing. But when she came back to life and recognized what fate had done to her, her soul was one pool of bitterness. They had carried her into Jensy's house— that house she had vowed never to enter. The threshold she had forbidden this woman to cross was a tossing bit of drift somewhere down the creek which had floated jamb and lintel of her door toward the Tennessee, carried chips and splinters of it no doubt into the Mississippi and toward the great Gulf, cradle of storms. She was lying on Jensy's bed; the food that nourished her Jensy cooked; the hands that tended on her were Jensy's.

And the unwelcome daughter-in-law was not long left in doubt as to her feelings. The flashing glance from those stern old eyes, the demand for Aaron's hand instead of hers, a swift inquiry as to the whereabouts of her various belongings, this taught Jensy where she stood and brought her to keeping herself and the baby in the outer room away from the invalid.

An injudicious visitor, from time to time, added details to the story that Aaron had told and Verona had listened to with incredulous ears. There was word of broken saucers and a battered milk bucket found in the far fields; of shreds of cotton, the very lining of her poor home nest, fringing the branches of forest trees. Her wash tubs and Aaron's fences, wrought so toilsomely out of stark timer, would never be seen again.

After the storm came ruthful, clement spring weather. Old Verona, growing better, lay all day, propped in her bed, gazing quietly out of the open window. Aaron would bring her breakfast and put everything to her hand; then he must go down with Harvey to where they were rebuilding the old home. Neighbors helped; the old man was still too crippled to be of much use, and Verona sternly bade him come back in time to wait upon her with dinner, since she shunned the favors of those detested hands that cooked the food. She could not hinder her own recovery, could not help gaining strength; but she was furious that she must be here and alive at all. Inly she raged at the storm, at nature, at herself, at Jensy.

It added poignancy to her sufferings that she knew, as the warm April days followed each other toward May, every old mother in the country was hunting through a collection of baking-powder cans and broken coffee pots for saved garden seed, or running out to look for eggs where the hens cackled in the log barn. Here she lay defrauded of the usefulness that had been hers since she could remember. That woman out there kept the child away from her, would not even offer her the smallest task of knitting or sewing. Life was pushing forward without her. The chirping of newly hatched "weedies" filled the yard; treetoads sang by night a long-trilled cool nocturne; wrens building under the porch eaves twittered a sunshiny warble for each hour of the day. The first mocker greeted the morning from the top of a hickory near Harvey's barn; the first ruby-throat hovered about the lilacs. She wondered how the bluebirds were faring who, each spring, hid four sky-colored eggs in a cleft apple-tree by her own kitchen door. Like her, they had lost their nest. From her bed she could see two lambs that lay in a sunny corner, their heads resting prettily and softly on each other's backs, and Harvey's colt gamboling awkwardly on long, unmanageable legs.

Gradually, her sense of desertion became intolerable. Many had lost by this memorable storm, but none so heavily as the old couple in the cove. There were intervals in the rush of repairing fences, roofing barns, and replanting the washed-out fields, wherein still the neighbors' part might be credibly done. The women came to sit with old Verona, observing all too readily her aversion to her daughter-in-law, judging promptly that it applied to Jensy's child as well.

One morning such a neighbor sat with Verona when the little fellow strayed tottering into the bedroom. His hands were outstretched, his feet eager to run forth across the world, the light of life's dawn was in his eyes. At sight of the world-old miracle— his likeness to what she loved most and had clung to closest— a brightness like the twinkling of split quicksilver ran over the grandmother's face. The likeness! All other inheritance must be but passing clouds to the blue depths of his perfection. Again she was a young mother with a babe on her arm; the little Harvey's clear eyes looked up from his son's face. When the neighbor arose and hurried the boy out with shrill reproof, Verona saw with a sort of terror that those who build a house of hate are sometimes forced to live therein.

All day, after the marplot neighbor had gone, Verona watched the doorway for the moth-flitting of a little figure in white, crowned with a folly of curls. Every echo of lisp and babble and crow that reached the dim room gripped her lonely heart, and summoned the unreasoning tears.

The afternoon brought no other visitor. Shadows stole caressingly across the pasture slopes; it grew later and later and still no one came. After dinner Aaron had hobbled down to the cove, where rebuilding of the old home went forward. When that home was ready she must leave this one whose roof covered the baby. The baby. . . Ah! Jensy in the other room, thinking Verona asleep, rocked the child and sang softly. Then she began to be worried; she must go to the spring, or the men would presently come in tired and find no supper ready; and here was no one to leave with "Ma" and the child. She stood for some time hesitating outside the room door, her brows drawn high above her pleasant eyes.

The westering sun opened a gate into an enchanted land— a cloud-canyon, dim in maize-colored air, with cliffs of cloud soaring on either side; beyond, a vista of a thousand places and temples, a rajah's dream, domed in golden-tinted alabaster. It was to the old woman a vision of the Promised Land. Gazing at it from her window, she found herself in a humbler frame of mind toward life, even the little green points that sprang between the clods— toward the fine ferns uncurling, reaching up to grasp at existence like the baby's hands. The baby's hands . . .

The gentle radiance of the west filled all the room as Jensy at last came softly in, her face expressing still some perturbation of mind, the sleeping child in her arms.

Verona's lids were closed; it was the usual defense in Jensy's presence; but they quivered as the young mother bent and made as if to lay the child in the place she knew to be safest, next the footboard of the four-poster bed.

"Let not the sun go down"— murmured the grandmother. Suddenly her eyes opened and rested full on Jensy's face. "Hit's about sundown, ain't hit— Jensy?" she inquired gently.

The young woman stopped, wistfully regarding the wrinkled face on the pillow, and then glancing down at the flaxen halo of curls against her shoulder.

"I'm sorry," Jensy said, in evident allusion to having waked her mother-in-law. "I was lookin' for somewhars I could leave the baby that he'd be safe. I want to get you a fresh drink from the spring."

"Safe," echoed the deep old tones. "Lay him up here 'side o' me so as I can see him, won't you— daughter?"

Jensy did as she was bid, stooping toward the pillows to hide her astonishment, and settling the warm little body, heavy with sleep, into the new nest with croonings and pattings such as mothers use. She was tucking the coverlets round both helpless forms when she stole a glance at Verona's face and found that it was trembling into smiles, and all of that deep, sad mother-heart of hers was in the smile.

There came a sound of footsteps outside. Jensy lifted a warning hand. Their two men, refreshed and cooled, after the day's work, by a wash-off in Harricane's waters, stood in the doorway. The plangent glories of sunset beat into the dusk of the room. Verona's gaze passed child and grandchild to look into Aaron's tired, honest blue eyes.

"Why, Mother," the old man spoke in the hushed voice which is our tribute to the holy presence or the sleep of a little child, yet there was an awakening ring of surprise and gladness in his tone, "you're feelin' peart, ain't you?"

"Yes, Pap," murmured Verona, catching at the hand that ministered to her: "Daughter Jensy, she's got both her babies in one bed now, whar she can tend on 'em, ain't you, honey?"

Published in
Pearson's Magazine - July 1911

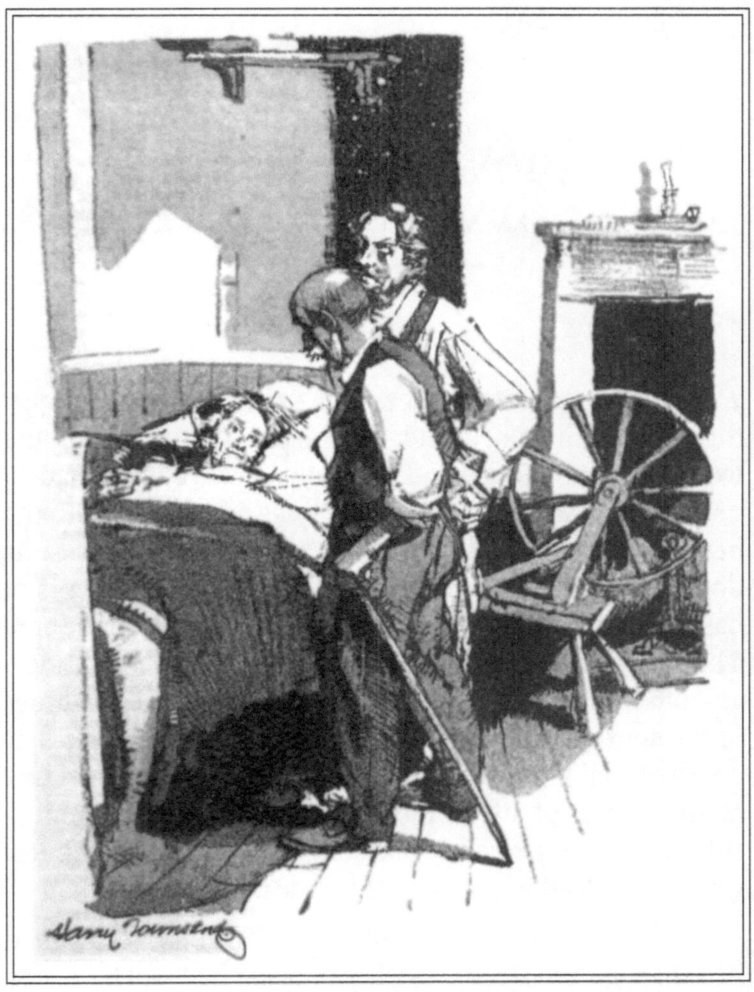

"WHY, MOTHER, YOU'RE FEELIN' PEART, AIN'T YOU ?"

Flower of Noon

EMMA BELL MILES

Although there had been for years a continual sly threading of the trails that led to his place of business in the woods, Harmon Ridge had never during his lifetime had so many guests as today. Most of the folks now gathered in the best room of the log house were voluntary strangers to its door. Women were coming and going clad in garments of hastily donned and ill-matched colors, with here and there a black waist, hat or skirt. Susan, the wife of Clifford Ridge, and old Mrs. Bivins were distinguished by whole costumes of the appropriate hue; the latter not through any peculiar depth of feeling, but because, having no kin of her own, she made a point of attending all the burials of the country-side, and for expediency had long since cast all her outer garments into the same pot of funereal logwood.

In the tidy kitchen Harmon's young housekeeper had not changed the steel-gray gingham she had worn the day before. She was occupied with straightening the dead man's accounts, which she had kept for two years. Fan Walton was a strongly built, energetic girl, standing firm in her broad shoes and breathing deeply as she worked. She always experienced a faint shock of surprise on the rare occasions when she faced a mirror, at not finding herself beautiful.

From under eyelids swollen with loss of sleep she looked up as a tall, sunbrowned young mountaineer stooped through the doorway.

"I've cut you a quantity of wood and killed them chickens for dinner, Fan," he said. He came forward and laid one hand on the table at which she was seated; his tone became almost pleading as he went on. "Now you let me start dinner for ye. You're werried out. My dad was cook for his company all through the war, and he learnt me how. I bet I can beat you makin' dodgers."

"I bet you can't," she replied; but putting away her book, she watched him deftly blow up the hearth-fire with a turkey-wing and hang a kettle over the blaze.

"I reckon," he continued presently, coming up the cellar-way with a pan of potatoes, "that's why Mr. Ridge always liked me to tend the still for him; I could generally git water to bile without burnin' it. Well— I got to look out for another job now. I'll never work for a man I like better. I do wisht I'd a-been there when— when— the rev's took him, instead of haulin' corn. Maybe if there'd been two on gyuard it wouldn't have ended that way."

She caught her breath with a great sob. "Oh, Byron!" There was something tragic in the cry that freed itself from her strained throat. "He was so good!"

The boy nodded without looking up from his pota-to-paring; the pathos of her position, or as much of it as was known to him, smote him to the heart. But Fan, impatient with herself for the moment's weakness, turned quickly, and rolling up her sleeves on her firm shapely arms, mixed a creamy mass of meal and buttermilk and began manipulating it into dodgers. They remained silent and busy until Grandma Bivins' shrill voice announced her entry: "Looky thar, Bar'n— that colt's a-gwine to break ever' one o' them crocks!"

The pretty, petted sorrel sprang back in a well-simulated panic at the wave of Fan's dish-towel, and an instant after was stretching an investigative nose toward the window again.

"Truelove's restless today," explained Fan as she patted the oval pones into their oven nest. "Take a chair by the door, Mrs. Bivins. I hate to shut the colt up, for I know how she feels."

"I'll go turn her in the pasture," said Byron as he put the potatoes in the pot.

In the barnyard, a half-dozen men sat around upon inverted feed-buckets, the chopping-block, the ash-gum, the bales of clapboards riven to roof the old barn— anything rather than go in the house before the activities and lamentations of the womenfolk had come to a standstill. A certain cautious restraint was perceptible in the conversation here, an edging around the subject that was inevitably the center of interest to all, of which circumstances forbade direct mention.

". . .That's a powerful fine orchard. Might' near all Limbertwigs, ain't they?"

"Harmon Ridge took as good keer of his land as he did of his team."

"I never seed a better quartered colt than that one Bar'n Standifer's a-leadin' yonder. Her dam was a fine pacer."

But no one asked in so many words how much Harmon Ridge was worth or who would inherit the property.

In the lane three men conferred a little apart from the others; Absalom Ridge, the deacon of the Borden Springs church; Clifford, justice of the peace at Belview, affable and prosperous beneath due decorum; and with them the preacher, properly punctilious and punctiliously proper, as befitted the master of ceremonies. In the mountains a funeral sermon is seldom preached in seed-time or harvest; it may await for months the convenience of the family connection. Clifford urbanely offered the front rooms and ample porches of his house for the purpose; but Absalom, loth to relinquish the one bit of prestige he had granted him, insisted that his church should be the chosen site.

The preacher agreed. "Let 'em all bring a basket and spread dinner on the ground, Brother Ridge, and afterward protract the service into a praise meetin'."

Clifford yielded the point with admirable grace, perhaps feeling that he could afford to. "That announcemint will bring out a good crowd."

"Then," continued the preacher, "how 'bout havin' it the third Sunday in next month? All crops 'll be laid by again' that time, and I haven't got no appointmints for that date." He cut a fresh chew of tobacco from the plug offered him by Clifford, and went on dolorously: "It's a hard thing to be called on to preach the funeral of a man that never made any profession of faith. I'd rather be called on for any other duty of the ministry than that."

"Hit's hard; yes," agreed Absalom sympathetically. "I'm afeared the one consolation you can set before our sorrowin' family is the fact that not one of us ac-chilly knows anything about pore Harmon's faith."

"You might jist mention," interrupted a new voice, "that he was honest as the open day, and the best-hearted friend a man ever had in time o' need."

They all jumped around, and came face to face with Byron; but ere they could frame a suitable reply he had passed on, the sorrel following. The very presence of Harmon's helper was embarrassing to the justice and the deacon, reminding them that the brother whose large well-knit frame and lionlike flow of beard now reposed beneath a sheet on the rude scaffolding had served the devil and defied the law for the past ten years.

Yet as they halted, staring at each other, those two suddenly remembered the warm-hearted, wayward boyhood of the rover— the brightness of his blue eyes, the reddish-brown cowlick that swept down over his forehead in correspondence to some unruly twist in his nature. After all, in those far-off days, of what had Harmon been guilty except just being himself? Only his earthborn strength had affronted the careful propriety and thrift of the one, the saintly demeanor of the other. Slowly and in silence they walked toward the group under the tree.

Indoors, the wives, under cover of putting the house in order, essayed an examination; but the attempt failed dismally as closet after closet was found to be already immaculate.

"I wonder if she does keep things like this all the time; or did she take 'n hustle everything straight because she knew folks would be in?" whined Absalom's wife, Marzela, between her prominent yellow teeth.

"Do you reckon he was prepared to go?" continued Marzela, piously. "I hoped, seein' he lingered on for some days after his injury, that he'd profess religion at the 'leventh hour— repent, and believe, in time. I even tried to git Absalom to ride over and talk to him; but he's always had trouble when he tried to git pore Harmon to think of his soul, and there was only them three days left of the dark o' the moon to plant in."

"The fact is we didn't none of us have any idy it was so serious; we would a-come, but we didn't look for the end so suddent; it come on us a awful shock." Susan began to weep in a ladylike fashion, rocking to and fro in the easiest chair.

The company had recourse to Scripture texts.

"And I know in reason," she continued presently, "that Harmon himself didn't expect it neither; 'r else he'd a-left some kind of a-will." There seemed some thought behind the speech which it was not advisable to put into words.

"He always thought so much of N'omi and Paul; he was good to all the children, but them two was his favorites." Marzela had awakened tardily.

The two women eyed each other for the first time with frank hostility. But Susan, feeling the necessity for making common cause against the enemy, resumed tearfully: "I wouldn't want to ask her anything about the 'last hours,' but Lucy, maybe, 'll know when the comes."

"Why ain't Lucy here, do you reckon?"

"She'll be here to set up," a neighbor volunteered. "She told me as I come on that she had been obliged to wash today; but she 'lowed to git here tonight."

"Late, I expect," said another, "for she'll have to carry that heavy baby. And she's been a-settin' up, her and Fan, ever since it happened."

A low voice sounded from the doorway, and at least eight earbobs swung as one.

"Come to dinner," Fan Walton bade them quietly, "and please bring out four chairs."

From early candlelighting the house was full. And then, led on by those first comers, the whole gathering began covertly to watch Fan. Whatever she did was commented on. Sometimes when she passed there were whispered conversations; again an uneasy silence fell. Strange glances followed her through the doors, and when she was gone the subdued conversation began to fly back and forth. At last she caught the words, "He never would trust a bank, but—"

The significance of that phrase did not burn its way through her heavy thoughts until after she had quit the dimly lighted rooms and gained the quiet of the dark kitchen porch. Then, her noble strength deserting her suddenly, she dropped on the bench beside the crocks and churn; her cheeks burned in the darkness, and her mouth straightened to a hard line of suffering.

On the front porch Byron, half asleep after days of work and nights of watching, was stretched out with someone's saddle for a pillow, when he became aware of a point of light too low for a star, and sat up.

"Some of 'em pokin' about tryin' to find out some-thing 'at's none o' their business," he decided, and roused himself with an effort. Visions of a lantern overturned in the hay hurried his feet across the lot. But it was no curious stranger; it was Fan, with her arms round Truelove's neck, crying as though her heart would break.

"Fan," he whispered, coming up, "don't— don't grieve so. . . . He was sure one good man; but he died about as he'd have chosen to, all alive and hearty, and hard at work. He didn't suffer but a few days. He'd much rather have gone this way than— behind the bars. He took his chance—"

She put out a work-hardened hand without speaking, and he led her to the piled hay in the midst of the wide shadowy spaces. "What did you come out for?" he asked, seating himself below her. "I fed everything. You ought to git some sleep."

"I wanted to get shut of all those folks," she answered, dabbing at her eyes with her apron. "Not you, Byron— you know they all talk so much. Oh, they're so— dirty! They shall not have Truelove, and the old man's team that he had so long, and the Durham heifer he raised: I'll kill the poor pets first!"

He nodded broodingly. "Fan— I don't want to push myself, but— you know what you told me oncet. If you still feel so— as soon as you can get consent o' your mind to let things loose here, why, turn 'em over to these folks. I want you to come to me. My house is a poor place— a poor home for a girl like you; but oncet you give me the right I'll make 'em careful what they say."

She shivered, and dropped her face into the cup of her palms.

[203]

"You're a dear boy, Byron. I could leave any time; but I—I don't know yet what I'm going to do. I want these folks out of the house, and I feel as if *he* does too "

Byron was slow in replying. At last he said, "Well— I'll be around, Fan, any time you need me."

In the house the night wore on; the lamp burned strangely in the thick, drowsy air. The watchers seemed gradually to lose their individual characteristics, appearing neither young nor old, like a row of images, presences vaguely unfriendly to each other and to the dead, they sat silent and grave, their shadows motionless on the wall. And still most of the men remained without, sitting on the steps, murmuring to each other in the desultory fashion of mountaineers; for death and birth are matters on which only women can bear to look.

"Mamma," whispered the young girl fresh from the Select Academy, "did you notice how short that Miss Walton's dress is made?"

The justice's lady nodded ponderously. "I wouldn't call it immodest exactly, but it don't, today, show a proper respect."

"What I want to know," intoned Marzela, solemnly, "is what she's a-*doin'* in this house all the time, day and night."

"You know she wouldn't let none of us feed the stock, nor do about in the house. It looks as if— "

"It does!"

". . . She might know we'd think strange of hit."

"Don't you?" The speaker addressed Lucy directly.

The dead man's only sister had just come in. She was a small, worn, faded woman in blue calico, nursing her baby in a corner. Lifting her red-rimmed eyes, she answered from a kind of remoteness, as if rapt in sorrow: "Don't I what?"

"Don't you think strange of this Fan Walton bein' here?"

"No, I don't," she replied with more spirit. "I'd certainly think stranger if he'd a-lived here all these years without nobody."

"Well," said Marzela, "we 'lowed you might maybe know something about her."

"I know she took care of him like a own sister. I couldn't a-done better if I'd a-been here all the time."

"Well, but hit don't look right— a young thing like her. I'm surprised at you, Lucy, upholdin such a— arrangemint."

"I'm surprised to hear all o' you'ns, that couldn't come about whilst brother Harmon was down and hurted to see how he was conductin' his house, come in now and take it all out on a defenseless gal!" cried Lucy. Then, remembering the presence of death, she rose hurriedly and carried her drowsy child out of the room.

The two in the barn looked up as the big doors swung a little apart, and Lucy glided like a mouse into the shadows which the lantern's rays only made more gloomy.

"I laid my baby on your bed, Fan, and come to see why you wasn't in it," she said in her gentle monotone.

"I can't sleep," protested Fan; but she accepted gratefully the homespun shawl her friend had brought, and wrapped it round herself and Lucy as they both rested on the hay. 'We better go get them folks something to eat."

"I set it on the table afore I come out. You go to bed," said Lucy.

"I can't. . . . I can't think what I ought to do. I'll tell you and Byron how it really is . . . "

But a disturbance in the stalls had called the boy away. He found the stable overcrowded, and as he led the stamping intruders out, but few of Fan's words reached his ear— scraps of which he could make nothing:

". . . And I thought I should like it better here, all quiet, with a whole house and farm to myself. I like to get out in the patch with a hoe— I like to make bread and wash clothes. So I wrote to him, and he said he'd be so glad to have me with him again. . . . ."

When he passed a second time Lucy's arms were round the girl, and Lucy's voice was saying: "He was the best brother I ever had. If he hadn't helped me I don't know what we—"

From the house came the long strains of "Away Over in the Promised Land." He distinguished the preacher's "lead" and Clifford's bass, and Grandma' Bivins' quavering "high tribble."

"I can leave it all to them— I can make my way," Fan was reiterating. "But he wouldn't have wished that."

"Then tell them, honey; tell all the folks," counseled Lucy.

"He didn't want it known here, because he always meant to wind up his business and take me away. But he put the day off too long."

"Well, if I was you I'd stay right here," said Lucy. "I always thought there was something— and I know in reason they would of too, if they wasn't already eat up with suspicions. You'll be obliged to let it be known."

Byron approached the pair under the tentlike shawl. "I've got three or four o' them strangers roped in the sheds," he told them. "I think they'll be quiet now." He sat at the women's feet, drooping over the lantern.

"Byron," said Lucy, "Fan's just told me something that makes a difference all 'round— "

"Hush," he bade her softly. "She's might' near asleep."

And so resting, they remained silent through the night. At last the gray dawn glimmered against the smoky lantern; the watch was over. Lucy and Fan awoke, and went back to the kitchen to get breakfast.

Afterward a little procession filed across the fields, Grandma Bivins warning each member not to break the line lest he be next to die; and Harmon Ridge was laid in the good earth's embrace under soughing cedars of his own planting.

Immediately upon the closing of the grave, a clatter of harness-chains and much whoa-ing round the stable announced the general departure. But after each neighbor had spoken his farewell with a murmured phrase of gracious feeling for the family, Lucy looked out of a window and made mild eyes of surprise.

"Why, there's Clifford and Absalom and all their folks still waitin' round. They've corkussed and plotted and talked out there for I don't know how long."

"I thought they was s-one long ago," said Byron. "Why, they're all a-comin' back to the house!"

Fan re-set the chairs in the strangely vacant-looking best room with a sinking heart that asked no questions. If it must come now, she would face it.

"Miss Walton," began the justice, clearing his throat, "we got a matter to bring up that we think needs namin'. If you— as you know all the house, and brother Harmon's ways, probably better than anybody else— if you can find— find— that is— unearth the money he left, you know-why, we'd be prepared to offer you a liberal amount of it— a share, in short."

The girl addressed lowered her eyes for very shame of his confusion. What a roundabout way he had taken to accuse her! She answered, "I don't believe he had any such amount as you all think."

She looked up. The silence was startling.

The next words were a veiled threat; they came from Absalom. "But we'd like to know what you— a young woman alone in the world, and without a home— proprose to do? We cain't leave you here. And there's certain facts, If— if a heap o' people was to tell about 'em, might not sound well— might not be the best start for a young gal that's got her living to make, in fact!"

"In that case" — Fan lifted her head proudly, and faced the room-full— "I expect I had better stay right here."

"Why— !" If they had held their breath, they caught it now, hard. "You don't imagine you can hold this farm against the man's own blood and kin, do ye?" Clifford had not intended to go so far today; but neither had he looked to encounter such confident opposition.

"And Harmon not cold in his grave!" gasped Marzela.

"Don't anger her," whispered Susan pacifically behind her black veil. "I do believe she knows where the money's at."

"Can't you explain yourself— tell us what claim you've got on the estate, anyway?" probed the questioner, his eyes troubled with an uncertainty that was growing in his mind. "It ain't possible that— air you— a relative?"

Fan sprang forward with flushed cheeks and flashing eyes, throwing out her open palms. "God's my judge!" she cried in a clear ringing voice. "Can't you all see?"

And in her strong features, her firm neck and square-set shoulders so like those on which they had looked their last an hour ago through the glass of a coffin, they read the answer.

Byron was not the only one present whose heart leapt at her stand. At bay before them all, so young, brave, sweet, she stood, telling in a few words the story of her upbringing in the other valley.

The blue of her eyes became brighter as she talked; she shook her head a little, and her rough reddish-brown hair came loose and swept down over her forehead in an unruly wave.

They did not ask to see the papers of evidence; not one but was glad to conceal discomfiture and mortal offense as inconspicuously and hastily as might be, on the road home.

"Well, I'm glad for ye, honey," was Lucy's parting word. "I'm a pore hard-run widder woman, but I'd rather have a niece like you than a share in what brother Harmon left. Now, run over to my house as often as you can, for you'll be lonesome."

"Don't say that, Lucy." Fan took the toil-worn hand and held it. "You come back tomorrow. As you say, I'll be lonesome; and I know he'd rather you'd be with me than anybody else. So you and the children bring this chap— " she stroked the baby's tow-colored head— "and move in with me, and help take care of the place and things. We'll keep 'em just as they was left—" A shade of her grief filled her eyes, and she turned away.

Byron was outside, drawing a bucket of water for the sorrel. Seeing Fan at the window, he came and folded his arms on the sill. "Well," he said, "I reckon you won't need me any more." The depth of his voice, the entreaty in his eyes, made her think twice of the words, though he tried to speak them lightly. "Not any more— ever."

She laid her hand on his head. "Why, Byron," she answered, "I'll need you more than ever now."

Published in
The Craftsman Magazine - January 1912

The Cook Stove

EMMA BELL MILES

THE DRANE FAMILY CONNECTION HAD JUST CELEBRATED, modestly but heartily, the china wedding of Cephas and wife. Their wagons and buckboards were now clattering away along the valley road, pursued by exchanged shouts of farewell. In the wagon of the elder brother, Lester Drane, whose family had been so decimated by marriages that for the first time in fifteen years it could be got into one vehicle, an animated conversation went on above the steady grind of the wheels.

"Aunt Phronie's a-failin'. " It was a grown daughter who brought up the subject.

"She is. Seems like she's breakin' fast," her mother replied soberly.

"Uncle Sam 'lowed"— it was a tiny voice piping up from under the seat— "he 'lowed she might have two perculo-cusses on her lungs. What is them?"

"I axed her," said the first speaker, "and she 'lowed she was jist tired. Said she always coughed some this time o' year, but she taken cold gittin' up to feed the colt in the night, and it come on worse 'n common."

"That's goin' to be a fine colt. Too bad its mother got killed."

"I heard Uncle Sam offer a hundred for hit," said Lester's tallest son, from his precarious perch on the edge of the wagonbed.

"I'd a-looked at hundred a long time afore I'd a-give hit for a colt," declared his father. "Wouldn't Cephas take hit?"

"Wouldn't say. You know, pa, he's sort o' closte."

"Yes, he's a closte dealer. He'll stand to a bargain, though."

"Oh, yes. He's honest; ain't none more so in the state."

"He raises good stock. Did you notice them two cows?"

"That colt's wuth 'em all. Best quartered colt I might' near ever seed." The road here plunged into a rocky creek bed and continued along it for half a mile, and the jolting put an end to intelligible talk.

"How'd it happen?" asked the schoolteacher, who for the first time occupied a coveted place beside the daughter and was finding it hard to make conversation with her— "how was it Cephas inherited all the Drane real estate?'

"Hit was this way," explained the head of the family. "When Pap died he left the farm, and but very little else, to be portioned out equal amongst the five of us. A'ter we talked it all over, Lucy and Myrtle and Myrie they each took a quarter of the quarter-section; Cephas took the quarter, the house and barn and all's built on, and give me his note for the difference, as we judged hit to be worth twicet as much as ary one of the others. Hit was a fair arrangemint.

'Cause I'll tell ye why: I didn't want to work the farm, and I did want the money to start me a store with. Then, you see, Myrtle— she was married a'ready— she jined her forty acres to Sam's— he's her man; and Lucy and Myrie rented theirn to Cephas. But once at a time he's bought them three forties back, till now he's got the whole farm into his own hands and free from debt."

"I think, myself, he's done mighty well, considerin' how hard he's worked and lived," commented the storekeeper's wife.

"So," mused the schoolteacher, "the farm stands intact now with the original hundred and sixty acres?"

Lester nodded. "Jist as the old man bought it from the gover'mint. I'm glad hit is all together that way. Hit feels like home to me still; and I like to come back to it about oncet every so often; but I do better keepin' store than I could farmin'. So we all of us turned our sheers into cash as fast as Cephas could earn and save hit."

"Law, yes!" agreed his wife. "I wouldn't live on a big farm like that for anything you could give me! Why I declar' Phronie has to live, looks to me, harder 'n one o' them Jersey cows. Gettin' up afore day the year round— washin' by the creek with her feet wet all day- and nary stove to cook on! Yes, sir, she's still a-bakin' her brains over that old hearth."

"She didn't get that good dinner on the fireplace?" cried the young man in astonishment. "Will you tell me how any one can bake a frosted cake on the fire?"

"She did," said Lester.

"She can bake a pone o' bread,
   With a skillet and a lid—
She's a young think and
   cannot leave her mammy-O!"

he sang, cracking the long whip at the team.

"And she was used to better ways afore she married," sighed his wife. "I sh'd think now she's so poorly, Cephas might make things easier for her. They got no children; he could if he would."

"He might anyhow dig a well," allowed her husband. "Phronie ain't able to fetch water up from the spring."

"He jist don't think."

"Why'n't you tell him?"

"Why don't you?"

"I wanted to, but I was afeared she might think I was meddlin' or dictatin'. You know, she thinks whatever Cephas does is all right."

It was even as Lester's wife said. Cephas' wife had on her marriage come into a comfortable home, although there was plenty of hard work, and entered with zeal into her husband's plans. But he never measured the depth of her longing for little comforts which he never could afford,— could not, first because he was paying off the note to Lester; afterward because he was buying in the remaining forties; and after that because the habit was upon him. The lifelong pinching and paring of every outgoing penny had worn no groove, but a sunless chasm, in the fabric of his mind.

Lucy, his sister, had come to the festival today in a new buggy; Myrie had told of her new carpet, and Myrtle had new beds throughout her rooms. Any one of the visitors was almost fashionably dressed beside Phronie. They had learned, as the country's standard of living rose with the filtering of civilization into the mountains, to account many things as necessities which formerly had been luxuries; but Cephas reckoned all such things as future acquisitions. He would get round to them some day.

He stood beside his wife after the departure of the company, gazing admiringly at the beflowered dishes that had been brought as gifts.

"Wouldn't they look sightly, Cephas," she suggested half timidly in her soft *[We apologize, but the text is missing from the original document. - Ed.]* "haf to git us a new eatin' table, and with glass doors to put 'em in?"

"Hit would," he agreed. "But—," he glanced round the bare room with its few sticks of battered furniture— "we'd hafto git us a new eatin' table, and then new cheers to go with hit."

"Wouldn't that be fine!" She clasped her work-roughened hands, smiling.

"Most too fine for the rest of the place. Wouldn't want the diningroom to be better fixed than the front house."

Her face fell. "You don't know how pretty they'd look, Cephas," she urged, gently."

But he shook his head. "Put 'em away for jist now, and I'll see about it," he told her. "Maybe next year we can go over the whole house and git new things."

"Next year. Oh!" Her chin quivered; but he was looking at the new bowls.

"There's one thing, Cephas, I do wisht we could have right away," she went on. "That's a cookstove. My head gits so hot a-bendin' over the faar, hit makes me right dizzy whenever I straighten up. An' it seem' like the smoke bothers me worse 'n hit uset to."

Cephas set down the bowl he was examining. "Huh— that's so," he nodded. He pursued his shaven lips in the direction of the kitchen, thrust one hand into his pocket, and rubbed his iron chin reflectively with the other. "That's so. Hit would be good to have. Well— we'll git hit along with the rest. I reckon we can make the faarplace do us one more winter." He faced about with the air of putting temptation behind him.

"I 'lowed maybe when you sell the colt you'd— maybe— you'd give me part o' the money," she pleaded. "I got up a many a night and went th'oo the straighten up. And seem' like the left you sleep. She ought to be part mine."

"Yes, I rickon she ought," admitted the man, looking guilty.

"And then—," Phronie hurried on, her eyes lighting, her voice trembling- "and then, you know, I could git' me a cookstove. Hit wouldn't come to a great deal."

"Well, Phronie, the fact is— the facks air—" he looked genuinely distressed. "Well— now— Sam he came back and offered me a hunderd and twenty for her, and I done taken him up; and what's more, I sent the money by him to pay my bill with the hardware men in town, and to get me some things I've got obleeged to have round the barn. I kep' out jist enough to buy my fertilizer and seed potatoes. You know you got to pay cash for them things."

She turned to set the new dishes out of sight, submitting, as she had done before, with no word of reproach. But the look in her eyes penetrated his complacency far enough to make him say to her patiently drooping calico back:

"But ef you feel that way about hit, Phronie, why— I'll try to make it up to ye some other way. A'terwhile things won't be so tight with us as they air now."

Next day, when the sound of the sawmill's whistle, thin and distance, pierced the noon hush of the valley, Cephas came up from the field to a house disconcertingly quiet. Phronie sat in the kitchen, bowed disconsolately over folded hands.

"Why!" he exclaimed, dropping his own broad palms on either side of the door frame, "what's the reason dinner ain't on the table?"

She coughed for some moments before replying slowly, "The forestick burnt in two whilst I was down at the creek a-washin', and the pot tumbled over and the beans put the faar out."

It had happened before. Cephas ejaculated "Dad-limb the luck," in more disgust than surprise. "Ain't they nothing to eat?"

"You'll haf to make out, I reckon, with what's cold from yistidy. Look like I'm so tired I jist cain't git another dinner now."

He turned to the water shelf that was built outside the door, and began to wash his hands. "All right, I'll make out. Ain't you aimin' to eat nothing?"

"N—no. I b'lieve I'll go lay down on the bed a while."

He glanced at her uneasily for the first time. "You sick?"

"No. I ain't sick." But she dropped forward.

"You ain't been eatin' enough to keep a chicken alive. I'm a good notion to git the doctor."

"Oh, no! Jist seems like again' I git a meal cooked I'm so werried and tired I don't want to eat it."

"Then go and lay down," he bade her; and after his solitary meal he returned to plowing.

But at supper time his wife had not risen, and he was again obliged to do for himself. Open fire cookery calls for ten times as much pure skill as getting a meal in a kitchen with modern appliances— skill that Cephas did not possess. That was a poor repast to which he sat down with scorched fingers, a flushed face, and short temper. Afterward he approached his wife where she lay curled up among the pillows in the huge four-poster and said: "Why Fronie, you— you must be sick!"

"I ain't," she insisted. "But I never was so tired in all my life."

"What ye want me to bring ye to eat?"

She shook her head slightly. Her worn hands lay out on the counterpane as if too weary to move; the lids drooped over her eyes.

"Ef you'll tell me anything you'd like, I'll try to cook it."

"No— no," she sighed, "I've been werried for years on in about things to eat— about buyin' 'em, and savin' 'em, and cookin' 'em. I'd rather starve as to think about 'em any more."

"Well, I aim to have the doctor here."

"No! No— don't! I'd only haf to werry over another ten or fifteen dollars."

"Why, I'm payin' for hit!" he replied impatiently.

"Yes— but I got to save for hit. I got to scrimp down closter and study harder for every extry ixpense, and I cain't bear no more jist now. I'm too tired."

He stood puzzled. Her eyes shut slowly as he looked; her face was death-white against the immaculate sheen of her pillowslips. Then her hands fell limply across each other on her breast. And at that sight his mailed heart was at last shot through and through with a bright shaft of fear.

"You ain't goin' to werry nor scrimp neither for one while!" he almost shouted. "Wait— I'll go hunt up some o' the neighbors, and then we'll see what the doctor says."

The doctor said it was serious; and none could have charged Cephas Drane with saving money during the weeks that his wife lay ill. He even tried of sending for a trained nurse at $20 a week, but this his sisters, who took turns watching by Phronie's bedside, would not allow. Lester's wife brought her every delicacy in the country store; the schoolteacher and his sweetheart walked to town for the first box of strawberries shipped from Georgia; but she persistently turned away from food, and day by day they saw her growing feebler.

One evening, when the doctor had been more than unusually uncommunicative, Lucy and Myrie both remained to watch. Cephas stood long by his wife's bed. Outside, the low moon looked through the blossoming apple boughs into the room; the soft breeze filled the open window with a flood of fragrance and the hum of great night-moths. He remembered that it was through an orchard coaxed into bloom too early by the treacherous wooing of a southern spring that she had come to the house a bride; she had worn a spray of the pink-and-white florescence, and its freshness had matched her own. He turned about. The kitchen door was wide open; the fireplace was visible, where so often he had seen without seeing Phronie's dun calico back stooping painfully over the smoky, ash-grimed hearth, ministering to his comfort with more of thoughtfulness and skill than he had ever realized till now. This was what he had made of her!

"Do ye blame me with all of hit, Phronie?" he gulped, his throat working. "Lord! don't ye even know me, girl? . . . No man could a-had better intentions. And hell's paved with 'em," he muttered bitterly. "Hit was all there afore my eyes, but I ain't never seed. Oh, I ain't never understood!"

She made no sign of hearing. In the mingling of lamp-light and moonlight the face on the pillow blanched to the hue of an ivory carving; the lids fitted closely over the sunken eyes like shells of wax; the skin under the jawbones was drawn back in fine folds like the skin of a plucked fowl. He held the little brass lamp directly over her head. The delicate shadows of the eyelashes lay softly on the thin cheeks. How tired she looked! How weak and old! And Phronie was only forty-seven.

He listened for her breathing and could not hear it. Did he imagine that her chest rose and fell gently as she lay? Her hands shook so that all the crouching shadows trembled in the corners. Fear gripped soul and shook it to and fro.

"Oh, Phronie!" he groaned. "Don't, don't lay there and die. You must open your eyes and look at me! Phronie! What is there that you would look at? What could I git for ye?"

The two women in the kitchen saw him set down the lamp and turn, with an air of having suddenly remembered something long overlooked. He passed them without a word or a look and hurried to the barn. They heard "Whoa," and then the jingle of harness slapped over the backs of the team.

"Lucy!" whispered Myrie, startled, "you don't reckon he's a-hitchin' up to— to go after—"

Lucy stared. "He couldn't!"

"He was always powerful fore-handed—"

They leaned down to peer out of the window, and then, as the sick woman appeared to be resting quietly, resumed their places in the kitchen, talking only in undertones.

The hours wore on; the air was thick with sadness, drowsiness. They sat silent and grave, their shadows motionless on the bare wall. An indefinable uneasiness, near akin to terror, began to grow within them. From time to time they rose, and tiptoed to the door of the next room.

The clock struck midnight. Lucy began to whimper.

"I b'lieve in my soul she's a-dyin', Myrie!"

"The Lord, what'll we do! Oh, he hadn't ought to gone off and left us this way!"

"Cain't you call some o' the neighbors?"

"Cain't make 'em hear this distance. You'll haf to go the nigh way to Mis' Bain's and git her."

"Oh! I wouldn't for anything to th'oo that piece of woods alone. They say they's a Ha'nt walks there— and dark as 'tis!"

"The moon's a-shinin'."

"You go with me."

"And leave her without anybody?"

"Hit won't take ten minutes. Besides— Listen! He's a-comin' back! Do you reckon he's got—"

As they ran to the door they felt their hair softly rising. Cephas was just driving into the barnyard. His figure, doggedly humped on the seat, showed plain against the blank barn walls in the moonlight, and behind him, protruding from under a tarpaulin thrown askew, was a bulk black and angular and strange.

Myrtle clutched her sister's arm, intoning in a voice deep with solemn import: "He's got hit!"

"He has!" cried Lucy. "I wish I may never if he ain't!"

"Ain't he got no feelin's?"

"He's my own brother, but"— Lucy sobbed hysterically—"don't seem like he can be any kin to me."

"I couldn't— not if they was to hang me. I couldn't take 'n' buy anybody's coffin afore they was dead!'

"Oh— oh— I cain't stand hit to stay here!" cried Lucy wildly. "Can you?"

"Let's go quick and fetch Miss Bain."

Cephas saw them flitting through the moonbeams and out of sight down the shadowy woods path, but he asked no questions. He was tugging to lift, all alone, the angular bulk from the wagon. At last he got it free and hoisted to his shoulder— a burden for two men, whose rigid inequalities bruised his flesh— and staggered beneath it to the house. The weight was as difficult to lower as it had been to raise, but at last it jarred from his straining form to the floor. Then he got stiffly and gingerly to his feet, and rubbing his bruised and aching hands together, stood off to view what he had so laboriously brought. It was a stove.

Back to the wagon he went, making several trips to and fro to carry in grates, lids and doors. He fitted everything into place with frowning and grunting, and mounted the thing on its four legs; he climbed on a chair and enlarged with his knife a hole in the wall, and thrust the pipe through. The stove was ready.

At last he stole into the room where his wife lay. She turned a little and sighed faintly, lying among the fragrant homely fabrics of her own weaving. He sat down and dropped his face into the great cup of his palms. The big wooden clock, under its pointed roof, ticked out the minutes slowly. No more than the woman beside him did Cephas care ever to rise. "Too late," he whispered; "too late!"

A stir among the coverlets, a squeaking of the cords that supported the mattress, made him turn quickly, the fierce anxiety of his heart leaping to his eyes.

His wife, who yesterday could scarcely move her thin fingers in a light caress of his own, now leaned hight upon one elbow, clutching at her throat with the other hand. Her mouth was open and her blue eyes had brightened and rounded with delight and wonder.

"The stove," she whispered, excitedly, "the cook stove! I ain't dreamin', am I, Cephas? Ain't that what hit is? Ain't that there—" And her momentary strength ebbing as suddenly as it had risen, she fell back on the pillows. "Tell me!" she gasped, her eyes searching his face.

He was up on the instant, bending over her. "Yes, yes, Phronie— honey!" he answered distractedly. "I got it for ye at last, but I'm afeared hit's too late. Phronie- honey! Don't ye try to raise up that way— you're too sick-"

"I ain't," she responded, wriggling toward the edge of the bed. "I want to see. I ain't much sick, Cephas— jist weak, because I ain't had nothing to eat."

"Want me to—"

"Ain't ye never put no fire in hit? Let's see how hit draws— go on! And you fix me somethin' on it right away!" She was using only the faint, clear echo of her usual voice, but it was eager and almost girlish with joy.

Awkwardly and with shaking hands he started a fire, warmed a cup of milk, and sat down to feed her with a spoon. Perhaps she did not know that she was sipping. She was counting the windows which he had left wide open in the stove's broad front. There were thirteen of them— seven narrow ones above and six wider along the opulent swell of the door; all glowing squares of scarlet radiance as the flames began to roar softly within.

"You're the dearest wife that ever lived," he told her between spoonfuls. "The sweetest woman— the best woman! And I always aimed to be good to ye. But I wanted so bad to git the place paid fur that I didn't consider as I ought."

Myrie and Lucy, breathless and dishevelled, came upon them thus, and stopped, astonished.

"Why— why, then— she wasn't dyin', " gasped Lucy, too wonder-struck to consider her words. Myrie began to talk rapidly, to make Phronie forget what her sister had said: "We got off the path and got lost, and been a-wanderin' all around! Air you better, Phronie?"

"Law, yes! I feel like gittin' right up and cookin' breakfast on my new stove. You go home to your children as soon as hit comes light, Myrie. I ain't sick." She smiled, weakly but joyously. "You lay down and sleep, both of ye."

"I'd give the whole farm today," said Cephas, when the two sisters, whispering, wide-eyed, clinging together, looking backward as at a miracle— had withdrawn. "I'd freely give hit if I'd a-bought ye that cook-stove ten year back."

The waxen mask of her face shown as though a new candle of life were lighted behind it. "Law, honey, hit's here, now, and I'll cook ye many a good dinner on it." She patted his hands.

Through the door stole the first pale glimmer of the dawn. She had finished her milk. And together they counted the windows in the stove's opulent front. There were thirteen of them.

Published in
The Chattanooga News - June 1912

[225]

Enchanter's Nightshade

EMMA BELL MILES

At a merrymaking in caney's cove two brothers were dancing. They were both in the early twenties, blond, well formed and agile. They had been known as "them good-lookin' Reedy boys" before they were grown, and although demure Fedelma had married the elder a year ago, the maidens pressing their best plumage softly together in the doorway whispered to each other, "Ain't he straight!" as Ransom took the floor, even while all their arts were directed toward attracting the still eligible Atlas. Ransom was a smaller and finer edition of his younger brother; he had clearer features, bluer eyes, and fair hair curling close to the scalp where Atlas' mop was sandy.

Ransom's partner of the moment was, as it happened, the very girl whom Atlas had brought to the gathering— Callie Drane, a girl large for her age, whose vivid coloring and thick waving hair bespoke abundant vitality. With a grace like that of a wild creature she bounded to meet the young fellow in the middle of the ring; her eyes and her teeth gleamed as she gave him her hand, unconscious of the strength of its clasp. Catching the air from the banjos, she began to sing as she danced.

"The ficety thing," murmured some of the women. But others took up the melody, a native composition, and carried it all together:

> "Some days seem dark and dreary,
>
>> As though it was likely to rain;
>
> Some clouds may float to center,
>
>> My love has gone off on the train.
>
> "Oh it's hard to be bound in prison,
>
>> It's hard to be bound in jail!
>
> To see iron bars around you,
>
>> And no one to go your bail!"

Callie moved to and fro lightly, her head high, her mouth well open, her face full of light, the song rippling from her throat as limpid and fresh as a streamlet from a mountain spring.

Her very antithesis was Fedelma, sitting mute and motionless by the wall. The bride of a year was not dancing this set, preferring, out of sheer pride in his appearance, to keep her soft dark gaze on her young husband. They were late in arriving because she had stopped to sew a patch inside the collar of his best shirt. Despite the meek grace of her neck and smooth brown head, she heard and rather resented the whispers; and at Callista's too eager advance she half-rose with a smothered exclamation. A little later she stood up, turning her head from side to side uneasily.

To a would-be partner she replied confusedly, "No—I—jist 'lowed to get me a drink; it's hot in here," and slipped out under the tranquil stars.

She had kept a beautiful secret to tell Ransom tonight; but something, some careless word of his, had postponed the telling until they should find themselves alone on the homeward road, and now— "I won't tell him a-tall!" she whispered fiercely, threading her aimless way through the undergrowth. "I jist won't! That big tomboy Callie—she came right into his eyes with that look o' hers, and he let her in— he let her in! . . . They act as if they knowed something I don't." Her throat ached with rising sobs. "They used to go together, didn't they? No telling but they think of each other still!"

Her feet found themselves in the spring path. Wishing only to be alone until this unwonted flood of feeling could spend itself, she went slowly down the hill and seated herself on the puncheon bench, placed there for the support of washtubs. Before her, in the white moonlight, stood Bivins' springhouse, its walls of heavy logs and stones crossed by a delicate vine whose leaves and clustered berries showed translucent. Having once noticed, she could not take her eyes from the exquisite thing. The moon was mounting into the sky; she heard the whispered counsel of the leaves like a warning, and the night's heavy moisture spilling from leaf to leaf. A faint pattering footfall rustled in the thicket. She felt so afraid of the lonely woods that she ceased crying, and leaned forward as if to rise; but she sat on, looking at the pretty slender vine, wishing she had not come here or to Bivins' dance, yet perversely assuring herself that, if Ransom were really bent on reviving an old affair, nothing else could matter to him or to her.

A heavy, tramping step and a splash roused her from the mood into which she had fallen. She rose now and stood, a white slim shape in the cavern of shadow beneath the big tupelo that overarched Mam Bivins' washplace.

The newcomer was Atlas. "Hello! what you doin' here, Delma?" he asked, surprised. As she made no answer, he entered the springhouse, dipped his bucket and began fumbling along the walls. "Do they keep ary gourd here, that you known of?" he inquired, reappearing in the moon-drenched doorway.

"I don't know," she answered mournfully, speaking with an effort over the lump in her throat.

Replying to the tone instead of the words, he came toward her. In the moonlight she saw his honest face touched with concern, its big brows wrinkling together. "Is the' anything the matter? Does Ransom know you're here all by yourself?"

In the darkness she found his soft Southern bass inexpressibly comforting.

"I— jist wanted a drink." And out of pure pique she added, "He don't hafto know every step I take, does he?"

He answered with a little laugh that meant nothing except the blessed readiness of youth for laughter. "Let's git us a drink, if we can find a gourd."

She caught the quick spurt of a lighted match, an ejaculation as its snapped-off head hissed in the water. To the mountain girl there was a fascinating masculine reckless-ness in this dashing waste of matches.

He struck another, and looking up over its glow in the cup of his hollowed palms, found her face crowned with its wreath of jade and coral unexpectedly close to his own in the doorway, and smiled.

Fedelma drew back. "Well, there ain't a thing here to drink out of except that big wooden bucket," she exclaimed petulantly.

"Would ye take my hat?" he proffered, scooping a drink in its felt brim.

She drank and thanked him, but did not at once set off toward the house. Something in the deferential gesture with which he waited on her, some vibration in his voice, filled her with a sudden overwhelming curiosity as to how he would make love. She wondered, with a thrill of terror at her own daring, what were the deepest and tenderest notes of his voice, what the falling, hovering motions of his broad hands. One man's wooing she knew by heart; could there be another as sweet?— But was that, perhaps, Ransom's feeling about Callie? The racking anger came welling up again; and before she was aware it rose to words.

"Atlas, what makes you go with Callie Drane?"

He laughed again, a rich, pleasant chuckle. "Don't you like her?"

"Oh— she thinks too much of herself, I b'lieve! Whatever makes you—?" She checked herself, realizing that her speech was open to misinterpretation.

"Why— because I couldn't git you, I reckon." It was an absurd compliment, awkwardly turned; but finding Ransom's wife so unlike her usual shy and gentle self had gone to his head a little.

"Oh, shuh! You and me—" She really hardly knew what to say. "You and me ain't never went together enough to—to— to make you talk like that."

"Why—" He made a gesture of protest. "You remember the Three Springs picnic, don't ye?"

Of course she did, but she had never been sure till now that it was worth remembering. Had he meant it, then—all the play of that merry time? Her pulses quickened; she stood silent, lovely and alluring in the dusk of the perfumed woods. The red berries in her hair seemed to burn like a desire.

They moved forward together, and Atlas, knocking accidentally against a sapling, brought down a shower of starry drops from the branches all over her.

She gave a little shriek, and then laughed, dancing ahead under the moving shadows of the foliage, bent upon reprisal. Tiny drops like diamond dust glittered on the stray curls over her forehead, and on the leaves and berries of her wreath, twinkling with the tremor of her laughter.

Atlas stopped, his hands closing into fists. They stood facing each other, eyes answering eyes with something roused and dangerous. He recovered himself by an effort and drew back a step.

"You goin' back to the house?" he suggested, taking up the bucket of water.

She trembled, balanced, hesitated—then compromised, "Not yit a while." How far she had drifted from this morning's austere joy in her secret, after the nights of terror and doubt!

Atlas set down the pail. "Then shall I stay too?" He came and bent over her. "Do ye want me— to— stay with you— Delma?"

She did not look up, as she made room for him beside her on Mam Bivins' bench:— "only don't ye forget, Atlas Reedy, that I'm a married woman!"

"I won't if you don't," he laughed, fanning her with the hat she had drank from. Something in her fragility and helplessness moved him in a different way from Callie's robust buoyance. He could not deny that he liked doing little things for Delma.

From the house up the hill the music of banjos came pulsing out upon the ancient night, powerful with associations to those two— a music indigenous to the soil as the scarlet-berried vine.

> "I have a great ship on the ocean,
>
>> All lined with silver and gold;
>
>> And before my true lover shall suffer,
>
>> My ship shall be anchored and sold.
>
> "If I had the wings of an eagle,
>
>> Or either the wings of a dove,
>
>> I'd fly over mountain and rivers,
>
>> And rest in the arms of my love."

Of a sudden her face crinkled miserably. "I reckon Ransom's done forgot it already."

"How's that, Fedelma?"

"Didn't you see, Atlas?" Insensibly a note of sincerer feeling crept into her voice. She looked straight at him without self-consciousness. "Ransom and Callie?"

The hat quivered, and stopped, clutched hard. "See . . . what? You tell me!"

"Nothing only— she looked at him, I thought. When they danced."

"Oh, she did, did she!" Atlas got to his feet. "I been afeared of it," he groaned. "Rans' was the first that ever went with Callie. . . . They say a gal never forgets." He strode forward and caught up the bucket without looking round. "Let's us go back!" His voice went strangely harsh on the words. "By jacks, I've whupped Rans' afore, and I can again if he gits to lookin' too hard at my gal. Condamn that curly head of his!"

She had no choice but to follow, flung into a gulf of doubt and anger by his ready acceptance of her suspicions as valid. She would hurry to see what Ransom was doing now— oh, she must! What had she been thinking of, to leave him to his own devices for so long? But it was Ransom who showed himself at the turn of the path, and demanding: "Been down to the spring, Atlas? Have you seed Fedelma anywhere? Oh, there she comes— "

Her heart at first expanded with relief; but she distinctly saw his start as he realized that she had accompanied Atlas. He stood before her, blocking the path, and did not speak for a moment. Atlas disappeared with the bucket of water; the dropping dew, the crickets and the katydids, possessed the stillness. They heard the banjos at the house, and the thudding feet of the dancers.

[233]

"Had you forgot you belong to me?" he asked at last. He stopped with his mouth open, and she smelt the product of Bivins' still.

"Rans'! Why, Ransom! had you forgot you wasn't goin' to touch whiskey tonight?" she countered. "Let's us go home right now, Rans'. Let's do!"

"Not till I've licked that— " Ransom's synonym for "cur" was polysyllabic but forceful— "for stealin' you out. And I'll see you afterward." He turned on his heel and moved away, a feeling of sullen resentment against her in his heart, suddenly estranged and isolated. He felt powerless to fight against the hideous doubts that took his mind by storm.

But his wife, following, clung to him, her arm round his shoulders.

"Rans', he didn't. He didn't. You wouldn't think so if you wasn't drinkin'. Wait, honey— wait a minute— let me tell you! Atlas come down to git some water for the folks; I'd done been there for some little time. . . . Don't you go to the house, Rans'. Take me home." She began to cry, stumbling along beside him. "I want to go home, Ransom! Hit's the best. I got something to tell you. You— you'll take another drink or two up there, and then first thing you know you'ns 'll all git in a jower and a jangle, and you or him, one'll be hurt."

"Sure will," he retorted grimly, moving doggedly forward. They came out into the open road, flooded with light. "But I want to tell you something! Listen—"

He flung off her hands. "If hit's what I think," he said, in a tense undertone, "you better never tell it." His light-weight figure was drawn erect; his eyes glinted like steel.

"You and them for it, then!" cried Fedelma, stopping short with a gesture of despair. Her secret! Had he guessed it, then— and was this the way he meant to take it? She made no attempt to follow him farther; she forgot Atlas and Callie entirely; her deepest feelings were wounded now. "His baby, his own little—Oh, dear Lord, what shall I do! I'm a good notion to go back to Marion County and stay with mammy!"

She wandered, sobbing and wiping her eyes on her sleeves, along the road home.

Ransom, hurrying to Bivins' house, looked through the window at the lighted room. The rhythmic swing of the music urged the pounding of the blood in his temples. He saw Atlas join the dance again, saw a little flurry among the girls, and heard without noticing Callie's laugh. The little children, who had been allowed to sit up late, now began to nod over in the corners; the usual contingent of bad little boys arrived and, growing obstreperous, had to be hustled out of the way. The fun waxed furious; the figures wheeled and swung and eddied; coats were flung off, hand-clapping and stamping increased, laughter was continuous. At every shout he glowered more darkly through the narrow pane.

"I'll take one more drink, and then I'll call him out," he muttered to one who stood near him in the yard.

"Who?" asked Homer Bivins.

"Huh? Why, Atlas,— dam' his impident looks."

"What's he done, Rans'? I wouldn't, Ransom. Better not call him out, Ransom," said several bystanders quickly. For Ransom and Atlas had fought ever since they were boys on the slightest provocation or none at all; their only peace lay in keeping apart, although there seemed no ill feeling between them other than the ancestral rivalry between males of the same blood.

Old Bivins came from the jug hidden in the althea bushes, all solicitude for the success of his daughters' merry-making. "Looky here, Ransom," he began in a conciliatory tone, plucking the young man's sleeve. "Some day when we'ns ain't got no frolic afoot we'll make a ring, somers out, and see fair play whilst you and him settles it for good, and finds out which is the best man."

"No, by Jacks, I'll have him afore I go home tonight," cried the little man, exasperated at the quivering of Bivins' long beard. What business was it of anyone's? "I feel like I could whup him right now; I b'lieve I can."

"You go fetch his woman," suggested Homer aside to another. "Maybe she can do something with him. Lord, what a temper Rans' Reedy's got! I'll go warn his brother."

But Fedelma could not be found; she was already whimpering to herself, far in the moonlight; and Atlas presently came to Callie with a very serious countenance.

"Callista, girl, I've got obleeged to quit and go, I reckon. Do you want me to take you home now, or— but I declar' I hate to leave ye to ary other boy! Go now, will ye— with me?"

"What time is it?" she parleyed, reluctant. "I'm havin' such a good old time! Has something happened?"

"No— not yit."

"Then what you leavin' for?"

"Well— Rans' has took one or two drinks too many, and he's lookin' for me. You know, Callie, how he always was."

Her eyes opened. "You ain't afeared of him, air ye?"

"What would I be afeared of him for? I don't want to fight him; ther ain't no sense in hit when we ain't got nothing to fight about, and him and me has both swore we never would again."

The girl considered, her face still flushed, her eyes gleaming; and then, even while her foot still beat time to "Citico," she gave in. "Wait, then, till I say good-bye to Sally Bivins, and I'll git my shawl."

The music swelled to their ears in an appealing crescendo and diminuendo as they made an unobtrusive exit. "I don't much believe Delma was right about him and her," he was thinking. "If I 'lowed he was, though, Rans' wouldn't hafto look far afore he found me."

They gained the road with a reassuring backward glance to where Homer, with diplomacy slightly mistaken, was plying Ransom with more liquor.

"I like to walk with you this way," he murmured as they swung into step. He drew her hand within his arm and kept it there, pressing and pressing it, the unlighted lantern swinging at his side.

"Why," said the girl, perceiving a glimmering shape moving before them down the road, "somebody's went on ahead of us."

"Hit's a gal," he supplemented her observation. "All by herself. Why, I'll swar!"

"Don't do it," she laughed.

"I won't. I just said 'I will swar.' But I b'lieve on my soul that's Fedelma. What's the matter, Dell?" he called.

The forlorn figure waited for them to come up, and they saw that she was crying.

"Did Rans' make ye go home? Did he scold ye? Air you waitin' for him?" asked Callie, all in a breath.

"We left," explained the boy, "because he seemed to want to jump onto me. I 'lowed it would be best to keep out of his way."

Delma nodded, but could find no words.

They were now all four at cross-purposes; and their hearts were all beating a little too fast.

"Well, walk on with us," said Atlas at last. "We'll sight you home; won't we, Callie?"

But as Fedelma joined the pair, Callie swung apart. "Why! you ain't aimin' to leave Ransom come home all by hisself, the way he is?"

"O' course; he'll be all right," answered Atlas. "Or, if he ain't, some o' them boys 'll see to him."

"How d'you know they will? He may go wanderin' about and break his fool neck."

"He wouldn't let me," protested Atlas; but he glanced back along the road uneasily.

"Dell!" The appeal was from one woman to another on behalf of an erring boy. "Ain't you goin' to wait for your man?"

"No, I ain't," declared Delma, speaking for the first time.

"After the way he talked to me back yon, he can go on and break his neck for all o' me— b-hoo-hoo!"

"Then I will!" cried the girl, stopping.

"You won't neither!" snapped Fedelma.

"Why, Callie!" Atlas stopped, facing her. A jealous wrath surged up in him and burst bounds. "By Jacks, if there *is* anything between you and your old sweetheart, hit's time I knowed it, Callie! I want the straight of hit; I can't stand this—"

"Don't you name such to me!" She sprang back and squared away valiantly, like a man, with heaving breast. "Why— why then, the straight of hit is, I wouldn't leave a dawg to blunder around in these here woods, and him full o' Bivins' pizen! You'ns go on, I'll wait." She knew perfectly that this was ridiculous. "Or else we all wait, right here."

"Won't hafto wait long," muttered Atlas, hearing swift unsteady footsteps. A second later Ransom, whom Homer's wit and hospitality had not availed to detain long, burst upon them, wildly swinging a lantern covered with blazing oil, and cursing.

"Look out, you'll set fire— Put that light down, you firebug!" shouted Atlas, leaping; and then it happened. Whack, whack, whack; crash went the two lanterns; a yellow oily flame shot up from the sand; the two girls, in momentary terror of an explosion that distracted even their terror of the conflict, saw in the bright light the brothers at each other's throats, struggling, kicking, reeling to and fro. Into the shine and out of it they drove, now trampling the sand, now crashing through the bushes, till Atlas tripped on a root and was down.

"He's got a knife!" screamed Delma, catching the glint of a blade.

"Oh, my God, he'll kill him!" cried Callie at the same moment.

Together by a great effort the women dragged Ransom back by the arms. Never had Callie's splendid strength and courage served her so well as while she held the furious little man and shrieked, "Run, Atlas! for the Lord's sake, run!"

A second later she caught up Atlas' hat from the ground and set off after him.

Ransom, the knife still in his hand, stood blinking foolishly at the last flicker of the spilt oil. He drew a long breath, like a gasp. "Let me have the knife, Rans," pleaded Delma. "Give it here. There, there, honey! it's all over; you won't need ary weepon." She approached timidly, feeling for his hand.

"Naw!" he said, and with a jerk sent the open blade whirling into the thicket. "Shucks! I never tried to knife anybody afore. . . . What's it all about, anyhow?" He seemed to have sobered all at once. "Shucks!" he repeated, looking down at the trampled road and broken lanterns. "Oh, shucks! Atlas. Oh, At!" There was no answer. "Done gone on, has he?"

"Let's us go, too," urged his wife.

He laid his hands on her shoulders and turned her to face him; putting both arms closely round her, he looked intently into her eyes.

"Tell me, Fedelma— was there anything to fight about? What was you down to the spring for?"

She responded gladly to his touch, as always. "Not anything. There wasn't no harm in that, was there?"

"What was he sayin' to you?"

"Not much of anything. . . . I— jist wondered how he *would* talk if—

"Fedelma!"

She tore the wreath from her hair and sent it flying after his knife. It caught on a twig and hung, swaying a little, all transparent against the luminous background, each delicate leaf-rib clear as if formed of coral and crystal and jade. It seemed not to be of earth, but the last visible fragment of a dream-world, called up by a magician and on the point of vanishing.

"I don't know what made me so silly— especially seein' that I'll haf to face death my ownself in a while,— for you and yourn," she added, so low that he did not quite hear. "Ransom, it wasn't— real. Nothing is real but you for me. You've made my life for me, every day for a year now,— and, look!" She fumbled at his collar and turned it down to show the patch she had sewed there. Her neat strong stitches caught the light as clearly as the delicate interlaced veins of the wreath. "That's mine— you're mine! Don't you see we've growed together— we belong to one another. Nothing can change that. Nothing else is real. Only I wisht— I wisht I never had gone with any boy but you."

He pressed his lips to her face, feeling it cool and fresh as a fruit just freshly plucked. "Let's be good people, and not quarrel. I reckon we better go home and stay there."

"Air you hurt?" She passed her fingers over the curls she had so resolutely clipped the day before.

"Just a bump. Atlas give me one good lick if he never gits in another."

"And listen, Ransom, she continued breathlessly, nestling to him, "I'll tell ye now. . . . "

Callie fled along the road, her breath coming and going audibly, her dress flitting mothlike under the gliding shadows. "Atlas!" she called softly. "Oh, Atlas!"

In a moment he answered from a darker core of shadows under an oak, his deep voice vibrating like a soft gong. "Here's your hat," she panted, coming close to him. "Oh, Atlas, air you hurt?"

"Not me. 'Magine he is. I fetched him one with the lantern, just afore I went down, that ought to a-stunded him if it hadn't a-glanced."

"Serve him right. Oh, Atlas, 1 always heared you was a beautiful fighter, but I never thought so well of you as when you jist wouldn't fight till you had obliged to."

"Then you do?" He put out his arm, still quivering with the strain of conflict, and she came within it. All the warm, splendid womanhood of her seventeen rough-and-tumble years thrilled to his kiss. "So you think much o' me, Callie?"

"More'n the world and all. Oh, I do!" Their untried hearts beat and plunged against each other.

"Sure there's nobody— none o' your old sweethearts, f'r instance— that you might come to think more of, sometime?"

"I never had— oh! If you mean Ransom,— why, I was a little bit o' gal then, and he's— he's married!"

"You— I thought you looked at him tonight—"

"How?"

"As if he wasn't, maybe."

"Why, you old jealous-hearted— You old fool!" Her voice broke with tenderness on the final word.

As Callie and Atlas went by Ransom's house a few days later, they stopped at the gate and called to Fedelma.

The young wife was rocking on her front porch, stringing beans. She rose, and came down to the fence, putting back a wispy lock and smiling. A new gravity and sweetness had come into her eyes since the night of the dance in the cove, and she, and Ransom singing in the field below, alone in all the world knew why.

"Come on in," she bade the pair.

"Can't," stated Callie. "We jist wanted to tell you that me and Atlas— that we was— " She flushed, looked down, and seemed unable to go on.

But the young man put his hand firmly over hers where it lay on the top rail. "We're a-goin' to be married a-Sunday, Delma, and we want you and Ransom to be there. Then we'll have a housewarmin' soon as I can git a shack ready, and you can tell him that's one dance where there won't be any liquor circulated."

Fedelma regarded them with a grave smile.

"We'll be glad to come and see ye married," she answered. "But if hit's all the same to you-uns, I reckon we won't be at the infare. If a body can't keep their heads at a frolic no better than we do—" the prettiest imaginable color crept up into her cheeks, and she did not look at Atlas— "I think they better not go. I never have jined ary church, but I ain't shore I b'lieve in dancin'. "

Published in
The Craftsman Magazine - July 1912

Love O' Man

CAROLINE WOOD MORRISON
AND
EMMA BELL MILES

THE SLOPES OF THE MAJESTIC KNOB THAT SHUT THE
high-hung valley where Isodene and Peter lived were astir
with tiny lives innumerable; the tide of spring washed over
everything in deep waves of beauty and life. The very fields
seemed unreal in the haze of spring bush-burning; the
dead branches tossed like gray foam against a smoke-faded
horizon. Here and there a single tree grew dark against
the sky as it thickened with countless little leaves, and its
shadow, falling, outlined contours of boulder and ravine.

Dimly on the face of the brown fields, a youth appeared
with a mule and a plow, advancing, turning, and retreating
along the dew-darkened rows.

On the lonely road that meandered between two farms a
girl walked slowly, swinging at her side a stout basket woven
of white oak splints. Here, among the fence-row weeds and
brambles, fine green films of spring were stealing over all
that was stiff or colorless. In the same way the girl's presence, homely though it was, and tiny in space and time,

seemed to nullify for a moment the stark and desolate facts of a sordid, lonely existence. For in her homespun garments blossomed some old pagan fancy; her shawl was saffron-dyed, her dress was the mellow old-gold hue of peach-leaves, and her neckerchief, which she had bought at the store, a deep, opulent yellow.

The plowboy halted his mule at her approach. "Howdy, Isodene! Where you goin'?" he greeted her with the heavy courtesy of a good-natured man dulled with toil.

For answer, she showed him the basket that contained her father's midday meal. "There's too much for one, Peter," she commented, looking straight at him with blue eyes that held always behind them a cloud of dreaminess, of other-worldiness. "Have a piece of pie."

"Ef it won't disfurnish your pap," he answered, accepting the proffered refreshment. She leaned on the top rail and silently watched him eat, sitting on the plow.

"Seems like I can hear a noise under the ground," he remarked, looking curiously at the earth beneath his bare feet.

She also bent downward and appeared to brood or to listen in a sweet melancholy.

"Like water a-runnin', or like somebody talkin' and movin' around," he continued, gesticulating vaguely with the half-eaten section of pie.

"I know what it is," she said, after a pause. "It's the *Sylvaines!*"

Peter scratched his head under his wide straw hat. "You mean one o' them ha'nts you're always a-seein'?"

"No— no ha'nts nor boogars." Folding both arms on the weather-blackened rail, she fixed her lack-lustre, indwelling eyes upon him. "The Sylvaines are—well, roots: the roots of plants and trees," she told him earnestly. "They have shapes somethin' like people. Ain't you heard tell of mandrakes and potatoes with faces? They move round and creep, soft and slow, in the earth when it's warm with the sun. This time o' year the sap runs in streams— they're all awake and reachin' deep in the ground. They have their own rules and laws; they can see; they can move back and forth; they can talk! I know! I know a heap they say— or that they think, anyhow."

"You know a heap!" he gibed good-humoredly.

"Yes, I do," she assured him. "My mother is Scotch-Irish. She's a seventh daughter of a seventh daughter, just like me. She can visit with fairy folk in the evenin'. I used to wake up and listen at her when I was a little chap. But Father 'lowed it might be resky in some way, and he made her stop. And I used to listen at the Sylvaines with her, but I don't any more now. Brother Lominack said for us not to— that it might be dangerous."

Peter laughed sheepishly and slapped the lines on the back of the drowsing mule, as though to move on.

"Let your plow stand still a minute, and I'll tell you what they're a-sayin' right now, if you don't believe I can," she challenged.

"Let's see you— ef you ain't a-feared," he answered, half daring, half hesitating.

She crossed the fence and flung herself on the newly turned earth, her ear close to the warm, dark loam.

"They must be havin' a meetin'," she murmured in a tone that caught Peter's interest and touched his imagination. "They're all talkin' at once. I can't understand when they mutter away so fast. . . . Oh, I can tell you! It's a new plant they're fixin' to set out right here. A young one— a Sylvaine has to hold it until the flower opens. They're makin' out to tell her somethin' particular— oh, somethin' wonderful! This is the seventh seed of a seventh bloom, and so it's got a blessing on it——"

"Huh!" grunted the listener, incredulous. How could there be a blessing on mere natural objects— on anything outside the church?

"I can hear them now," the interpreter continued, "sayin' that if two mortals, two that love each other, try to pick the flower at the same time, the Sylvaine will come to life and be like us"— she seemed far away— "so long as she can hold to the flower, so long as she can keep it in her hands. It will give her a chanst, they say, to find a soul of her own; but it'll have to be before the flower fades. . . . They're *all* talkin' again," she lamented plaintively. "I can't catch a word." She rose to her feet and shook the clinging fragments of soil from the dull gold of her gown as she seemed to shake herself free from a spell.

"I don't believe a word of— of that!" Peter cried passionately. " Yes— ef I was your brother Lominack, I'd see to you! I sure would!"

"*Ffttt!* He don't know nothin' about me— and you won't tell," she replied, but the blue eyes widened uneasily.

"Have you ever said anything about— this here —to anybody but me?" the boy asked.

[247]

"No; and I ain't liable to name it to you again, nuther," she retorted.

"I'm tellin' ye for your own good. Where do you expect to go to, holdin' with such?" His voice was harsh. "I wisht you had n't been born with a veil like they say you was. Ha'nts don't do nobody no good. The Bible names them, and says not to have nothin' to do with 'em. They'll wither your time. But it don't name no Sylvaines, nor them fairies nuther. I don't believe in no such— a-tall!" His voice rose almost to a shout.

Half ashamed and half angry, she turned away to cross the fence and regain the road. Awkwardly, Peter reached a helping hand; yet when she touched him he snatched it suddenly away.

The boy was half afraid of the girl.

She gave no sign, but caught up her basket and walked steadily on. He stood grasping plow and lines, watching until the warm-hued figure was far away in the shortened shadows and quivering air of noon. It was always this way with Peter. She had forgiven him many a rudeness in the past; but this she resented smoulderingly. For days thereafter, until the spring plowing and planting were finished, she went and came silently on her lonely road between the fields. And though, later, she made friends with him, she would never discuss the sylvan mystery of which she had once spoken so boldly, putting aside his tentative questions.

"It brings bad luck to name them things, just like you said. It made us quarrel that time."

Singularly, he felt no triumph in this admission. "I named Sylvaines to my mother," he said sheepishly. "She 'lows they're gypsies. I've heared they live in the open and cooks outdoors. Pappy traded horses with 'em oncet."

Isodene maintained obstinate silence.

They were standing on the spot where the end of Peter's furrows brought him near to Isodene's path, and she swung the pail with the daily luncheon for the husband and father of a seventh daughter of a seventh daughter.

"Pappy says," continues Peter, "there's a bunch of 'em camped now down the river a piece. Folks that's been missin' their chickens lays it onto them."

Isodene's lips parted; but before she was ready to speak a storm-wind drew across the knob in enormous, shivering sighs. The woods, the blades of sprouting corn, moved, fluttered, and whispered together. Eerie shadows leaped forth as from hidden lairs, and flung their formless duskiness across the fields. Thunder rolled, deep and ominous, in the clouded west. In their flight for shelter, neither Peter nor the more observant Isodene saw that a brilliant scarlet flower had opened at their feet.

Again next day they failed to see it. Isodene had trudged faithfully in draggling weeds to carry her father's dinner. Both countrymen were afield in spite of threatening weather, for the summer was wet, and they utilized every moment of sunshine.

There had been a quilting in the settlement, and Isodene was accusing Peter:

"You walked right through the room without speakin' to me. You never even looked at me."

"I looked," said Peter meaningly, and turned red. "I seed your pink dress. It— it was powerful pretty."

His unaccustomed tone and manner made her eyes droop. She twisted the corner of her apron, dropped it, reached vaguely for its support, and looked about for a new subject of conversation.

"Oh!" she cried, perceiving the blossom and coming closer to it. " How pretty— like something alive!" The flower on its tall, slender stem, wafted by some vagrant breeze— or impulse, was it?— leaned toward her. Peter reached for her hand as it slipped below the scarlet cup. Both, startled, stepped back and half turned away. The dank mist, rolling up from the creek, enveloped them closely. Conscious, embarrassed, they stood perfectly still for its passing.

When the wind lifted the fog, the sun shone clear on a group of three where but two had been.

In place of the blooming plant an elfin shape clothed in tints of browns and grays swayed slenderly; dark hair curled over slim shoulders and around a dark-eyed, pointed, wonderful little face; all brown and gray save red, red lips and the scarlet flower clasped tight—a flower whose petals shivered with vitality, of a color rich as blood of youth and bright as flame of desire.

"It's the Sylvaine! It's the Sylvaine! Let's run away quick before we-uns is bewitched."

Peter did not hear. He had forgotten Isodene. He saw only the beautiful, bewildered stranger, who, meeting his admiring eyes, smiled timidly and moved towards him.

The boy held out both hands. His shyness even was over-borne by the rush of new emotions, whirled away and lost like a dry leaf in the flame of the hearth as the boy, under the influence of beauty and mystery, became a man.

"Don't be afeard," he said in tones new to Peter's tongue. "Come home with me— to Mammy's house."

The other murmured words in a strange language, looking at him with her great eyes. She seemed not to see the shrinking Isodene. Peter pointed to the smoke rising from his father's house, and she let him take her hand and guide her toward the gray roof.

Isodene, alone and forgotten, ran after them a little way, but they did not glance back and would not heed her appeal. Pride came to her aid. She would not follow, though she could not force herself to go home. The bitterest drop in her cup was that she herself had evoked this apparition!

From afar now, she saw Peter with the exquisite stranger, pointing to various objects, already trying to find some method of communication, to teach the new-comer his rough, earth language.

Doubts as to Peter's safety mingled with Isodene's anger at his desertion. That night she stole by his window, where the red fire-light streamed forth, a square shaft, into the thick mist and flying rain. She was spared the sight of Peter's rapt, adoring eyes; the narrow pane showed the stranger only, framed the lovely form and spirituelle face, like some painting. She was dancing. Without music, without other rhythm than the swift, resonant patting of Peter's hands, she was dancing as Isodene and Peter had never seen any one dance before— dancing all over, alive with poetic grace to the tips of her fingers, to the swift, soft pressure of feet no larger than might set firm on a man's heart. Not the loose-jointed swinging, tossing, bounding, of the mountaineers, but a bending, melting, swaying movement that went weaving to and fro on the homely braided rug, her dark eyes flashing, the flower of her mouth parting to disclose heart of pearl.

Isodene, out in the rain that was falling again, shivered and turned away with a sob. The loneliness of unshared gayety struck into her heart. Peter's voice held her:

"I don't want nothin' better than to pet you and wait on you!"

The Sylvaine laughed aloud. Peter dragged forward a chair, and she threw herself down, panting, quivering, a-glow, in a pretty abandon.

"You shall always be waited upon," said the young mountaineer, with unexpected eloquence. "I'll spend my life bein' your slave. And when Pappy and Mammy come back from town there won't be nothin' too much for you to ask. They'll be proud to do hit!"

Isodene pressed closer to the window under the streaming eaves. She must watch lest the Sylvaine do him occult injury. And now she saw him bring fresh milk, newly baked oval pones, services and wild berries drowned in cream.

As she ate, the Sylvaine's eyes blessed his ministry. Always her left hand clung to the flower.

"Oh, but you're fine!" jubilated the boy. "There never was anything like you in this world till to-day. Smile, you pretty child! I never will make you cry. I won't have no aim but to make you happy. It don't make no differ now whether it raines or shines. Ef you smile, I'm jist plumb content!"

That his words were not comprehensible by her appeared not to trouble him. Only once was his mood shadowed. Bringing a vase for the flower, he met with a shaken head and frown of refusal. But he had so completely forgotten Isodene that even her story of the Sylvaines and the magic red bloom was obliterated from his mind. He felt only that he had erred in one effort to please, and tried another, bringing a drinking-cup.

Isodene, outside, in misery, thought that the girl, unaccustomed to light and love, drinking from the cup he held to her lips, letting her hand rest in this big, fine lover's, must feel like a spirit newly received in heaven. Surely one so happy could work no harm to the mortal that loved her.

"I ain't needed, not even to take keer of him," Isodene told her heavy heart.

The two rapt beings in the firelit room heard soft, swift sounds, a pattering as of heavier drops— it was Isodene's feet fleeing from the window, out into the wet fields, the drenched night, the lonely road. Her eyes, aching with unfallen tears, saw at last into the little cabin where her mother held hard-bitten lips to deny the "visions" that came to her wild, Celtic blood in midsummer nights like this.

The next day Isodene, hidden in a fence corner behind a tangle of undergrowth, saw him come, leading his horse, whereon perched a small brown and gray figure holding against its breast a brilliant flower.

Very tenderly and carefully Peter lifted the little Sylvaine off at the field's edge.

The music of bird and insect thrilled all the opal summer air. A gurgle of clear water sang in the dell. Peter bent his head above the stranger's happy, eager face.

"I love you," he murmured, "I love you!" and leaned yet nearer to illustrate his meaning with a caress. The soft dark eyes widened, then suddenly changed to a look of alarm.

There was a sharp cry of jealous pain; Isodene flung herself across the low rail fence and snatched the "red flower of life."

The lips that Peter would have kissed vanished! The slim young form in its dull grays and browns, the little pointed face with the big eyes, disappeared like a wraith of the mist out of which she had come. Where her bright young life and loveliness had delighted the earth, there drifted now but a passing cloud of golden motes that were slowly drawn up in the long afternoon sunshine.

Peter and Isodene faced each other, alone. Dazed and perplexed, they waited each for the other to speak. At first there was a space between them— where the Sylvaine had stood. The breeze blew Isodene's full skirt forward and bridged it.

On Peter's yokel countenance a great wonder erased his first expression of horror and grief.

"I— I t-told you it was bad luck to name the Sylvaines!" panted Isodene, her apron to her eyes.

His mind adjusted itself. He had been in love— beauty had set his thick pulses to fluid ecstasy. That beauty he suddenly suspected of being insubstantial, not natural. But another woman was here in place of her whose lips he had been about to press! Strange! Still, there was the mitigating fact that the other woman was Isodene, whom he would have liked to kiss long ago, had he not been afraid. Since her eyes were hid in her apron, he lost the old timidity. His big arm went naturally around her sob-racked form.

"We-uns has been bewitched, Isodene Deever," he said in tones not free from fright.

By accident his broad sole trod on the flower Isodene had let fall.

The vision had faded— the red, sweet flower was perished— the man's foot was set on its perfumed ruin!

From a fence-row clump of bushes that shook, a face, pale with the sudden fright of Isodene's onslaught— a pointed little face with pathetic eyes—peered forth on the reunited pair. A moment it glimmered there— a moment long enough to stamp and fix upon it the cruelty of love's lesson— and then was withdrawn. A low sob came to their ears; in the drone of June meadows soft, pattering footfalls mingled with the hedgerow voices and whir of filmy wings.

"What was that?" cried Isodene, leaping to Peter's arms in terror. "I heared somethin'— somethin' run! "

" 'T ain't nothin'," he assured, his manhood conquering superstition as he felt the weaker woman-girl clinging to his brawny neck. "We ain't a-goin' to be bewitched no more from nothin' from the underworld. As long as we live together, Isodene, don't never say no more the word that done hit!"

As long as we live together! And but an hour ago she had been forgotten! But Isodene saw in a confused way that such is the love of man— and, such as it was, her nature cried out for its possession. Perhaps it was never to be hers in its entirety— perhaps she could never utter the same appeal to his fancy as the vision lost. Perhaps all women would hereafter seem to him large or dull or heavy. But she clung to Peter, murmuring over and over the sweet assurances of her faithfulness and her love.

"Them gypsies is gone," said Pappy Bell, returning with his spouse from an excursion into civilization. " They 'lowed in the valley that one of the youngest gals— she peddled 'pressed flowers' they called 'em— was lost up yere on the mountain and come back nigh about dead. They air queer folk, a-wanderin' an' a-wanderin' to and fro. 'Pears like they jist simply ain't human. An' the jargon these talked! Some of 'em didn't know a word o' real langwidge like we-uns speaks. 'Pears like they ain't scasely human!"

"Don't you listen to no such, Isodene," warned Peter, catching the last words only, and dragging his promised wife out of ear-shot, "I don't want you to have no dealin's with any such truck as Pappy's speakin' of."

Isodene lifted to his, humble, wistful eyes. "I won't, Peter," she promised. "As long as we live together I won't never no more talk erbout nothin' strange or— underground"— she whispered the word— "or that ain't like other folks. Well jist be content with what we can get our hands on— us women-folk has to anyhow— and not try to know nothin' else. I'll do jist what you tell me, Peter," she said; and he gave her a kiss and the promise:

"I'll make ye a good man, Isodene, an' allus aim to see atter you the best I know how. You're the onliest woman in the world for me!"

And the little red flower lay dying, and the summer drifted a few leaves— not having many to spare in the season's busy heat— above its lonely bed. Its episode had been a fairy tale that is told.

Published in
Lippincott's Magazine - March 1914

At the Top of Sourwood

EMMA BELL MILES

THE LOG HOUSE THAT WAS THE CHADWICK HOMESTEAD, as well as the general, store, sat perched like a cliff-eagle's nest on a jutting shelf of rock just where the old corduroy road went down a break in the mountain wall. By those who dwelt above its level, no less than by the five or six inhabitants of the sweep of mountainside that fell sheer away from its back windows, the shelf of rock was called The Top; and few were the articles required by their daily living that it did not carry in stock. The summer population, whose residences gleamed white along the "brow" heights bought provisions for the season here; girls native to the coves and ridges came hither in search of print and ribbons for weddings and frolics, and young bucks in quest of the girls, as also of knives and ammunition, gathered on its cluttered stoop to exchange tales of prowess; grandmothers from remote cabins here bartered eggs and hominy for quilting thread and knitting needles; the housewife obtained here her salt and spoons, her spider and hearth-oven, and an occasional "chaney" dish to be cherished all the way home like a captive bird. Men bought leather for half-soles in autumn, axe-helves in winter, and hoes in spring. The steadiest of staples was tobacco, which sold the year round to both sexes and all ages. Next in importance came powder and lead; coffee followed a close third; after them the salt pork and corn meal that were the mainstay of existences too thriftless to support a shoat or a patch of corn.

As the business throve and old Noah Chadwick found his hands overfull, he insured himself good service by taking on, instead of a single clerk, two youngsters of the same surname, Cairo and Cephas Plank. These boys were supposed to be cousins, although, in fact, no native of that intermarried district could say exactly what kin he was to any of the others.

"Sort o' half-Brindle to Buck, as your mam used to say about my yoke o' steers," old Noah remarked to his daughter Rosabel. "And so nigh the same age that when-ever Ceph dies of old age Cairo can burn his hat. But they ain't no more alike 'n a sourwood and a black-jack. Cephas don't kill the timber a-bein' pretty, though he's some peart and soople when he's dressed up; but that there long-legged Cairo— he's ugly as home-made sin." He wanted Rosabel to say so, too; but she merely arranged the budding come-liness of her features to an expression of preternatural composure. "An' he walks around here with his head up like a steer in a cornfield, as if he owned the store!"

From the first day of employment the boys had thrown their weight into the collar like a gallant team; but Chadwick's satisfaction in his advantage was moderated by some uncertainty as to his daughter's possible interest in either of the helpers. As a precautionary measure, he took to ridiculing both lads in her hearing. It ought to be easy, he thought, to show her that there were better and more prosperous men awaiting her notice. His hope was that she might incite them to continue the rivalry by favoring neither beyond his fellow, maintaining an even balance of smiles and friendly words from day to day.

On a morning when the sweet, keen breath of the first frost was in the air, and the gold and azure of September was inclining toward the rich October purple and scarlet, Cairo was sent to the valley for a load of freight from the way-station. As the wagon came rumbling and clanging forth from the lot, Rosabel threw on her sunbonnet and ran out on the porch, calling to the driver for a ride as far as her uncle's house at the foot of the mountain.

He bent down and drew her to the high seat beside him; and Cephas, sorting late potatoes by the window, watched them ride away through the dreaming shadows that lay across the corduroy road.

When in the afternoon they returned, Rosabel's hat wreathed in flame-colored vines and her lap full of tart wild grapes and sugary persimmons, he became sullenly furious.

"Ol man 'll be apt to fire you, Cairo, 'f he ketches you takin' Rosie with ye round the country," he warned his yokemate.

"That's all right!" Cairo's voice was half friendly, half derisive. His steel-gray eyes held a genial light, but his chin was like the point of a flat-iron, and there was something square and grim, possibly from a faraway Cherokee ancestor, about his wide mouth. "You can stay and court the old man whilst we're out, and maybe beat my time a'ter all."

Cephas glowered across the crates they were unloading and found nothing to say. As for the girl, she had run into the house the moment she alighted, and sought her own room. She had something to tell her father— something that required all her resolution.

The next day Cairo was not surprised at being summoned to the back room, where the kerosene and sorghum barrels, the tubs of lard and sides of pork, the bags of feed and salt, lay in dim rows along a windowless wall. He entered with quickened pulses; but the old fellow only adjusted his spectacles and motioned his clerk, salesman, driver, and factotum to a seat on a bag of cotton-seed meal.

"Cairo," he began, "you've worked around this store a right smart while, off and on."

"Yes, sir; goin' on two years."

"And I've been a-payin' you regular, over 'n' above your board."

"I ain't never complained about that," said the young man, wondering whither this oblique approach might be tending.

"Now, then," challenged Chadwick, "I want the truth out o' you— how much have you got saved up in that time?"

Cairo's eyes narrowed, and he thrust his hands deeper in his pockets. "How much would you expect a man to save out o' three dollars a week?"

"I ain't sayin'. Though I made out to save on less, when I was a youngster. I'm wantin' to know how much you got, and where hit's at."

"Why, hit ain't a great deal, but hit's in a good safe place," Cairo countered, grinning.

"You've e'en-about butted your horns off, if ye did but know it!" Noah admonished him sharply. "I'm axin' because Rosie told me last night— something I'd as leave not a-heared for a good while yit. Anyhow, I aim to know something about the fellow that gits her."

"Don't ye know enough about me yit?"

"Not till I'm satisfied whether you're able to take keer o' my gal. I do know there's ne'er a foot o' ground yourn, nor a stick o' timber. There's room in my house for the man that's good enough for my Rosebud; but you, Cairo, you're a-makin' too pore a start." He was silent a moment, and then repeated a mountain proverb: " 'There's more marries than keeps cold meat.' "

"Well, Mr. Chadwick," replied Cairo, sobered, "I don't aim to give ye a short answer, but looks to me that's my business. *I* never inquared round what you was worth nor what you was liable to give her."

Noah drew himself up. "You didn't have to ax what everybody knows."

To this Cairo seemed to have nothing to say. He opened his knife and began whittling— a tacit admission that the argument might reasonably be prolonged. The dim and dusty room, lighted only by two thin rays of afternoon sunshine through the chink of the heavy oaken door hinges, was still— so still that they could hear the high squeak and chatter of a bat incensed at the wasps that circled over the drip of the vinegar barrel.

Noah's eyebrows began to work up and down on his forehead. "You dad-limbed cymblin'-head!" he burst out at length. "Got the imperence to marry my gal and set 'round waitin' for the old man to leave ye well off, have ye? You'll see in a minute where ye drapped your candy! Not a cent have you got only what you was lookin' to git from me; now, ain't that so?"

"I've got a right to say I won't answer! You've knowed me, Mr. Chadwick, ever sence I was as big as your fist. That ought to be enough."

"Well, hit is enough!" retorted Noah, now completely antagonized. "And you kin leave my store if I ketch ye talkin' to Rosebud a'ter this."

"All right. I aim to wed her, though— and then if you give me and her ary thing, I'll be jist as good as you air, and give hit back to ye." Cairo shut his knife, and, getting to his feet, turned away.

"She'll never have my consent to wed ye!"

"She may do without it," was Cairo's parting shot, as he quietly left the room.

A few days later Rosabel's mother, a meek, hardworking woman who did as her husband bade her on all occasions, approached the assistant thus cast into disfavor as he was preparing to take his place in the store after breakfast, and began hesitatingly: "Cairo, I hate to tell ye, but pap, he 'lows I cain't feed ye no more." She wrapped her worn hands in her gingham apron and stood regarding him almost sadly.

"Cain't? What for? I know I hide white beans and biscuits as if my laigs was holler, but Cephas eats me a match every meal— or did until right lately," responded the young man, laughing.

"I— I reckon pap's afeared you and Rosebud's a-makin' it up to run away," she explained, trying to smile in response to his jovial bearing.

"He better watch closeter than what he's been a-doin', " chuckled Cairo. "Well, that's all right, Mis' Chadwick. I'll go and talk to him a'ter while. Maybe he'll decide to keep me around."

In the slack of the afternoon he came out on the high back porch overlooking the valley, where in the shadow of the house two buckets of spring water sat on a puncheon shelf, and a pair of gourds swung gently in the breeze, since neither Noah nor his wife liked to drink from a dipper. The old man was standing before a second shelf that upheld a tin basin, a towel, and an eight-inch square of "bubbly" mirror, laboriously removing from his countenance a week's growth of gray stubble. He prided himself on shaving regularly once a week, "whether his face needed hit or not." He was contorting his features into more extraordinary grimaces than a school-boy behind the teacher's back, and took no notice of Cairo's advent except by grumbling to the mirror, "Dad-limb this old razor! If I cain't hone it into better shape again next time, I'll have to give up and grow a beard."

"You aim for me to leave, Mr. Chadwick?" asked Cairo, closing the door softly behind him.

"Have to board somers else!" was the gruff reply.

Cairo, being disposed to grant the naturalness of his employer's resentment, would not make too much of this. "You mean you don't want me to work here no more?" he pursued.

"I ain't anxious either way." In truth, Noah could ill afford to lose his most wide-awake assistant, but was in no humor to say so.

"Then," the young man continued, under his voice, "I've got a thing to tell you afore I leave."

"More out o' your sass-box!"

"No, no; hit's somethin' you ought to hear, and nobody else."

"Dad-limb this here razor— Hit's dull as a frow! No, I've heared enough about ye and out of ye, you high-headed Two-by-Four!"

"This here's different; hit's about—"

"I've done told ye I don't want no words with ye."

"About the store—"

"You've made me cut myself three-four times a'ready. If you stand there a-jowerin', you'll have me scored, ready to be hewed. May do for Planks, but I'll be jiggered if I—"

"Well, I'm a-leavin'; but there's a word to say. Hit's about the store; and I miss my guess if hit don't find ye where you're at home," Cairo maintained with significant firmness.

"I'll run my store without any ad-vice. There! *Cut again!*" Chadwick turned. "Now, you git!"

[264]

Cairo flushed darkly as he turned away. "Well— if you was to happen to want me for anything next week, I'll be down at Sis' Marthy's," he remarked as he went forth.

No sooner was the storekeeper alone than he began to regret his "tetchiness." This was not what he had intended. He wondered and wondered again what the boy could have meant to tell him. Some impertinence about his daughter, perhaps. Let him go!

"Shoo! Thinks he's a whole dime's worth o' nickels. With the town folks gone down for the winter, and trade gittin' below profit mark, me and Cephas can certainly mind the store without him. He'll be ready enough to come back again when the summer trade commences," Noah declared to his chin-lathered reflection.

Yet he could hardly eat his supper. He preserved a dignified and stubborn silence, as befitted the proprietor of the only store in that quarter of the county; but night fell with the clouds riding swift and low across the sky, and found Noah in an unapproachable temper, Rosabel in tears, Cephas unaccountably absent, and the mother going heavily and silently about the evening tasks of the household.

An hour after dark Cairo stood on the platform of the little valley way-station, just out of reach of a cold drizzle that was beginning to fall. He examined, without appearing to do so, each member of the group that awaited the coming of the south-bound train. Two loafers and a drummer, besides an old lady whose daughter kept reassuring her as to the safety of traveling by rail, he let pass with hardly a glance; a country preacher carrying a handbag, and after him a mountaineer with a jug, he regarded more closely as they passed under the dim and smoky wall-lamp; and at last his attention became fixed on a kerchief-muffled individual who stepped unostentatiously onto the extreme end of the platform a few moments before train-time. There was nothing remarkable about this newcomer, although the home-woven basket of oak splints, bulging with clothing and tightly roped, might in other regions have occasioned some amusement.

Cairo sauntered to and fro, softly whistling "Texas Rangers" between his teeth, and finally came to a stop directly behind the other and looked him over from head to foot, staring longest at the fringe of hair that remained visible above the coat-collar turned up to meet a low hat-brim.

The traveler, feeling the scrutiny, glanced furtively around, started at sight of Chadwick's employee, and moved nervously away from the dim light that struggled through the door and the window.

Cairo greeted him without receiving a reply, and added: "You're uncommon skeered of the toothache. Look like you had a bad cold and was afeared to ketch another on top of hit." As the other still made no answer, "You didn't 'low you could fool me, did you?" he continued, following a step. "Why, Cephas, I'd know your hide in the tan-yard."

The discovered Cephas, finding retreat no longer possible, faced the situation with a stuttered "W-what you— what you want, then?"

"Jist whatever you got in that basket."

"My—my clo'es?" Cephas glared, and involuntarily tightened his grasp on the stout receptacle.

Cairo laughed a little. "The money's in there, sure 'nough, then! I won't be hard on ye," he persisted. "I'll let ye have thirty dollars o' my own— enough to land ye safe in Florida, or Texas, or wherever ye was aimin' to go."

"You— you jist better let me alone, now—"

"Make up your mind, quick," urged Cairo in a half-bantering tone. "I seed the sheriff in the saloon as I come on by there. 'F he was to ketch ye with all that on ye, hit'd be all-night-Isom."

The train, after a long preliminary rumble rising to a roar, dashed out of the tunnel. The whistle screamed aloud; the two notes of its cry, falling one into the other, were caught up by the crags of Sourwood, echoed and re-echoed till the night was filled with its floating, flying tremolo, blown with the rain through the dark— a sound unwonted and disquieting to a country boy with senses already guiltily perturbed. Cephas stood confused and reeling.

Cairo advanced, holding forward three ten-dollar bills. And half mechanically, even while turning his head from side to side, as though still seeking a possible alternative, Cephas accepted them and gave up the basket. Then, realizing his mistake too late, he broke into wild and incoherent cursing.

"All abo-oard!" sang the conductor. As the fugitive obeyed the suggestion, he saw Cairo diving rapidly through the contents of the basket, making sure of his capture. He sank into a seat and did not look up when the train began to roll slowly forward, until some one knocked on the open window, and there was his late comrade running alongside.

"Here! take your clo'es," cried the half-friendly, half-mocking voice. "You'll need them shirts afore you git another job." And the runaway snatched the basket-handle just before the gathering momentum of the train swept home and friends out of his ken forever.

Next morning, on the store at the Top, consternation fell like a blasting wind. It was found that Cephas, their dependence, had not slept in his room, and, further, that the key of the strong-box which held the store's and Chadwick's available capital was missing. The same little boy, whose untimely purchase of snuff and boss-ball thread for his mother's quilting precipitated the discovery, was despatched in haste to Cephas' aunt, who recalled that the missing man had borrowed a basket of her the previous noon. She quitted her house immediately with a square of homespun thrown over her head, and in an incredibly short space of time, considering the distance between neighbors, rumor was abroad and active.

It was clearing colder after the night's rain; the broken clouds, as they sailed over, gleamed against a brilliant sky; the air was crisp. Leaves from the painted forest went swirling out across the valley, borne on the wind almost to the flying clouds. On such a morning every one must needs be astir on one pretext or another, and a crowd soon gathered at the Top, each man babbling of a theory and a plan of procedure that conflicted with all the others. The road was blocked with ox and mule teams and "tar-grinder" wagons, some laden with "spun-truck," fruit, and logs on the way to the valley, others coming up with lumber, "roughness" from lowland fields, and manufactured articles from

Macklimore's shops; for not a soul was able to drive past the scene of so notable a robbery.

Hours were spent in discussion and argument before the blacksmith broke the lock of the box and the worst was known. Noah Chadwick was one of those old-fashioned people who distrust banks. He had long contemplated hiding his hoard as had his father before him, under some boulder in the breaks of the creek; but he had put the day off too long. Now, stunned by the knowledge that he was robbed, the old man simply cowered, shrunk into a heap on a cracker-box, his face drawn, his arms shaking, and allowed his neighbors as they assembled to offer consolation or encouragement unheeded. He would not be roused even by suggestions for borrowing the county bloodhounds or sending for the neighborhood wizard, who divined secret waters and treasure by means of a wand or a cup and ring.

"I'm a' old man and a little man," he shrieked once in a high, febrile voice of impotent rage, "but I can kill the sneakin' hound that stole my money!" And he felt the emptiness of the threat even as it was uttered.

His wife walked to and fro, whimpering, "Oh, I wisht Rosabel was at home! She'd know what to say to her pap if anybody could." She was not thinking of his loss or her own, although she had toiled as heavily as her husband for the slow accumulation of the lost two thousand. "Oh, Rose might understand how to ease his mind! I wisht she was here!"

"Where's she at?" inquired a sympathizing woman whose hands were still pink from washing breakfast dishes.

"She went to stay all day with her uncle's folks. Oh, I wisht—"

"Some of you'ns ketch out my ol' Soapstick and go a'ter her," proposed the other. And a lad was ready with a neighbor's buckboard to go in search of Chadwick's daughter, when a shout went up from the small-boy contingent watching by the roadside, and she and Cairo came in sight, driving up the corduroy road in a cart hired from Macklimore.

Questions were called excitedly down the steep approach as the pair ascended; but Cairo merely laughed, and waved his hand. On reaching the store, he leaped to the ground, passed the file of waiting teams, and hurried in without a word.

"Cairo," the blacksmith hailed him as he entered, "do you know— know anything about this here calamity?"

"What time did you leave the store yesterday?" asked another.

He replied to the latter: "Right after I was fired:"

"Fired, was ye? How much money did you take out?"

"Five dollars that was comin' to me," answered Cairo.

"Yes, I let him have that," corroborated Mrs. Chadwick, "and he went right off. Oh, Cairo, he'p me and pap to find out—" Her face crinkled distressfully.

"I will; don't you worry," he bade her, a reassuring seriousness and warmth coming into his tones.

"You didn't have no more here your own self?" pursued the smith.

"Naw; I had thirty dollars in a safer place." He lounged against the elbow-polished counter. "I jist 'lowed this store might wake up some morning and find its cash gone."

"What fur?"

"Well, I been with Cephas Plank long enough to know in reason what he'd be apt to do whenever Rosebud turned him down."

At these sensational words, the circle swayed and jostled, while a tremendous chattering and whispering went up from the outer group of shawled and aproned women.

"Shoo!" The smith was first to recover himself. "You ain't got nothing to go on— that's jist your guess."

"That was all at first; but I noticed him git some things together yestidy that he wouldn't 'a' needed without he was goin' away; and I judged, too, that he'd whirl in and do some devilment whenever I wasn't here to sort o' keep a eye on him."

"Why in time couldn't ye 'a' said something about hit, seein' ye knowed so much?"

"I did try to," explained Cairo equably, "and Mr. Chadwick wouldn't listen to me. He got so mad, I looked for him to throw me over the bluff."

He had missed the psychological moment for this laughing disclosure. The circle narrowed imperceptibly; the men growled in their bearded throats, not half liking his light-heartedness.

"Maybe you know more'n you've told."

"Maybe I do."

"Was hit Cephas, then, sure 'nough ?"

"Sure 'nough hit was."

"Know where he's gone, do ye?"

"He's half-way to the Indi'n Nation by now."

Chadwick groaned, and got to his feet. "You holped him git away!" he groaned. "You ought to be hung in his place! You knowed all the time, and you let him git away with every cent I got! I'll see what the law—"

"Oh, no; he didn't git away with a cent o' your'n," pronounced Cairo deliberately. "Hit's all right out yender in the buggy with my wife."

"In the buggy— with your wife!"

"You didn't think we was goin' to stand round waitin' for your say, after you'd done told us we wouldn't git hit? We was married at her uncle's house this morning."

The little bride was already tip-toeing on the threshold, and now ran forward as the people made way. "Don't feel so bad, pappy," she pleaded, reaching toward him a care-fully tied packet. "Take 'n' count the money— look, hit's all here. Don't be mad at us; don't, pappy."

Chadwick looked into her sweet, flushed face a moment before he took the packet from her out-stretehed hand. "No, I won't be mad, honey," he said at last, slowly. "And— and don't you and him be mad at me. A man ort not to hold to all the contentious things he says, and— Cairo, ef the money's here— and hit is— why, you and her'll have enough out of hit to start ye to housekeepin'. You will, won't ye? — something for Rose? I always aimed, whenever she got married—"

"I'm proud to," said his son-in-law heartily.

On each dour and stolid mountaineer face approval struggled forth like the sun through clouds. Every watcher drew breath as the package was opened and found to contain the money and every least security that Cephas had deemed negotiable. Rosabel and her mother were crying and laughing in each other's arms.

"Well, hit's my treat, boys," Noah came to himself as he closed his strong-box on its wonted contents. "And I ain't got a thing but cider, so I cain't ax y'uns what you'll have." He turned to the counter. "Some of you boys make on a fire. Cairo, you he'p me about these here glasses and cups; and say, Cairo; wait a' hour or so and I'll ride back down to Macklimore with ye, and he'p ye git your things. I cain't do no business to-day. Let's all turn in and give this here couple a ch'ivari."

Published in
Lippincott's Magazine - August 1915

The White Marauder

EMMA BELL MILES

ILLUSTRATIONS BY R.F. TANDLOR

Waked in the night by a sound of trampling hoofs, Letty Kindred sat up and the creak of the bedcords under her movement aroused 'Bithie, her husband's twelve-year-old sister who slept beside her. They were not in the least afraid, although they were alone in the little cabin and only a wooden latch, rude and flimsy, held the door between them and the world. But when the trampling was followed by a swish as of ripping silk, they were aroused.

"Hit's that ol' rogue of Cap'n Charley's in the corn agin. You git the broom, 'Bithie honey, and I'll take the poker."

Out they dashed into the early April night, and gave chase to a white mare, gaunt and ghostly under the stars. Impudently the creature flung up her heels, and trotted twice around the clearing, sporting defiance; then, being hard pressed, she sailed lightly over the fence and disappeared into the woods.

"Now that's the fou'th night she's broke in sence we planted. And last summer you ricollect she never stopped till she'd eat up mighty nigh the whole patch. Lawsy-massy, I jist wisht you'd look here how I've tore my skyirt!"

"Yes, and I e'en-about ruint my feet, when I took out a'ter her th'oo them briers along the fence," complained 'Bithie.

"My feet's a-bleedin' too; but I don't keer for that," said Letty. My feet'll git well and mend theirselves, but my dress won't. Nor the corn won't neither, ef she's tore hit up much bad. I aim to light into Cap'n Charley about this, right soon in the morning."

"I like to busted her ol ' jaws with a rock, anyways," crowed the younger girl. "Let's go make a light and see what she's et this time."

Too anxious to wait for daybreak, they kindled a sliver of pitchpine by some coals that were buried in ashes on the hearth,

OUT THEY DASHED INTO THE EARLY APRIL NIGHT AND GAVE
CHASE TO A WHITE MARE, GAUNT AND GHOSTLY UNDER THE STARS

and inspected the damage. The young corn indeed was considerably torn and trampled; a whole row of beans was gone entirely; worst of all, the tender mustard was ruined.

"I wouldn't a-hated nothin' so bad as losin' that there mustard," lamented the wife, who was but a few years older than her companion. "Hit had leaves over a inch long, mighty near big enough to eat. And I'm so hongry for green I declar' I'd go and pull me some brier leaves and weeds ef I wasn't afeard they'd pizen me. Jist a handful o' green and drap o' vinegar would piece out our cornbread and pork into full rations; but we ain't had nary mess, nor any gyarden-sass only 'taters, sence away last fall." She was thoroughly angry as they trudged, shivering in the chill dew, back to the cabin where they warmed their feet on the hearth. "Now, ef Mansell had only fixed that fince afore he went off to work in the valll'y! He had plenty of time durin' the winter. Or ef he'd a-notified Cap'n Charley to put up his critter!"

"Cap'n Charley's had a plenty of notice from other folks to put her up," said 'Bithie shrewdly. "She's a ol' rogue. He knows good an' well she can jump ary fince in the county."

" Well, I aim to take it out of him and Mansell, too; come down on 'em like a hen on a June-bug, I will. You see ef I cook a bite, now, when Manse comes a-Sunday! Not till that there fince is mended."

"On a Sunday?"

"On a Sunday! The better the day, the better the deed. Ah— ho— hum! I ain't goin' back to bed for this little piece of a night. You can." And 'Bithie did, while the young wife sat beside the hearth alone, considering what she should say to the Captain.

[276]

"I hate to raise a fuss with him; Aunt Minar Bushares was good to me when I was sick. And she's a own sister to him, though nobody'd think it. But thar's all our truck spiled!"

By the earliest light she prepared breakfast—corn cakes baked on the coals, coffee and a wee rasher apiece of the salt fat which is the regulation meat of the mountaineer. Then they ate, hurriedly washed the two plates, made haste to redd up the house, and set forth— florescently sunbon-netted though the sun was not yet risen— for Captain Charley Bushares'.

A morning mist hung over the budding woods, shaken with all the sounds of April— frog trills and bird song, and the hum of honey-lovers' wings. But the two girls did not notice these things. They walked with nods and gestures and quaint posturings, making threats against the Captain and his mare as their warlike mood dictated.

The old soldier's habitation was not a hollow tree, though a glance at his beady eyes twinkling from out a thicket of furry gray might have led to that supposition; he lived with camplike simplicity and neatness in a cabin by the Gap road. Almost from his door the mountain side fell away in a magnificent sweep of unbroken forest. Behind the house was the spring, where they found the old fellow filling a bucket.

The ceremonious greeting, with its usual "Toler'bles," and the customary invitation to stay to breakfast, were far off the key Letty intended to strike, but for the life of her she could not see how to omit either. No, they had just been, she said; and no, they couldn't stay long enough to set, even on the puncheon bench by the spring-house. She hesitated in great embarrassment and finally plunged, trembling a little.

"Your mare she went 'n' got into our corn again last night, Cap'n Charley. I do think on my soul you ought to do what's right about it. Hit's— now— hit's jist more'n I aim to put up with, her a-roguin' this way every summer."

The grizzled Captain eyed her a moment, then set down his bucket and dropped into something like a fighting crouch. As if by instinct he made straight for the weak point in her battle front. "Now, here-here, Miz' Kindred, let me remind you, the woods is free in this part o' the State. Has your corn got ary fince around it?"

Letty thought best to evade this point. "You know how last year she come in and eat up the whole patch—"

"Oh, Miz' Kindred; not the whole patch— no-no-no-no! And for what she did eat I paid you with my 'pologies— now didn't I so'?" He began to prance about in a semicircle. "That's what I done, wasn't it, Miz' Kindred?"

Letty was a little disconcerted by the formal "Mrs.," and more than a little anxious to keep the conversation off the condition of the fence. At the same time, she wasn't going to be diverted from her claim.

"You paid us a dollar, Cap'n. But I never come over here a'ter no dollar this morning. Hit ain't right and hit ain't fair, the way you let that mare run over folks' places, and I want you to stop hit and pay for what she's done. I jist wisht you'd come over to my house and look at our gyarden."

"I don't see how I'd stop her without you'ns built a fince. I cain't keep her in the stall all the time." He came to a stand, with the air of being ready to listen. "Now, I ain't a onreasonable man, Miz' Kindred. What do you hold the rights of the matter to be?"

She was not clear on this point either. Oh, if she could have consulted Mansell! But now she had come she must say her say, and coerce this old man and his mare, alone. If only he wouldn't crouch and stare like a wild creature about to spring! She put up one hand to her burning cheek uncertainly.

"Two dollars, tell him," whispered 'Bithie, plucking at her sister-in-law's sleeve. "Let's take hit and go."

"Two— two dollars," stammered Letty.

Captain Charley jumped as though on the release of springs, his stubby forefinger emphasizing every word: "Two dollars! *Two* dollars! Why, Miz' Kindred, you surprise me. I don't believe there's a truck patch on Sourwood Mountain wuth, as hit stands to-day, two dollars for everything in hit; I don't for a fact."

"You owe me two dollars for that mare's damagin', " insisted Letty, but feebly.

The agitated finger came closer. "I do not owe you a cent, madam, not a cent. I'll give you two dollars ef you air in need of hit; but I won't be held up for no sech amount—" He recoiled a step as if from the attack of a "flog" hen defending a brood, and the overset water-bucket rolled down the hill unheeded.

"You won't neither give me— You won't do no sich a thing, you great big ole—" she hesitated and used no word

"TWO DOLLARS! WHY, MIZ KINDRED,
THEY AIN'T A PATCH ON SOURWOOD MOUNTAIN WUTH THAT."

at all. "You talk about givin' me ary cent only my dues—
why—" Her little fists were clenched, her eyes flashing; she
stamped her foot.

"Oh, well, I'll take that back— I'll take hit back ef you
say to." Instinctively he made shooing motions with both
hands.

"You better!"

She found that she couldn't, to save her, think of another
word. Nor could he. But neither disputant was standing still.
To the sole onlooker it seemed they were dancing round
and round each other like a pair of belligerent bantams;
and so absorbed was 'Bithie in the spectacle that all her ten
fingers stood out in ten different directions.

The old soldier was first to recover the thread of argument—probably because he and his mare had already figured in several court-rooms.

"Now, here-here, Miz' Kindred. As I'm a livin' sinner, madam, I didn't know nothing about this— didn't know you'ns had a gyarden even. And I may say I don't like to be jumped onto onexpected this way, let alone threatened."

"I ain't aimin' to threaten ye," said Letty more mildly. "But ef I was you I *would* be keerful how I talked and went on."

"Ef you, or either your husband," he began judicially, "had a-come to me in the first place, and told me the mare was breakin' in; and ef then I had refused and neglected to keep her up; and ef then your fince was showed to be in fair good order and condition at the time she jumped hit— why then, Miz' Kindred, you might have reason to fault me with your troubles, and you might recover damages accordin'. That's the Law. That's how the Law reads. *But* you come and jump on a gray-headed ol' soldier disabled sence the Wah, for somethin' he knows ab-so-lute-ly nothin' atallabout— I tell ye, madam, and you'll find hit so, there ain't a court in Tennessee that'll sustain ye."

"Ef I had a Bloody Sixth record endurin' the war the less there was said about hit the better I'd be suited," retorted Letty in the heat of the moment. She had not meant to pour such vials of contempt upon her antagonist; for the Bloody Sixth had been a disreputable bushwhacking company, never proved to have taken part in a single genuine engagement, although the Government, after some litigation, had given its surviving pensioners the benefit of the doubt.

Locally, the whisper of "Bloody Sixth" was accounted the bitterest of taunts.

"That ain't the p'int; that ain't got nothing to do with hit," argued the Captain unabashed. "I ax you, Miz' Kindred, why didn't you come to me the first time you seen the mare in your field; or else why didn 't you ketch her and put her up, as the law requires?"

His calm refusal to be crushed by her heavy ammunition daunted Letty, who was sure his war record ought to be at least as sore a spot as Mansell's fence. She felt her courage flagging, and knew that she was going to cry. "Aw, *I* ain't got no time to run around; and you know I cain't come within bridle-reach of that mare's heels."

"Then where's Mansell ?" he pursued.

"Why, he's a-workin' in the valley."

"Workin' for my brother, too, ain't he? Now look here. My brother's give Mansell a job that's kep' him all winter; and ef you was to count up all that my folks have done for you and him, at one time and another, hit would 'mount to more'n a dozen truck-patches— ain't that so? What do you think Minar Bushares'll say when she hears how you've talked to her pore ol' brother?"

He had missed the psychological moment for this. Letty had retired some paces, but now whirled and flung off her bonnet. "That's every word true," she exclaimed. "Your folks air good folks, Cap'n. I ain't got a better friend on earth than Aunt Minar; and ef you tell her what I've said to you this morning. I want you to be shore and put in what-all you've said to me, too. 'Cause ef you don't, I will. They've done for me time and again, your folks have; but ef ever you've done ary thing for anybody but your own self, Cap'n Charley, I never did hear of hit. And what's more, I don't believe you've got a brother nor yit a sister that would keep stock that bothered the neighbors."

The Captain tossed his head as she got breath, and sneered: "Then I must be the only scoun'l they is in the family." But he felt the need of a more effective reply.

'Bithie, fearing that her side was getting the worst of the encounter, shrilled forth unexpectedly: "I thest aim to maul the ghost out of that ol' nag anyhow, ef she jumps in to-night."

He turned on her: "Air you the malicious little whiffet that raised sech a welt on my mare's jaw? I seen she'd been hurt, when I fed her this morning. Now I let ye know, that's more'n ye dare do, whatever she eats. You understand that! Jist you lay a hand on her again, that's all!"

"Then you pay for what she's eat and tore," cried Letty. "My mustard— all pulled up and trampled. You never was hongry— you've got your pension—"

"I don't owe you nary—"

"Tell that to Mansell a-Sunday; I bet you don't shake your finger in *his* face!"

The old fellow looked at the offending member with compunction, really sorry to have forgotten his manners; but he seized the opening for a new line of attack. "Mansell he comes home of a Sunday? Was he there last Sunday?"

"Yes; he brung some provisions."

"Well, had the mare broke in afore that date? Did he know—"

"I told him, and so did 'Bithie, but—"

"Then—" the uncontrollable finger emphasized the point— "what's the reason he didn't come to me last Sunday?"

Letty, white and trembling, laid one hand over her racing heart as if to cover a wound. Whatever was said or left unsaid, she must not admit Mansell in the wrong!

"Because— because, she stammered, Manse is jist like everybody else round here— he thinks there ain't no use comin' to you for any rights or fairness between neighbors; and I see now he was edzackly right!"

It was but a Parthian arrow, and the last in her quiver. She turned, and holding 'Bithie's hand, took the road along which they had come— defeated. The younger girl looked behind at the turn and saw the gray figure still prancing with extended forefinger and still vociferous.

"Letty, Letty, he's a-callin' us."

"Oh, I don't want to talk to you!" Letty sent back wildly, and burst into tears. The two went home slowly, under drooping sunbonnets.

Once inside the quiet cabin, however, Letty seated herself on the edge of the bed and talked over the situation calmly enough. Her wrath against the Captain had well-nigh expended itself; she was half-laughing as she commented.

"Well, I've always mistrusted them fine manners of his'n, and now I'm glad to know what they're wuth."

But her resentment against Mansell's neglect went deeper, ached cruelly. He knew that she had worked hard planting and hoeing that handful of truck. What did he mean, leaving things in this shape? He might at least have kept up the fence; there was plenty of rail timber in the woods. Hadn't be spent half of last month picking the banjo?

'Bithie, casting about for comfort to offer, suggested that they go together to seek a mess of "wild sallat" or "sissles." The hardy rosettes of this humble member of the dandelion family would not replace the lost mustard, but would be a bite of green. An abandoned field near by was chosen as the likeliest hunting ground, and the two girls set forth once more, this time with a half-bushel basket woven of oak splints.

The lines of long-vanished fences yielded few "sissles" to their eager scrutiny, but there were also tender shell-shaped leaves of plantain, bunches of speckle-john and narrow-dock, Indian lettuce, bear-grass, and silvery tips of lamb's-quarter in the old field, among dry sedge and last year's leaves. They patiently culled every least sprout; but the final result scarcely covered the bottom of the basket. The season was so late at this altitude— and far below them spread the kindly valley, visibly and luxuriously green!

On reaching home they washed their precious hoard at the spring, and hung it over the fire in a pot with a tiny cube of pork for seasoning. Neither spoke of dinner, though the sun was past the noon-mark on the floor.

Their hunger grew with the passing of the hours. A catbird sang in the garden over his meal of cutworms; a drift of dogwood petals blew across the porch; a yellow "news-bee" hung round the door and buzzed off into the world again. There was nothing to do but wait, from time to time putting a handful of chips under the pot. As the shadows lengthened they mixed and baked a dodger in the hearth-oven. At sunset they turned the handful of greens into a dish.

"Don't that smell good!" exulted 'Bithie. She took a mouthful and looked up, puzzled. " Why— why, Letty this here sallat— hit's bitter!"

Letty, who was breaking the steaming pone on a plate, made haste to investigate the strange flavor. They looked at each other in consternation. The child had by mistake gathered some leaves of bitter dock!

Letty did not scold her; instead, she comforted when 'Bithie showed a disposition to cry. But she cried herself, after the young girl fell asleep and night had closed on the cabin. Oh, why couldn't Mansell provide better— give them just enough to eat!

Again a sound of trampling, thrashing feet brought her instantly upright, straining forward, hunger adding to her exasperation. She seized a billet of firewood and opened the door.

"I certainly will brain ol' Soapstick this time— Why! Manse! I wisht I may never! Ef you hadn't a-spoke I'd a-knocked your head off."

She took his basket that he might have one arm free to put round her, and they entered the cabin together.

"I was tired enough to have waited till morning," he admitted, throwing the bag of provisions off his shoulder. "But this mornin' we was clearin' around a ol' burnt shack, and I come on a patch o' poke. Everything's forwarder in the valley, and I 'lowed you and 'Bithie hadn't had ary mess o' poke yit. So I brung up a basket afore the leaves had time to wilt." He laughed.

"I started 'bout a hour by sun, and could a-made hit home for supper, but I come by ol' Cap'n Charley's and nothin' would do him but I must go in and eat with him. He given me a big bunch o' them early shallots o' hisn. Said he owed 'em to you'ns. I couldn't make hit out— he talked funny, like he'd been drinkin'— but here they air in the basket. They'll go good with pork and greens. What's the matter? You sick?"

Letty went limp all over as though fainting. "Hit ain't nothin'— nothin' at all, Manse. Only— I'm so glad you brung me somethin'. Our supper was all spiled. And I thought— I thought shore the ol' Cap'n was mad at me and maybe Aunt Minar Bushares would be, too, and then maybe you'd lose your job— and hit would be all my fault." And she told him all about it.

"Oh, well," was Mansell's conclusion, "hit ain't as big as all that comes to; but ef you was to werry yourself sick, now, that would be a whole dime's wuth o' nickels." He laughed again, with huge enjoyment of the Captain's manner. "I reckon he jist didn't want to turn loose two dollars."

Next morning the gray mare, edging round and round the clearing, a glimmering shape in the gold and green of the shadowless April woods, distinguished a new odor among those issuing from the cabin chimney. Mingled with sharp frying fat and richly browning meal was a savory tang of boiling pokeweed. And cocking an ear, she caught a sound of singing. Letty was recalling a ballad of her scarce-past girlhood:

> "Oh, green grows the laurel
>   and so does the rue,
> So lost was I, Polly,
>   at parting with you."

None of this interested old Soapstick much, but another sound, close at hand disturbed her so that she shook her head till her shaggy ears rattled impatiently against her bur-encrusted foretop. It was a noise of maul and wedge, of hammering and splitting. Mansell Kindred was risking the disapproval of the neighbors and the probable condemnation of the Recording Angel, defending and maintaining the welfare of his house and home by Sunday labor in main strength and awkwardness.

He was mending the fence.

Published in
The Mothers Magazine - August 1917

Turkey Luck

EMMA BELL MILES

ILLUSTRATIONS BY SEARS GALLAGHER

OLD DARTUS RHEA AND HIS WIFE, WHOM EVERYONE knew as Aunt Lucy, lived on the road that climbs out of Puncheon Camp Creek up to Moccasin Gap and crosses Sourwood Mountain.

Their house was a convenient stopping place for the tanbark men and drovers who came up the mountain from the far valley on the way to Watauga. From the road a man could see the roof spread out like an old hen's wings among the apple trees, and the bee gums round it like little chickens; but if he wished for something to represent a rooster, he must have strained his fancy to make one of the log barn, or of the great rock, from under which flowed the spring where Aunt Lucy kept her piggins of butter and crocks of cream.

From their back porch the Rheas could see all over three counties, and the view was equally wide from the middle entry, where the loom sat all summer. There also, from the

[289]

time the peachblows cast a shadow and the coral honey suckle budded out. Uncle Dartus used to sit, listening to his bees and the running spring branch and telling tales of the war. To look at him you would never have thought that he had been with General Miles in over a dozen battles. And he never spoke an ill word of anyone.

Uncle Dartus and Aunt Lucy never felt lonesome although the nearest neighbors lived in the coves and ridges far below. For it was known to the country round about that their coffeepot never went dry or got cold by day; and any stranger who lost his way between the last cabin above the gap and the first in Red Gully Cove was always directed to Uncle Dartus's.

"Come right in and wait for supper time," the old man would say. "Lucy she'll make up some good biscuits; and we'll go in the smokehouse and cut a ham." They always had honey and apples.

One fall it happened that they both felt unusually well and hearty. They had done fairly well for old folks that season, what with their truck patch and trading and a few pigs and sheep that ran over the ridges. A heavy mast of acorns and chestnuts fed the pigs fat and all three cows brought heifer calves and the chickens turned out well. Aunt Lucy thought that her luck with the chickens was because she had invited old Ann Goforth to stay with them on New Year's Day and had given her a poke of dried apples and eggs. Old Ann was part Indian and never was good company, but if she had not come early to sit by the fire that New Year's morning the first visitor of the day would have been Preacher Drane— and that according to local superstition would have caused all the settings of eggs to hatch out roosters, and might also have hindered Aunt Lucy in her soap making.

Aunt Lucy's luck held in other ways. She sold a six months accumulation of spinning truck and received cash for it. She could no longer see to weave the old-fashioned coverlets and counterpanes, although she made all her dresses of linsey-woolsey and "checkerty-plaid" cotton, dyed with copperas, indigo and madder and peach-tree bark and walnut leaves; and her good honest blankets were warm and lasting. They came to the notice of some people from Watauga, who bought all she had made up.

Then Dartus's nephew, Timon Poe, brought his young wife, Cynthia, to visit them in the early summer, and while they stayed, he and Dartus lined bees. They found three or four rich honey trees and added the wild colonies to the home stand. So what with one thing and another the old man and woman had reason to feel contented and comfortable.

When the frost came, ripening the muscadines and nuts and making persimmons sugary, they sat by the fire talking things over; but they did not let each other know that they were in high spirits, for they believed that it is bad luck to boast of good health and bad manners to boast of good living. Dartus, however, rubbed his hands together and said: "I'll be limb-juggled, Lucy honey, ef I ain't in-about minded to git us a turkey for this Christmas."

Perhaps the turkey would have been more appropriate for Thanksgiving, but, although they had heard of such a holiday, they were not sure of its date and would not have known how to keep it.

[291]

Dartus talked on the time when he was a little boy and his people sat by the fire Christmas Eve with whatever company had gathered and sang songs until after midnight. He had honestly believed, he said, that the elder bushes bloomed out in the snow at twelve o'clock and that all the cattle went down on their knees round the manger.

"I don't know but what they do too," he declared. "Because I've waked up on a bitter cold Christmas Eve and heard 'em a-lowing and a-mooing; and I've seen the elder buds all busted out and frostbit the next day. Oh, yes, a body always ought to try to keep Christmas!"

Then Aunt Lucy told how her father's family generally killed a deer and baked a great apple cake nearly two feet high, or else roasted a shote with sweet potatoes.

"Now, you and me, Dartus, we couldn't make out to eat a whole shote, without some of my folks to come from Meigs County to help us," she said; "but I aim bake us a little small cake."

"And maybe I can polish up Old Sister," said Dartus, as he looked up at the long muzzle-loader that with its six shot pouch and powder-horn had hung over the fireboard since they were married, "and I'll kill us a wild turkey or a pheasant, or anyhow a mess of quail."

The reason that they had fallen out of the habit of keeping Christmas was that they were both good church members and did not approve of the misrule that some people in the mountains set up from the new Christmas Day to the old, which falls twelve days later, They might have joined in the usual round of visiting, but it happened that all their near relations were away at one distance or another. Roistering with gunpowder and moonshine whiskey and cards was not what they wanted. But as the winter deepened over Moccasin Gap they felt more and more like celebrating in some way.

All the week before Christmas was dry, clear weather, crispy cold. Old Dartus was out with his rifle every day on the mountain side and in the breaks of Puncheon Camp Creek. But he was not, at his time of life, as quick with "Old Sister" as a frightened turkey hen can be with her legs and wings; and all he brought in was one opossum, tolerably fat, that had lived on stolen corn and chickens. He put the creature, grinning and snapping, into a coop; and the next day he hitched his mule to the spring wagon and set out for Watauga.

It was the Saturday before Christmas— the country people's day for going to town. Every wagon that came down the gap rang loud and far on the frosty air, for the road was hard as iron. Aunt Lucy heard them and stood by the fence with a homespun square pinned overhead, saying, "We're jist toler'ble. How's your folks?" to everyone that passed. She was kin to nearly everyone in the far valley, and some stopped and talked a long time with her.

When Eph Latiner came by she was glad to have him stay and tell her all the news from Blue Springs and Carson's Cove. His wagon was piled with holly and mistletoe and club moss and cat brier that he was carrying down to sell along the streets; but underneath the green he had a coopful of fat young turkeys that he was taking to market.

The way Uncle Dartus had spoken made Aunt Lucy believe that he was more than half joking about having turkey for Christmas dinner, and she thought it would be an excellent idea to surprise him; so she bought a fat turkey from Eph with her own blanket money.

But when Dartus drove into the lot that evening, with the provision of salt and water-ground meal and lamp oil and coffee and a little sugar, which was about all that they ever bought, he, too, had a turkey.

"Well, Lucy, we cert'n'y surprised one 'nother." he said. It was more'n we really ought t' a' spent, but never mind. I b'lieve the one Eph raised is a leetle the biggest. Fat, ain't they?"

Dartus locked the two birds in the henhouse together, and gave them all the corn that they could eat the next morning.

On Christmas Eve the weather turned colder, and a sharp wind blew down the valley. Everyone that passed was glad to stop and get warm by Dartus's fire and drink a cup of Aunt Lucy's coffee. Coldest of travelers on the road was poor Timon, Dartus's nephew, tramping home with a pack of meagre supplies on his shoulder.

"What you-uns goin' to do for Christmas, Timon?" inquired Aunt Lucy.

"Mighty little, Aunt Lucy," he answered, spreading his hands to the blaze. "Cynthy's poorly, and the baby, it favors a little picked bird. I ain't got to work at nothing all fall for havin' to take keer of them. I reckon me and her'll jist set and look at one 'nother for our Christmas."

She noticed then how thin his clothes were and how out of heart he looked; and she went into the kitchen and made haste to pack a bucket of honey to send to Cynthia. By the time it was ready she thought of something else and looked

SHE BOUGHT A FAT TURKEY FROM EPH WITH HER BLANKET MONEY

about for Dartus, to consult with him. But Dartus was not to be found at the moment, and Timon was in a hurry; so she ran out to the henhouse and, groping in the dusk, found a turkey. Tying his legs handily with a soft rag strip, she presented it to Timon.

She felt reluctant to tell her husband of what she had done on impulse— "me a-givin' away all that good turkey meat, and it so high! He'll be apt to read me the parables about it." She put off telling him until the last minute on Christmas morning; when he came in with a blank expression ftom a trip to the henhouse, she knew that she must make her confession.

When she had finished, Dartus said sheepishly, "I toted one of them birds across the hollar yestidy evening to pore old Aunt Goforth."

"You did!"

They looked at each other across the scalding water and carving knife that she had got ready.

"Well, there goes our Christmas dinner," he said ruefully. But he crossed the kitchen and kissed Aunt Lucy's withered cheek. "Old honey girl, I wouldn't 'a thought of you doin' that; I didn't 'low you thought that much of my kinfolks."

"So it's you and me, instid of Timon and Cynthy, that will have to set and look at one 'nother Christmas Day." she answered; but she said it happily.

"Well, by jings, Lucy, it wouldn't be so bad ef we was to," he reflected, noticing her mounting color and her smile. "But there's the possum. I'll go out and skin him whilst you fix a potful of sweet taters, and I reckon we won't go exactly hungry."

Published in
The Youth's Companion - October 1921